Don't Fancy Your Chance

The Chances
Book 12

Emily E K Murdoch

ARE YOU SIGNED UP FOR DRAGONBLADE'S BLOG?

You'll get the latest news and information on exclusive giveaways, exclusive excerpts, coming releases, sales, free books, cover reveals and more.

Check out our complete list of authors, too!

No spam, no junk. That's a promise!

Sign Up Here

www.dragonbladepublishing.com

Dearest Reader;

Thank you for your support of a small press. At Dragonblade Publishing, we strive to bring you the highest quality Historical Romance from some of the best authors in the business. Without your support, there is no 'us', so we sincerely hope you adore these stories and find some new favorite authors along the way.

Happy Reading!

CEO, Dragonblade Publishing

Additional Dragonblade books by
Author Emily E K Murdoch

The Chances Series
A Fighting Chance (Book 1)
A Second Chance (Book 2)
An Outside Chance (Book 3)
Half a Chance (Book 4)
A Chance in a Million (Book 5)
Not a Chance in Hell (Book 6)
An Eye for the Chance (Book 7)
A Sporting Chance (Book 8)
Any Chance You Can Take (Book 9)
Chance Would Be a Fine Thing (Book 10)
Take a Chance on You (Book 11)
Don't Fancy Your Chance (Book 12)

Dukes in Danger Series
Don't Judge a Duke by His Cover (Book 1)
Strike While the Duke is Hot (Book 2)
The Duke is Mightier than the Sword (Book 3)
A Duke in Time Saves Nine (Book 4)
Every Duke Has His Price (Book 5)
Put Your Best Duke Forward (Book 6)
Where There's a Duke, There's a Way (Book 7)
Curiosity Killed the Duke (Book 8)
Play With Dukes, Get Burned (Book 9)
The Best Things in Life are Dukes (Book 10)
A Duke a Day Keeps the Doctor Away (Book 11)
All Good Dukes Come to an End (Book 12)

Twelve Days of Christmas
Twelve Drummers Drumming
Eleven Pipers Piping

Ten Lords a Leaping
Nine Ladies Dancing
Eight Maids a Milking
Seven Swans a Swimming
Six Geese a Laying
Five Gold Rings
Four Calling Birds
Three French Hens
Two Turtle Doves
A Partridge in a Pear Tree

The De Petras Saga
The Misplaced Husband (Book 1)
The Impoverished Dowry (Book 2)
The Contrary Debutante (Book 3)
The Determined Mistress (Book 4)
The Convenient Engagement (Book 5)

The Governess Bureau Series
A Governess of Great Talents (Book 1)
A Governess of Discretion (Book 2)
A Governess of Many Languages (Book 3)
A Governess of Prodigious Skill (Book 4)
A Governess of Unusual Experience (Book 5)
A Governess of Wise Years (Book 6)
A Governess of No Fear (Novella)

Never The Bride Series
Always the Bridesmaid (Book 1)
Always the Chaperone (Book 2)
Always the Courtesan (Book 3)
Always the Best Friend (Book 4)
Always the Wallflower (Book 5)
Always the Bluestocking (Book 6)
Always the Rival (Book 7)
Always the Matchmaker (Book 8)
Always the Widow (Book 9)
Always the Rebel (Book 10)

Always the Mistress (Book 11)
Always the Second Choice (Book 12)
Always the Mistletoe (Novella)
Always the Reverend (Novella)

The Lyon's Den Series
Always the Lyon Tamer

Pirates of Britannia Series
Always the High Seas

De Wolfe Pack: The Series
Whirlwind with a Wolfe

Noble titles throughout English history have, at times, been more fluid than one might think. Women have inherited, men have been gifted titles by family or gained them through marriage, and royals frequently lavished titles or withdrew them as reward and punishment.

The elder Chance brothers in this series agreed to split the four titles in their family line during the Regency era, rather than the eldest holding all four. It is a decision that defines their brotherhood, and their very different personalities.

Now with the next generation, two Chance fathers have allowed their sons to inherit their titles before their own demises, echoing kings and queens who have abdicated their titles throughout history. Perhaps their brothers, the uncles of this next generation, will follow suit...

Get ready to meet a family that is more than happy to scandalize Society...

Chapter One

March 4, 1841

"ALL I'M SAYING," Lady Marjorie Dalton said, in what she hoped was a delicate and non-carrying whisper, "is that I would not have shown my face again!"

Her heart raced, her gaze flickering over to the woman on the other side of the Pump Room, as her friend Miss Harding nudged her elbow.

"You will have to tell me all, for I have been sorely left out of the entire affair," her friend hissed. "My papa has forbidden all scandal sheets, and Mama refused to tell me anything!"

And Marjorie hesitated.

Oh, it was not that she did not enjoy a little gossip. There always seemed to be something scandalous happening in Bath; that was why, after all, she had begged her parents to spend the spring in the city.

London grew so dull, and the very idea of disappearing off into the countryside to Dalton Manor, a thousand miles from anything—no, it would have been quite unsupportable. Especially after her wayward sister, Rose, had returned, and had married, and was now a marchioness.

Besides, Miss Harding was in Bath at the moment with her parents, and after attending finishing school together two years ago but only corresponding since, it was a delight to see her.

Even if the girl was… Well. *Naïve.*

The Pump Room was heaving with people, as Marjorie had known it would be, but she could not have imagined that the rumored courtesan to the Comte di Frechetti would be here in the…well, in the flesh, as it were.

Marjorie's cheeks burned as she glanced up once again at the lady in question. She was beautiful, yes—but wearing a gown that skimmed so low, and in the afternoon, too!

"Marjorie? Marjorie, what happened?" persisted her friend, seemingly unaffected by the scandal of it all. "What did the lady in question do?

Do?

Well, that was the question, wasn't it? Marjorie had been raised to be polite, genteel, and most of all, respectable. She had been raised not to ask questions, and to believe what she was told. That, perhaps, had been her downfall eight years ago. Her father, just last year the Earl of Burnell but raised in rank by her grandfather's passing, was only the second marquess of his line, and for his only unwed daughter to do something outrageous… No, it would not be borne.

Even *thinking* about the scandalous position in which the lady before them had been found…

It was enough to turn Marjorie's stomach.

To be found in such a situation: in a man's arms, in a quiet lane, of all places!

"Your face is red."

Marjorie's hands immediately lifted to her face. "No, it's not!"

"Getting redder," said Miss Harding with a grin. Her full lips complemented her cherub cheeks when she giggled. "You really are intrigued, aren't you?"

"*Intrigued* is not the word," Marjorie returned as haughtily as she could manage, opening her fan and fluttering it before herself in an attempt to ward off both heat and stares.

No, *intrigued* was not the word.

Fascinated.

How long had Marjorie lost herself in novels, novels in which the hero boldly rescued a maiden from a danger worse than death, only to lose himself in the embraces of the grateful lady?

How many novels had she devoured, sitting in the library not receiving visitors—her mother considered that *forward*, after what had happened to Rose—and escaping to Arabia, or deepest Russia, or the moorlands of the West Country?

How often had she wondered, sitting there in the armchair, a novel half-open on her lap as she dozed, what it would be like to be seduced by a man like that...

Marjorie cleared her throat.

Far too long, far too many, and far too often, as it happened. But she wasn't going to let Miss Harding know that.

"I do think the fashions for embroidery along the cuffs is most ingenious," her friend said eagerly, her attention following a pair of ladies who passed them in their promenade around the room. "It enables one to update one's gowns with very little expense. Don't you think?"

Somehow, they had managed to drift from scandalous courtesans to...sleeves.

Well, it wasn't the *dullest* conversational topic, even Marjorie had to admit. There was always the weather.

She forced a smile. "Most agreeable."

What *was* agreeable was that her parents had permitted her to leave the house in the company of just one singular friend. Marjorie could not recall the last time that had been allowed; an elderly chaperone or five had always been expected, and as Marjorie had such a small acquaintance here in Bath, she had spent the first two weeks never leaving the house at all.

And now here she was, in the Pump Room with Miss Harding, her mother a whole ten feet away, sunlight soaring through the windows and the smell of that unpleasant-tasting water drifting by them, and she was...free.

Well. Free up to a point.

Free to attend the Pump Room for an hour, then return immediately.

A smile crept across Marjorie's face. It was freedom of a sort, and she would take it.

She would take anything at this point…

"—and so many eligible bachelors!" her friend said brightly, staring eagerly over at a trio of young men who had halted their conversation to look over at them.

Marjorie tried desperately not to flush as she lifted her fan higher. "Not so loud, please!"

It was bad enough that her own sister had made such a scandalous marriage but months ago.

Well, the marriage itself was not so scandalous. Marrying the young Marquess of Aylesbury was in fact a coup for the family's elder daughter.

The fact that she had run away from home almost a decade ago, married a wastrel, become both his widow and a famed Italian actress, and *then* married the Marquess of Aylesbury…that was all Society could talk about.

"Oh, they are only minnows. I will not be casting my net in their direction," Miss Harding said blithely, though even her cheeks did pink at the boldness of her statement. "No, I have a different catch in mind."

Despite herself, despite knowing that such a topic of conversation was outrageous to have at all, let alone in public—a lady did not attempt to *catch* any gentleman; she was genteelly pursued—Marjorie leaned closer.

"A different catch?" she whispered, excitement fluttering in her lungs. "You have a particular gentleman in mind?"

It was not exactly scandalous—a young lady may have a preference, Marjorie knew. But to speak of it, and in public…

Miss Harding flushed. "Well, not a particular gentleman. A set."

Marjorie dropped her fan.

"Whoops, careful now, that looks expensive," said her companion.

"'A set—a *set* of gentlemen'?" hissed Marjorie, dipping down hurriedly to pick up her fan and wishing her cheeks did not go quite so red so instantaneously. "I'm sorry, 'a *set*'?"

"I didn't mean it like that—not quite like that, at any rate," said her friend, her own cheeks remarkably clear for having said such an outrageous statement. "I meant a particular family. I like the family."

"'The family'?" Marjorie repeated, hackles calming.

Well, she was hardly a prude—almost certainly not a prude, although she was not sure what a prude was compared to a genteel lady of Society. As far as Marjorie could make out, they were the same thing.

But her friend was right. A set sounded far more disgraceful than a family. Admiring a family's position was acceptable...for the most part.

It really depended on the family.

Miss Harding sighed, a dreamy, faraway look in her eyes. "The Chances."

The Chances. Of course.

Marjorie attempted to force a smile. "The Chances."

"You must have encountered them while you and your parents were in London. They are truly the most exceptional family to have ever lived," gushed her friend in an undertone. "I have heard that the ladies of the family are all beautiful and virtuous—"

"Well," said Marjorie warily, thinking back to a few scandals that had not quite been covered up.

"—and all the gentlemen of the family are all handsome and respectable—"

"Well," said Marjorie weakly, thinking back to a few scandals that no amount of effort would ever have covered up.

"—and they are all so charming," Miss Harding finished with a sigh. "Oh, I would love to meet one of them."

Marjorie blinked. "Wait a moment. You haven't actually met any of them? You are mightily certain in your opinions, considering you have never made any of their acquaintance."

Her friend shrugged as a quartet of people entered the Pump Room to much muttering and intrigue. "One does not need to have actually met these people to know that they are truly wonderful, Marjorie. I thought everyone knew that."

Everyone except me, Marjorie thought ruefully.

Or at least, the little interaction she had had with the Chance family had been relatively…pedestrian.

Her parents had hosted a ball, a few dinners, and members of the Chance family had attended. True, it was a large family: four brothers, each of whom had married and produced a great deal of children who were now fully grown. Almost no one in Society could claim to be intimately acquainted with the entirety of the Chance family; there simply wasn't enough time in the day.

But Marjorie had been introduced to all of the Chances at one point or another but had only said more than a few words to a few of the Chance ladies, who were brilliant and beautiful, as Miss Harding had said… and that was it.

The Daltons were not a smart enough or a prestigious enough family to attract the notice of any Chance sons. Her sister had married her Chance in quite a roundabout way—he hadn't even known she'd *been* a Dalton.

"I am absolutely certain I would recognize the Chances if I saw them," her friend was saying in a light whisper. "After all, such breeding, such excellence in manner and taste… They must be obvious."

Marjorie's focus fell on the four people who had so recently entered the Pump Room, and her stomach twisted. "Yes. Obvious."

"I mean, one could hardly fail to spot them," Miss Harding said loudly as Marjorie attempted to clear her throat pointedly. "It would be a fool, indeed, who was ignorant of—"

"That's them," Marjorie muttered behind her fan, unable to bear her friend's continuation.

Miss Harding almost fell over in her haste to whirl around. "What—where?"

"Try not to make it too obvious that you are staring," begged Marjorie, the embarrassment of it all already starting to spread up her neck.

But it was no use. The eye of everyone in the Pump Room had been dragged inexorably to the quartet who were, Marjorie had to admit, exactly what her friend had described.

Two ladies of exquisite beauty and refined taste, their gowns the latest fashions and yet understated, as though they did not hope that their attire would distract from their inane conversation. A gentleman who was smiling, nodding agreeably with something that one of the ladies had said—his wife, from what Marjorie could remember.

And her stomach jolted.

And a gentleman so handsome, she could never set her eyes upon another and see his equal.

Oh, dear Lord. Marjorie had never felt so…so unsettled. As though the boards beneath her feet were on a ship and she were being tilted from left to right in a storm. As though a great wind was blowing through her, stripping away all resolve and all manners. As if—

"Goodness, what a striking gentleman," Miss Harding uttered in a whisper that surely had to carry all the way over to the four of them. "Have you ever seen the like?"

Yes, was what Marjorie would have said, if her tongue had been operational and she was not afeared of the Chances hearing her. *But only when he and I were introduced.*

But it did not seem to matter that she had said not a word. Somehow, painfully, the gentleman nearest them—the Chance gentleman nearest them, that was, the one who made Marjorie's eyes hurt and her pulse skip a beat—turned to look at them.

And the smile he gave the pair of ladies was wolfish to the extreme.

"Oh, no," Marjorie said weakly, even as her hopes leapt.

"Oh, yes!"

"Do not look over," she ordered her friend, hoping to goodness no one had noticed the brief, momentary gazes meeting.

Across a crowded room. Honestly, if this had been happening to a heroine in a book, she would have been cheering her on,

Marjorie could not help but think ruefully. As it was, it would be a social disaster to be seen conversing with a gentleman of that particular ilk—and without her parents!

Oh, Miss Harding was a dear friend, but she was two months younger than Marjorie herself, hardly a suitable chaperone at the best of times. Certainly not a suitable buffer between her and a man who made all women sigh with delight.

Despite herself, Marjorie allowed her eyes to flicker back to the gentleman. Tall and handsome, yes, but that could describe almost all of the Chance cousins. Even some of the ladies.

But Lord Alexander Chance... There was something about him.

She had noticed it the first time they had met. The only time they had met, in truth. One of her parents' balls, a hasty celebration of her elder sister's marriage. Marjorie had been out, officially, for the first time, and the fact that the Cothrom Chances had accepted the invitation...

It had not been the magical night she had hoped. Her mother had adorned her in the frumpiest gown Marjorie had ever seen, she had been forbidden from leaving her sister's side—to their equal disgruntlement—and Lord Alexander had barely noticed her.

And he was even more handsome than she remembered, worse luck. A strong jaw, a smile that appeared swiftly yet seemed warm and genuine each time. Hair that appeared dark or light depending on the time of day. A style, an air of standing that suggested delight was just around the corner, if one were willing to accept his advances...

Marjorie allowed herself a small, slightly petulant sigh.

A man like that does not notice ladies like myself. He was the sort of man to have a mistress in every town and know the best courtesans of London by name. He was the sort of man to gamble money he did not have and wager on horses that he did not own. He—

He was smiling at her.

Marjorie turned away hurriedly, but the damage was done. Even out of the corner of her eye, she could see that the absolute worst was about to happen.

"Oh, goodness," breathed Miss Harding beside her.

"Oh, no," whispered Marjorie, her pulse quickening.

"Just be respectable." That was what her mother had told her. *"Stay at the edges, do not speak to anyone even if an introduction is offered, then come straight back home."*

Speaking to one of the most immoral and therefore most ineligible Chance cousins, and in public, had not been on her mother's agenda.

"He's coming over here!" Miss Harding grabbed painfully at Marjorie's arm. "He's coming over to speak with us!"

"We need to leave," Marjorie said sharply.

Her friend stared in utter confusion. "You cannot be in earnest."

"We must leave. Now," whispered Marjorie, her pulse quickening with every step the man took toward them. *"Now—"*

"But why?" Biting her lip and glancing around, Miss Harding looked bewildered, and quite rightly.

Marjorie swallowed. "Because that isn't just any Chance gentleman. That is—"

"Lord Alexander Chance, at your service." The charming man smiled as he swept into a low and decadent bow. "And I have the pleasure—the very great pleasure—of addressing?"

He didn't remember her? She supposed there was no helping that. There had been a great number of Chances at the ball that day.

Well, this was it. Her mother had trained her for this; the elegant and socially acceptable sweep around a gentleman who had been so bold as to introduce himself. Yes, she had been introduced to him before, but he clearly didn't remember that, so he was being rather forward. Marjorie readied her skirts, preparing to storm away from the man who had been so presumptuous as to—

Miss Harding simpered and curtseyed low, ensuring her gown dipped at the front. "La, sir, do you not know it is most improper for a gentleman to introduce himself to a lady?!"

"Then I find myself most improperly enchanted," Lord Alexander said smoothly, his smile widening. "And I have the pleasure of being enchanted by…?"

"We should go," Marjorie hissed, half to herself more than anything else.

She had to leave. She knew she did; Lord Alexander Chance was the most rakish, most roguish, most…most unsuitable gentleman in the whole of Bath.

The man was a known liar and a scoundrel, and although Marjorie could forgive a certain amount of scoundreling, lying was perhaps the one fault she could not abide.

Not after—

Focus, woman!

Yes, there was a rake before her and she must absolutely not converse with him. Her mother would not like it. Her father would most certainly not like it.

And if she did not leave right now, in this moment… Well, she would never leave.

"Miss Catherine Harding," said her companion, fluttering her eyelashes and looking the young man up and down with the most obvious of delight. "And this is—"

"We have met," Marjorie said curtly, trying not to flush at the man's inexplicable charm.

Charm and attraction. Why, just standing before him was enough to raise the hackles of her neck, and for her fingers to warm, and…

And a whole host of other things that Marjorie was most certainly not going to think about.

That was the trouble with the Chance men. *They have no idea, do they,* she thought ominously, *just how much of an impact they can have on a lady merely by standing by her.*

And not just within her.

Within Society.

"Listen," Marjorie said sharply, tugging her friend away and hissing low in her ear. "We need to go. This man is... Every scandal in London is somehow attached to his name! Even to be seen *standing* near him could ruin us."

"But he's so handsome, Marjorie," Miss Harding said in a far-too-carrying voice. "I don't know why you don't like him!"

Marjorie swallowed down a litany of reasons, including but not limited to, seduction of widows, a potential elopement with a young lady thankfully rescued by her family, and that small matter of the lions of the Tower of London and a dip in the Thames.

And those were the scandals her parents had permitted her to read about.

Despite herself, Marjorie felt her attention flickering over to the gentleman in question.

Lord Alexander Chance was grinning.

Of course he was. No gentleman ever had to face consequences, not true consequences, for his actions. *A man of that ilk likely never has to worry about a thing in his life*, Marjorie thought darkly. A lady of any standing in Society had to watch carefully for even a *hint* of impropriety.

It's so different for them.

"Your friend does not appear to wish to make my acquaintance, Miss Harding," Lord Alexander said lightly, a teasing air in his voice that Marjorie did not like. "What on earth have I done, I wonder, to lose such favor?"

Oh, he is charm itself, Marjorie thought joylessly. At least, he would have been.

If they had not already been introduced.

It was not offensive, exactly, that he had obviously forgotten her. It was merely aggravating.

Incredibly aggravating.

Fine, it was offensive.

"I cannot make your acquaintance, Lord Alexander," Marjorie said quietly, holding herself up as upright as she could and hoping to goodness her mother would never hear about this.

The man's expression flickered. Just for a moment—but she was almost certain it flickered. For a moment, he was displeased.

The smile and accompanying charm returned almost immediately. "Oh, to be wounded in so public a manner—"

"I cannot make your acquaintance because we are already acquainted," said Marjorie stiffly, wishing to goodness—and for the first time in her life—that her mother was with her. "We are, in a way, related."

Dear Lord, that it has come to this.

Lord Alexander's smile really did waver this time. "We are? Goodness, I have no memory of you at all."

Blast, but that hurt. Marjorie attempted to speak calmly as she said, "My sister is married to one of your cousins."

Not that any of the families had been at the wedding, of course—Rose and the Marquess of Aylesbury had reappeared in Society already married, which had caused some consternation of its own.

Lord Alexander was still grinning. "I think I would have remembered seeing you at a wedding."

"And on such an appealing note, I am afraid Miss Harding and I must depart. Good day, my lord," Marjorie said swiftly, tugging her friend's arm away from the blaggard.

"Marjorie!"

"It's for your own good," said Marjorie sternly, sounding painfully like her own mother as she marched Miss Harding past Lord Alexander, past the other three Chances—his sister, one of his brothers, and the brother's wife—past all the other current inhabitants of the Pump Room who were now staring and muttering in their groups, which did not bode well, and out into the bustling Bath street.

Miss Harding wrenched her arm from her friend and glared. "What on earth did you do that for?" She turned over her shoulder. "What about my mother?"

"Trust me, it was the right thing to do. And we'll send someone in with a note for Mrs. Harding, tell her I didn't feel well and we took a hansom cab home."

"Why? Why lie? Why *leave*? I just made the acquaintance of Lord Alexander Chance—the only unmarried son of the Duke of Cothrom!" Her friend looked genuinely upset. "That could have been my opportunity to marry a title. Even if just a second son."

"Third son," Marjorie corrected, wincing at the revelation that she knew so much about the man. "And his father goes by the 'Dowager Duke of Cothrom' now. The eldest son inherited the title prematurely." She paused. "Honestly, you need to trust me," she said darkly, glancing over her shoulder and swallowing, her mouth suddenly dry as she looked back and saw that the gentleman in question was staring after them. "The woman who marries Lord Alexander is to be pitied, indeed."

Chapter Two

ALEXANDER COULD NOT recall ever being this bored.

"I do not wish to be pitied," snapped a bejeweled Maude, in a most pitiful condition.

"No one is pitying you," Alexander said calmly, lying directly to the second of two women he had ever trusted and hoping his sister never discovered his falsehood.

She did, after all, have an impressive right hook.

"Yes, they are. Everyone is!" his sister said cheerlessly, just about managing to keep her voice quiet enough so that the entirety of the Pump Room did not hear. "Everyone is looking at me and pitying the old Chance *spinster*."

No one would dare call Maude that except Maude herself. At least not within her earshot.

Besides, she was Lady Maude Chance. She'd be well cared for her entire life, first by their parents and then by her brothers if need be. She did not need a husband. Alexander certainly wouldn't have recommended any of the scoundrels of his acquaintance for the position. She was fortunate she, unlike so many ladies in Society, did not *need* to marry.

But he'd keep those thoughts to himself.

"No one is pitying you," repeated Alexander's older brother Thomas, though even Alexander would admit—if forced—that he did not appear to be entirely truthful.

Maude snorted. "You are both terrible liars."

"No one even knew about your engagement, Maude," said

Victoria, their brother's wife and the Duchess of Cothrom, in a calming voice with her dark hair swept up into a resplendent braid, which impressed Alexander. The calming voice, that was. Not the braid. It took a great deal of patience to be this calm around Maude. "And now that it is over—"

Thomas winced. "I still cannot believe—"

"I do not wish to talk about it," hissed Maude as the four of them walked elegantly around the Pump Room, smiling and inclining their heads at acquaintances as they went. "It is not to be talked about!"

That was what their mother had said only an hour before, over luncheon.

"It is not to be talked about!" The Dowager Duchess of Cothrom—her husband still lived, but he had rescinded the title officially to his eldest son in a manner that had scandalized the whole of Society—tried to smile as she spoke. Her sparkling, blue eyes were exactly the same shade as Maude's. "The engagement between Maude and—"

Maude had growled. "Do not even speak his name."

Alexander had hidden his expression behind his cup of tea. It had had brandy in it, but his mother was not to know that.

"The engagement between Maude and the man who we will not name—"

"Oh no, that only makes him sound even more fascinating," Maude had snorted. "We shall have to think of another name for him. The idiotic one. The shamefaced liar. The—"

"I liked him," Leopold, the second-eldest brother of the Chance family with the widest shoulders and the one who always managed to say exactly the wrong thing, had chimed in.

His wife, Kathleen, had clearly agreed. "Leopold!"

"How can you say that?!" Maude had flared up, as Alexander had known she would, and he'd leaned backward from the table carefully in case she decided to wrench the tablecloth. It would not be the first time. "To take *his* side?"

"I'm not taking anyone's side!" Leopold had protested.

"I don't think you should be taking his side," Thomas had said gravely, his serious eyes matching his taut jaw.

"Does anyone want another side of potatoes?" Alexander had asked cheerfully.

Everyone around the dinner table had glared at him.

"What? They are remarkably good—the rosemary must have been particularly fresh," he'd said lightly, rolling his eyes. "Come on—we are the Chances. Scandal doesn't stick to us, and as you say, no one knows the blighter—"

"Yes, yes, the blighter. I like that," Maude had said, immediately cheered.

Their blue-gowned mother had sighed and dropped her head onto one hand. "You four will be the death of me."

Which Alexander had thought a tad harsh.

After all, his brothers, Thomas and Leopold, had married well. Nice ladies, a little dull, but fine enough for the pair of them. Maude… Well, at two and thirty, she was well past the age at which she was technically a spinster, but she was beautiful and rich and well-born, and was a spinster really ever any of those things?

And then there was him. He hadn't done anything wrong.

Nothing his family had found out about, anyway.

Oh, it had seemed like a good idea at the time. He had been young, inexperienced, coddled by his parents and treated like a child by his siblings…the baby of the family.

Viscount Gascoyne had suggested it. Or had it been Sir Percival?

"Look, the next time I'm chatting to a delightful widow," the cleft-chinned viscount had said with a shrug, "I'll give her your name. Your reputation as a distinguished lover will only increase."

"And I too," the lanky Sir Percival had said with a grin. "It can't hurt to keep my name out of widows' bedchambers, anyway!"

And it had all gone so well. Alexander's friends had bedded

ladies across town, and Alexander had gained a reputation for being a rogue, his popularity only increasing.

It was only now, five years in, that he was starting to tire of the ruse.

"The only thing we can do is to continue with our stay in Bath as if nothing has happened," Thomas had sternly over luncheon earlier that day.

Alexander had tried not to snort into his brandy. That was the trouble with Thomas; he was always trying to do the right thing, the best thing, the most appropriate thing.

It was fortunate, indeed, for his brother that Alexander was fond of him. That sort of behavior in anyone else would have been considered downright dull.

"Nothing has happened," their mother had said lightly.

Maude had snorted again. "Nothing except betrayal of the greatest kind!"

"We were thinking of visiting the Pump Room after luncheon," Victoria had said lightly, her gaze kindly as she looked over at her sister-in-law. "You would be very welcome to join us. Bit of fresh air. Disgusting water. That sort of thing."

This time, Alexander had not bothered to hide his smile.

That was one of the things he did love about his family. Even those who joined it understood that Chances stuck together. Even in the strange and bizarre moments.

And quite honestly, this engagement that hadn't been an engagement that had been a secret but now was over...it was strange, even for Maude. Why, she hadn't even told him who the gentleman in question was, which was probably a good idea.

The man wouldn't have both his arms after jilting his sister, if Alexander had his way.

"The Pump Room! An excellent idea," their mother had.

Maude had groaned. "I have no wish to take the water."

"A walk and a little Society will do you good," their mother had said brightly.

"A little Society is what got me into this mess," Alexander's sister had muttered, but only so he could hear her.

For a moment, just a flickering moment, unease had settled within him. Maude hadn't—after all, it would be most scandalous if she *had*…and if she and the blighter, whoever he was, had…had done so, the engagement could not be broken.

Surely, she wouldn't—his sister… It was a terrible thought to even consider, but she hadn't… She hadn't let the man…

Alexander had swallowed, but he'd known he had to do something. He'd leaned closer to his sister. "Maude."

She'd glared at him. "What is it?"

Damn, his mouth had been dry. How, precisely, did one delicately inquire as to whether one's sister's virtue was still intact? He couldn't recall the lesson at Eton.

Having said that, he'd barely paid attention at Eton. Or Cambridge.

"I…" Alexander had cleared his throat. There would be a way to ascertain this, wouldn't there? Surely, there was. Maybe he would have a moment at the Pump Room and he could delicately… He could carefully… He could inquire as to whether… "I will accompany you to the Pump Room."

Maude's glare had not dissipated. "I don't *want* to go to the Pump Room."

"So that's settled, then. The four of us will go," Thomas had said cheerfully. "How nice. A family outing."

Maude had glared at Thomas, then her mother for good measure. Her mother had glared back. Alexander had glared at Thomas for ignoring Maude's protests. Leopold had glared at Thomas too—presumably because he had not been included in the invitation. Thomas had glared at Maude, Maude had then also been glaring at Victoria, though Alexander had had absolutely no idea why, and Victoria had calmly sipped her tea with a beatific smile upon her face.

"A family outing," she'd said blithely. "How lovely."

And that brought them to now.

Alexander sighed. That was the trouble with being the

youngest brother, even though he was five and twenty. He never got much of a say in the matter. That, and the fact that he had no independent income, keeping him tied to his parents until…well, until forever, as far as he could make out.

Yes, some third and second sons found themselves occupations. No Chance ever had—there was enough wealth to go around.

It was just that the fathers and then the eldest sons were the only ones to control it.

Not that he was going to allow himself to get irritated about that again.

The Pump Room was packed, as he had supposed it would be, though there did not appear to be an interesting person in the place. Other than the four Chances, naturally.

There was the old Duke of Axwick—goodness, he had to have been a grandfather by now. A great man in his youth, his father had said. And there was the Duke of Dulverton, leaning a mite more on his cane now that age was rapidly overcoming him. And hardly any ladies.

Well. There were a few.

Alexander's eyes fell onto a lovely-looking pair. Both pretty, from what he could tell from this distance, and both gazing over at him in the most intriguing manner.

The taller could not have been more overt. She desperately wished for his acquaintance and clearly had no compunction in revealing that fact to the whole room. Now that in and of itself was most fascinating. A woman who was so willing to throw her virtue about the place was worth knowing during a dull sojourn in Bath.

But the other lady—she was perhaps more interesting still. She appeared now to be carefully *not* looking in his direction.

A young lady, not wishing to catch the eye of Lord Alexander Chance?

"Absolutely not," came a stern undertone. "Do not even think about it."

"Oh, Thomas, when did you get so dull?" Alexander said with a bark of a laugh as he turned to his elder brother. "You used to be so—"

"Reckless, yes," said Thomas sternly. "But I've grown up these last few years, man, and I would advise you to do the same."

"When I wish for your advice, I will ask for it," said Alexander as he tugged at the lapels of his coat. "After all, what is the harm in some unreserved conversation?"

"It is not some *unreserved conversation* that you wish to enjoy with those women and you know it," Thomas hissed, his cheeks scarlet as he glanced over at the ladies. "We have come to Bath to *avoid* scandal."

"Yes, yes, I know," Alexander said with a wave of his hand.

Yes, to avoid scandal—his *sister's* scandal.

What was the story there, anyway? He was never really one to pay attention much to family happenings. They appeared to happen whether he was involved or not, and so Alexander merely allowed them to happen and joined in when it appeared necessary.

Usually through wedding attendance. The family was getting awfully matrimonial in these last few years.

But Maude was not the sort of person to court such scandal.

Technically the brothers' half-sister, she had been adored by them from the moment each of them had been born. They would…well, perhaps not *kill* for her, Alexander considered as his attention flickered over her. Maybe seriously maim.

And the idea that out there was a man who could callously promise matrimony, then rescind such an offer…

"You're getting angry again," Thomas's wife observed in an undertone.

"You're damned right I'm angry," Alexander said menacingly. "Maude, just give us the name of—"

"Absolutely not," Maude said decidedly. "I told you before, if anyone is shooting that man, it's me."

"Please do not talk of shooting a man so loudly!" begged Thomas, glancing left and right in the clear hope that no one had heard them. "The Chance name—"

"—is spotless and shall remain so, yes," said Alexander with a roll of his eyes.

That shorter woman was looking at him again—and not looking, so swiftly that he almost wondered whether he had imagined it.

But no, he could not have dreamed up the heat that was so clearly rising in her cheeks. *Interesting.* She wished to know him yet wished to hide that fact.

Very interesting.

"—not going to discuss—"

"Well, if you three are going to bicker, I'm going to seek out some more interesting conversation," Alexander said lightly.

Thomas, Victoria, and Maude all halted in their conversation and considered him with a healthy dose of skepticism.

Which was rude.

"You don't have any acquaintance here," said his brother quietly.

Alexander clucked his tongue. "Then I shall make some."

"Zander, no—"

But it was too late. Alexander had had enough of family drama he was not properly told about, baby talk with his brother—Victoria and his son was but months old, but apparently was greatly advanced and the whole world must know about it—and attempting not to murder the man who had broken his sister's heart.

Whoever he was.

No, he needed a distraction, and these two ladies were going to provide the perfect one.

So, how should he approach this? Play the two against each other? Hope against hope that they were not related, and he could kiss each of them without the other getting offended?

It did not matter, not really. He had such little real experience with the ladies that anything, even quite frankly a pleasant conversation, would be delightful. Alexander knew that the moment he stopped before them, like so, and dazzled the pair of them with a smile, just like that, they would be clay in his hands, ready to be molded into the willing widows he so hoped they would be.

Right. How to begin?

"Lord Alexander Chance, at your service." Yes, that was just the right amount of charm to make a lady hitch up her skirts. Alexander bowed deeply, probably more deeply than was required. "And I have the pleasure—the very great pleasure—of addressing?"

Both of the ladies were pleasing to look at, and Alexander decided that he would flirt with the both of them. After all, the evenings were still long at this time of year, and it would be pleasant to—

Ah. Yes. He had promised his father he would not even be thinking of such a thing, not even a delectable widow.

What a shame.

At least Lord Gascoyne and Sir Percival were not in Bath. That had to help matters.

The taller of the two ladies curtseyed low, so low that Alexander was gifted a rather generous look down the front of her gown. "La, sir, do you not know it is most improper for a gentleman to introduce himself to a lady?!"

Oh, to hell with Society's rules. "Then I find myself most improperly enchanted," Alexander said, making sure to widen his smile. "And I have the pleasure of being enchanted by...?"

"We should go," the other woman said in a low voice.

Now *that* was interesting. It was rare, indeed, for Alexander to discover a woman who did not delight in being in his presence. In fact, other than his sister, Maude, and his lady cousins, there was almost no woman he had ever encountered who did not eventually simper like the taller of the two here.

But this woman was different.

Beautiful, yes. One could not ignore those large eyes and those eminently kissable lips, all rosebud with cherub aspects, framed by dark-brown, almost black curls.

But it was the sharpness in the eyes and the firm line of the mouth that gained Alexander's attention.

Was it possible she did not...like him?

"Miss Catherine Harding," said her companion, clearly delighted to be conversing with him. "And this is—"

"We have met," the more petite woman said, her cheeks pinking at her words.

We have met?

Alexander stared. It was not good manners to stare, he knew that, and in almost all cases, that was not too difficult. Most ladies were the same, in the end, and it was merely a question of enjoying their company until he felt the tendrils of boredom once again curling around him.

He would surely have to wait a great deal of time for that to occur with this woman. She was startlingly beautiful, but it was not her beauty that was so dazzling.

It was her utter disdain.

"Listen," the woman said, pulling Miss Harding away from Alexander and speaking in a low voice which nonetheless carried. "We need to go. This man is... Every scandal in London is somehow attached to his name. Even to be seen *standing* near him could ruin us."

Well, that was quite the review.

"But he's so handsome, Marjorie," Miss Harding said petulantly. "I don't know why you don't like him!"

And neither did Alexander.

It was most perplexing. He could not recall ruining any young lady, not really. Oh, to be associated with him had, for a time, been to call a woman's virtue into question, but he had never actually—oh, a couple of widows. Fine, more than a couple.

But they had known what they'd been getting: a few wild

nights of hedonistic bliss, the likes of which they had never known before, and thereafter polite nods in public.

Everyone gained something.

He'd never had any complaints.

It had been old Gascoyne and Percival who had done the truly outrageous things, and in his name, yes—but what lady did not wish to be in some way connected to a reprobate?

A slow, languid smile crept across Alexander's face. Whyever this woman, Marjorie—oh, that was a name he'd love to utter aloud, should Society deem it respectable of him—had taken against him, he was not abashed. He would charm her.

How hard could it be?

"Your friend does not appear to wish to make my acquaintance, Miss Harding," Alexander said, making sure his voice was teasing, mischievous, flirtatious. "What on earth have I done, I wonder, to lose such favor?"

It was a wonderful opener, yet she slammed the door in his face.

"I cannot make your acquaintance, Lord Alexander," the woman with the rosebud mouth said quietly, stiff as a board, as though she were a widow in her seventies rather than a ripe, young thing in what had to be her early twenties.

Alexander swallowed. To be denied, and so publicly... It was not something a Chance had ever experienced.

Well, it was certainly something *this* particular Chance had never experienced. And Alexander did not like it.

But then, perhaps it was a ruse—an attempt at flirting from a shy, retiring sort. Yes, that had to have been it. Perhaps she had been little in Society and was protesting a tad too much just to ensure no one could blame her for making the acquaintance too quickly.

That has to be it.

Alexander smiled brightly. "Oh, to be wounded in so public a manner—"

"I cannot make your acquaintance because we are already

acquainted," said the woman curtly. "We are, in a way, related."

Now his smile truly did fade. "We are? Goodness, I have no memory of you at all."

Acquainted? Already? Related?

No, surely not. He would have recalled such a delectable mouth, those large eyes, that impressive bosom—

Alexander had never forgotten a bosom he liked.

But hells bells, if this is another distant cousin, I can't be gadding about admiring bosoms!

"My sister is married to one of your cousins," the pert, little woman said stiffly, as though this were a great personal disgrace and she was not yet over it.

Oh, well. That was a relief.

"I think I would have remembered seeing you at a wedding," he said with a grin.

"And on such an appealing note, I am afraid Miss Harding and I must depart. Good day, my lord," the woman said, pulling her friend away before Alexander could do or say anything.

"Marjorie!"

"It's for your own good," the woman said sternly as the two of them marched away without even a second glance.

Well. The forward Miss Harding glanced over her shoulder twice, one of them a long, lingering glance that told Alexander in no uncertain terms that if he were to follow, she would be quite amenable to another conversation.

But the enigmatic Marjorie…she did not even pause for breath.

Alexander stared, his lips slightly parted. To be dismissed in such a manner, to not even wish to gain his acquaintance—dear God. What was the world coming to?

And as a prickle of discontent curled around his heart, another question rose in his mind that Alexander did not like: Was he truly no longer able to entice a young lady?

Heaven forbid.

"I see you have been abandoned by your potential conquests," said a sharp voice behind him.

Alexander turned on his heels and glared at his sister. "You're one to talk."

"We are not to talk of such a thing in public," their brother Thomas said sternly. "You know how I said. No scandal."

"Yes, yes, you say a great many things," Maude said enigmatically. "You're worse than Papa."

"I am not worse than our father!"

The debate raged, in refined whispers undeniably, around him. Alexander was not listening.

His attention was fixed on the door to the street. Marjorie. Marjorie who? It was not a very common name; there could not have been many of them in Bath.

Stepping away from the furious argument occurring in an undertone—and in public, something their father would not like—Alexander reached the book and glanced down today's entries.

The Baileys, the Ainsworths, the Duke and Duchess of Axwick, the Duke of Gilroyd, the Earl of—ah. There they were.

Miss Catherine Harding…and beneath that, Lady Marjorie Dalton.

Dalton. Surely the daughter of the Marquess and Marchioness of Dalton, until recently the Earl and Countess of Burnell, if he remembered correctly.

Oh. *Oh.* Lady Marjorie Dalton.

He'd recommended her as a suitable bride to Thomas not two years ago. She'd been a pretty thing then, but she'd vanished from Society for a while last year and she was back… looking utterly *transformed.* He would not have known her at a glance. He *hadn't* known her.

And to think, but for the flip of a coin, she might have by now been his sister-in-law instead of Victoria. The thought made him shudder.

But had there been two Dalton daughters? Had one been at finishing school all this time? Which cousin had married a Dalton?

Aside from his brothers, only one of his male cousins was married, and recently so, but had Samuel's new wife's name been *Dalton*? She'd been an actress, hadn't she?

Oh. Oh, yes. Now he remembered. The Daltons were not strangers to scandal themselves.

His sister's voice interrupted his thoughts. "You look distract-ed."

Alexander looked up and forced himself to smile. "I am al-ways attempting to be distracted when Thomas is speaking."

"Oh, he's not so bad. But don't tell him I said that," Maude said lightly. "Looking for the name of your next conquest?"

And in that moment, Alexander's smile became not forced, but utterly genuine.

My next conquest.

Well, why not? He was forced to stay in Bath for the next few weeks while his father conducted some business, and there were only so many games of cards he could play with Maude before he wanted to shove the deck in his ears. True, he was not one to ever actually seduce anyone—he left that for Gascoyne and Percival to enact in his name, and his own willing widows had approached *him* first—but this woman intrigued him, and very few women did that.

Lady Marjorie Dalton. She would be an excellent distraction.

Oh, he wouldn't actually seduce her. That would be a scandal that even the Chance name could not weather.

But tease her, charm her, entice her into a few kisses stolen in libraries or up against a dining table…duck around corners to avoid chaperones and give her a few weeks of ecstasy in Bath before parting forever?

Yes. Oh, that would be a most delightful way to spend the dreary spring in Bath.

"Maude," Alexander said quietly, trying to stifle his smile and not look too wicked. "I have a favor to ask."

Chapter Three

March 5, 1841

MARJORIE HAD BEEN careful, for the duration of breakfast, to be vigilant with her cutlery.

Until now.

"Marjorie!" gasped her mother, her rosebud mouth gaping. She looked utterly scandalized by the sheer nerve of dropping a teaspoon. "Honestly!"

"Your mother and I have raised you to be better than that, Marjorie," said Marjorie's father sternly from the other side of a newspaper. His thinning hair exposed his wide, furrowed brow most pointedly.

"I apologize," Marjorie said softly, keeping her gaze lowered.

They meant well. She knew that, had always known that—well, had known it for most of her life. Her parents had always been stifling, always been well-meaning, had always wished for her betterment and the betterment of the family.

And that meant doing what she was told and not complaining.

Most of the time, Marjorie was able to do just that. She hadn't complained when she had been sent away to school just after Rose had vanished. She hadn't complained when she had been sent abroad last year to Switzerland to be *finished*, her mother complaining that she'd needed a break from London and ought to try something new during the Season of 1840. She hadn't complained when she had been brought back and trotted back out into Society the moment that her older sister had wed.

And she certainly wasn't going to complain that she had received the letter that was now in her left hand, unfolded and only partly read.

Marjorie's eyes widened and her cheeks burned as she took in the very last line of the letter, the place her gaze had moved to understand who could have written to her.

Your very own,
Alexander Chance

Alexander Chance.
Lord Alexander Chance.
He—He had written to her.
Outrageous. *Scandalous!*
Gentlemen did not write letters to ladies to whom they were neither related nor engaged. She was certainly not related to the man, not really. And as for engaged…

Marjorie swallowed, her breath catching in her throat at the very thought of it. *Absolutely not.* The man was a rake! A scoundrel. The very worst sort of cad.

At least, that was what the scandal sheets she had managed to buy with her scant pin money had called him.

"I see that Lady Romeril is back in Bath," said her father, still from the other side of the newspaper.

"How pleasant," her mother said politely. "We shall have to invite her to tea."

"Yes, we shall."

"Indeed."

"Yes."

Marjorie worked hard not to roll her eyes. Her parents were not bad people; at least, the one thing they had done that had been unforgiveable, she had managed to forgive. But they were…good.

That sounded harsh. *They are good people,* Marjorie thought quickly. But they were also very…placid. Calm. Nothing exciting ever happened to a Dalton, and it never had. Other than her sister, who had lost the name of Dalton as soon as she could manage. They permitted Marjorie to attend Society events in the hope of finding her own match.

Presuming that he was an eligible and appropriate young man, obviously. And rich. And titled, ideally. Marjorie had a substantial dowry of her own, but her parents didn't approve of fortune-seeking husbands. Not unless they had something of their own to offer their daughter.

Perhaps, then, if they hadn't wanted to contend with fortune-seeking husbands, they shouldn't have given her such a large dowry. The sum mattered little to Marjorie. After all, it wasn't going to be *she* who got to make use of it.

How nice that would have been, to have the freedom to do with her dowry as she pleased. But nothing so exciting ever happened to her.

The Daltons' days sauntered past from card party to dinner party, nothing ever happening, just…just life.

And Marjorie knew she should have been grateful. It could have been so much worse, of course. Her father could have been a tyrant. Her mother cruel. Their treatment of her sister before her second marriage had been cruel, she could admit, in a fashion, but they had never extended such coldness toward her. She had never done anything to deserve their ire. Her parents could have been short of money, like poor Miss Harding, or they could force her to marry someone she did not like, as that poor Lady Sutherland—the elder Miss Ramsay as had been—had endured last year.

It was just—Marjorie wasn't asking for adventure. Adventure would be too much, even for her, after such a sedate and cloistered life.

Perhaps just a *small* adventure.

"You have received a letter, Marjorie?" her father asked.

Marjorie dropped the letter onto the breakfast table, then hastily snatched it up. The last thing she needed was either of her parents to discover that Lord Alexander Chance, rakehell and rascal, had done something so shocking as to write to her.

"Interesting, is it?" asked her mother blandly, sipping her cup of tea.

Marjorie tried to smile. "I...I haven't read it yet."

Well, that was true. She was not one to lie, and there was usually a way around these things.

"I did not stay above two hours!" She had stayed three.

"I did not speak to a single gentleman." She had spoken to them in pairs.

"I'm not even sure that there was dancing." Fine, that one had been a stretch.

Her mother smiled mildly. "Do not let me interrupt you."

Interrupt me? Oh, something, someone interrupt this dull life, Marjorie thought listlessly.

Then her eyes fell on the letter in her hand. Not him, though. Obviously.

My lady,

I have discovered your name and address from my sister, Lady Maude, who would be pleased to take tea with you at your earliest convenience.

I will admit that I was transfixed, utterly, by the beauty of your demure silence yesterday at the Pump Room and wish to make your better acquaintance. I beg your pardon; I mean, renew your acquaintance. I had not forgotten the shimmering light of your eyes, the way your—

Marjorie snorted.

Yes, that was just like the man. To be sure, she had but a passing acquaintance with the man. How intimate could one be with a gentleman who had been introduced to her, who had barely noticed her, who'd dined with her in large groups twice, and who'd smiled once at her in Hyde Park?

Well—obviously, she was not intimate with *any* gentleman.

"You look a little flushed."

Marjorie's head lurched up. "I'm fine, Father."

Her father looked at her sternly over the newspaper, which he had finally lowered. "Are you certain? That letter isn't too engaging, is it? There is not a new shocking play in town, or a new selection of startling books in the circulating library?"

It was all Marjorie could do not to smile. Or weep. "No, Father. Nothing as wild as all that."

Again, not technically a lie. Good.

> *I had not forgotten the shimmering light of your eyes, the way your very presence rendered me almost speechless—*

Marjorie snorted. *"Speechless,"* indeed! The man had surely never been short of words in his entire life!

"Amusing letter, dearest?" Her mother smiled innocently.

"Some parts are a tad silly, yes," Marjorie said brightly.

Well, she had not lied again. Best to read the rest of this ridiculous letter and be done with it.

And she was most certainly *not* enjoying it.

> *I had not forgotten the shimmering light of your eyes, the way your very presence rendered me almost speechless, yet I wish to repeat the experience. Call me transfixed, and you will not be half wrong.*
>
> *I await your letter of acceptance to tea with my sister and myself at your earliest convenience, and I hope that you do not keep me in suspense overly much.*
>
> *Your very own,*
> *Alexander Chance*

Her very own, indeed. Oh, Marjorie knew what he was up to. At least, she was almost certain she knew what he was up to. She rather hoped she knew what *she* was up to, she realized feverishly, just so she could deny him from having what he wanted to have. If he wanted it.

If he wanted *her*.

It was a wanton thought, and one Marjorie would never dare

to voice aloud.

Besides, *she* did not want *him*. Did she?

"And what are your plans for today, my dear?" asked her mother quietly.

The sound of her mother's teacup being carefully placed in its own saucer somehow seemed to rattle around the room. Marjorie's father looked up, his nose wrinkled and displeasure painted across his face.

"I am sorry," said his wife quietly.

"I plan to do very little," Marjorie said quickly, suddenly conscious that Lord Alexander Chance was not one to wait about. Why, he could be right outside the house at this very moment! "Read, and play the pianoforte, and…and rest."

Her father frowned. "'Rest'? You are ill, then."

"No! No, I… I find myself a touch fatigued from the excitement of attending the Pump Room yesterday." Marjorie smiled, congratulating herself silently for the technical truth she had managed.

"Rose always used to—I mean…" Her mother halted, her nervous eyes flickering to her husband. "Headaches. Very bad."

Marjorie pressed her lips together and said nothing.

Rose.

It was not often her elder sister's name was mentioned in this house. The day after she had run away, leaving a fairly snide note, if Marjorie recalled correctly, her father had declared that Rosemary Dalton's name was never to be spoken again. And it hadn't been.

Until she had returned to polite Society as Rose Chance, Marchioness of Aylesbury.

"Have…" Marjorie swallowed. "Have you seen her?"

Her gaze darted between her parents and saw precisely what she had expected. Her mother longed to see her eldest daughter. Her father would not permit it.

And this, Marjorie thought bitterly, *is why I hate lies so much.* She would not acknowledge the irony, considering her own small lies. But that was it. Hers were *small*.

Liars, all of them! All three of them had conspired to make her believe… It was not worth dwelling on. It simply wasn't.

But she would never suffer a liar—a liar who did more than merely stretch the truth, as she did—in her presence again.

"You look fine," her father snapped, rustling his newspaper as he folded it.

Marjorie smiled weakly. "A quiet day will see me right."

And it was quiet. Very quiet. Painfully quiet.

Dull was not part of the Dalton vocabulary, but it should have been. Boring, uninteresting, staid… Marjorie could think of a great many ways to describe the way she spent the morning and the early part of the afternoon. Luncheon was a quiet affair, just herself and her mother—Lord Dalton was at his club—and Marjorie had resigned herself for a similarly dull rest of the afternoon when Sackville cleared his throat before her.

Marjorie looked up from the book that she'd not been reading. "Yes?"

"A letter for you, Lady Marjorie," the robust butler said. "Brought by a footman."

"'A footman'?" Now that was most odd. Miss Harding's family would not have sent a footman for such things. They had a small staff. But Marjorie was not aware of any other friends in town. Why, so many of them had ventured off to London, where the real excitement was happening.

Sackville proffered the letter on a small silver platter. It was, indeed, a letter. Her name was written on it in a bold hand that made Marjorie's spirits sink.

Oh, dear.

"I… I do not think I should read it," said Marjorie quietly.

She did not need to look up to see Sackville's look of astonishment. "But, Lady Marjorie—"

"Burn it please, Sackville," she asked the servant politely as she resolutely looked away from the enticing letter and back to the volume in her hands, before remembering just how dull it was.

Still, she did not look up until the butler had left the library and closed the door behind him. Only then did Marjorie groan and place the open book across her face.

Another letter from Lord Alexander Chance? Two letters in one day? What on earth did the man think he was playing at?

Fine. She wasn't entirely gormless; innocent and untouched she may have been, but Marjorie was fully aware of what a lady and a gentleman could... Ahem. *Enjoy together.* That was what he wanted, wasn't it?

Wasn't it?

By the evening, however, Marjorie was certain she would go absolutely be mad—or at the very least, be stifled half to death with conversational topics as riveting as button choice, the favored embroidery pattern of the queen, and whether or not tomatoes were truly poisonous. The latter topic had promised at dinner to be at least mildly interesting, but the instant Marjorie had proposed it, her father had stated that gentlewomen did not eat tomatoes, and that was that.

"And where do you think you are going?" asked her mother as Marjorie rose from her seat on the sofa in the drawing room.

"To take some air," Marjorie said, adding hastily, "in the garden, Mama. I will not depart from the house."

"Yes, well, you have been a little caged in today," Lady Dalton said lightly as she stared into the fire. "Get some fresh air."

It was freezing, the night air, but Marjorie inhaled great lungfuls of it just to...just to feel something.

Feel *anything*.

This was to be her life, then. Days after days of doing nothing, saying nothing, thinking nothing, feeling nothing—

A hand grasped her arm. "Marjorie."

"Aarrghhh!" Marjorie whipped around, viciously attacking the brute who had attacked her in her own parents' garden, fists flailing, scream echoing into the night—

"Damn—woman, stop it!"

Marjorie froze.

Oh. Oh, no. Surely not.

Lord Alexander Chance was unfolding from the half-crouched position he had descended into the instant she had started to defend herself.

Defend herself…against the man touching her arm.

Marjorie sniffed and held her head up high. Yes, well, she had not expected such a thing, had she? What woman would expect a stranger's hand on their arm, in the dark, in her own home, from behind?

Despite the frantic beating—well, mostly hand flapping—she had just subjected him to, Lord Alexander did not look in any way offended.

"Goodness, you could give my sister lessons," he said with a chuckle in the darkness. "And that's saying something."

All Marjorie could do was stare.

Lord Alexander. Lord Alexander Chance. In her garden. Her family's garden. At night—at half past ten in the evening!

What on earth did he think he was doing?

"You," she said stupidly.

Lord Alexander gave her a charming smile she was almost certain had rid several widows of their drawers. "Me."

"But—goodness, as if my sister's disappearance and reappearance with a fortune and a title of her own weren't bad enough…"

"Yes, I heard tell of Cousin Samuel's luck in both bridal and the bank account departments." Lord Alexander grinned. "I suppose I can only hope I will be so fortunate."

Heat burned Marjorie's face. *This is not happening. This cannot be happening!* "You can't be here!"

"Hush, no one will ever know of our assignation."

"Assig—this is *not* an assignation!" hissed Marjorie, outrage and surely nothing else heating her as she pulled her shawl tighter around her shoulders. "This is not even a planned meeting!"

Lord Alexander blinked as though she had said something most strange. "It… It is not?"

The nerve of the man! "It most certainly is not!" Marjorie

whispered, hoping to goodness no one from the house was likely to look out of the window and see what could only be described as… Well. *An assignation.* "What on earth are you doing here?"

"But my letter," Lord Alexander said, his furrowed brow a picture of puzzlement. "I said, in the second letter I sent you—"

"I didn't read it, you dolt!" whispered Marjorie irritably, though mostly at herself for not being brave enough to read the thing.

The smile finally left Lord Alexander's face. "You didn't read it."

Marjorie sniffed. Yes. That was right. She had not done anything so scandalous. "I didn't read it."

"I can't believe you didn't read it," Lord Alexander said, his voice full of wonder. "I wrote it in my best hand."

"Well, I didn't read it," Marjorie said coldly.

"I am astonished," he said, and he truly did sound astonished. "You really didn't?"

"For goodness's sake, man, I didn't read it!" snapped Marjorie. Honestly, as handsome as the blaggard was—and he was truly very handsome, especially in the moonlight, which was painfully romantic—he was not particularly quick on the uptake. "I had it burnt."

Lord Alexander stepped toward her, and all of a sudden she was reminded not only of his height, which was significantly greater than hers, but also of his presence.

Commanding. Not domineering; she was not afraid of what he might do.

Only afraid perhaps of what *she* might do.

"You had my second letter *burnt*?" Lord Alexander said quietly, his gaze flickering to her mouth in a most disconcerting way. "And yet you still came out here to meet me?"

"I came out here for some air," Marjorie said defensively, sweeping a hand in a gesture along the terrace. "For a short walk. For some air."

For a moment, he just stared. Then a slow, languid smile

crept across his lips. "We are so in tune, you and I."

Marjorie stared. "I beg your pardon?"

Was the man short of his wits? Was he lost?

How on earth had he managed to get into the garden at the back of the house, anyway?

"Even without reading my letter, we are so in tune that you simply felt within your soul that you had to be out here to meet me," Lord Alexander said with a sigh, clasping his hands to his chest. "Oh, I could not have imagined such intimacy so quickly!"

"It is not—we are not being *intimate!*" Marjorie hissed the last word, hoping beyond hope that her father would not come out to smoke his cigar, as he often did before bed. Lady Dalton had never appreciated cigar smoke in the house. "You must go!"

"Ah, lest our love be discovered—"

"We—We are not in love!" It was all she could do to contain her astonishment.

The man was deranged; at the very least, he had totally lost grip with reality and would need to be taken into the care of his relatives. What did the fool think he was doing?

Speak with calmness, Marjorie told herself. *And kindness.* The poor dear couldn't be blamed for his lapse of reason. "You must go, Lord Alexander. You cannot be here."

Evidently, she was unsuccessful.

"Ah, even the fates will deny us!" Lord Alexander said dramatically, raising a hand to his forehead as though he were about to faint. "And yet our love—"

"Are you utterly idiotic, or is this just a part of your personality?" Marjorie had not intended to snap, but the man had honestly pushed her far beyond the limit.

Handsome sons and brothers of dukes did not turn up in gardens at midnight—fine, at half past ten—to declare love to ladies to whom they had barely spoken in their lives!

It did not happen.

Except for now. Apparently.

Lord Alexander breathed shallowly, taking her in with a

sweep of his heated eyes. "I am always idiotic when in your presence, Lady Marjorie."

Despite herself, despite her better nature, better judgment, and better manners, Marjorie allowed herself just for a moment to believe that all this was real.

Here she stood, on a midnight terrace—almost midnight—with a very handsome man. He was charming. He was tall. He was rich. He was well born. He had a scent to die for and lips that promised diversion. She was standing before him utterly in his power, and if he should choose to lean forward and kiss her most heartily—

Control yourself, Marjorie!

This was not a novel. This was real life, and if someone were to find her out here with a man, any man, there would be a scandal.

To be found with Lord Alexander Chance, rogue of the first degree, would incite a marriage.

Marjorie could not help but smile at the very thought. Well. There were worst things in life, she supposed.

Though she wondered if he would be a faithful husband, considering his reputation. Her smile started to falter.

Clearly, Lord Alexander had failed to see her smile slip and presumed her joy had been elicited thanks to his suave manner, for he leaned forward and cupped her cheek with his hand. "I know you will think this sudden—"

"Sudden and foolish," Marjorie breathed, looking up at him.

"Who has not been a fool for love?" Lord Alexander asked lightly.

And it was that question that, finally, brought her to her senses.

She had not. She had not been a fool for love, had never been a fool for love—and she would be a fool, indeed, if she were to let a flutter of flattery from a man who barely knew her turn her head.

Marjorie Dalton was a lady. She was well bred, well educated, and well on her way to spinsterhood, but she would be damned if she allowed her first kiss to be with a man who clearly knew nothing about her.

Besides, her thoughts raced as Marjorie took a hasty step back and out of the intoxication of Lord Alexander's presence. The man before her had been, if not a fool for love, then been foolish enough to get caught making love to more than one fine lady.

She was not going to be a one in a long line of fools.

"I think it best if you depart," Marjorie said primly, hating how much she sounded like her own mother in that moment. *Dear Lord, that is never a good sign…*

"You are right. I must not play with your honor," Lord Alexander said with a sigh.

Burning heat scalded Marjorie's cheeks. "I should think not!"

"But when can I come to you again?" he continued, earnest beseeching in his eyes.

Oh, it would be so pleasant if I could just forget everything I know of the rogue and enjoy this adventure, Marjorie thought desperately.

Such a shame that she had all the practicality of her mother and the entire lack of imagination of her father.

"You may address me in public, suffice to say, and that is all," she said sternly, hiding swiftly behind the formality with which she had been raised. "That would be proper."

"'Proper'? Yes, a proper way to hide our love."

"Don't be ridiculous," Marjorie snapped, stepping back toward the door now and hating how easy it was to step outside of his lure. "Lord Alexander Chance, you forget yourself."

"I could never—"

"And besides, you forgot me for quite a long time," she added, forcing herself to point out the shame of the not-quite introduction of the Pump Room.

Had that only been yesterday?

A shadow flickered across the man's face. "Yes, and I am sorry for that. You are so changed from when I first saw you years ago."

Changed. So that was his excuse? She could not believe it. "I am not sure you have ever been sorry in your whole life," Marjorie said tartly, her pulse now thrumming. "Not really. I have no interest in—in being wooed, or laughed at, or whatever this is."

Now Lord Alexander's face was serious. "Marjorie—"

"*Lady* Marjorie, and I will thank you to depart the way you came. Whichever way that was." This was a mistake, and she knew she would regret it the moment she got into bed and could finally think clearly—but Marjorie could not allow him to compromise her.

Lord Alexander Chance did not marry the women he compromised.

And she would accept nothing less.

"You are the most beautiful, the most spectacular—"

"If there is one thing I hate more in all the world," Marjorie said coldly, "it is liars. You, sir, are a liar. Goodnight."

She was not going to think about her frantically racing pulse. She was not going to think about it.

"But wait—Lady Marjorie—"

"Goodnight, my lord," Marjorie managed to say. Well, mostly breathe.

As it turned out, the moment she stepped inside and closed the back door—throwing the bolt home for good measure— breathing became rather difficult. Breathing became, in fact, almost impossible.

That man. That odious, handsome, irritating, charming man.

What on earth did he want with her?

Chapter Four

March 8, 1841

"**I**'M JUST SAYING," Alexander hissed, while doing his best to retain a smile, "you don't need a chaperone."

His chest was whacked by a reticule.

"But I may need a bodyguard."

He winced, rubbing his chest and perhaps finally figuring out why his sister had been jilted by her betrothed. "That hurt!"

"Good," said Maude lightly as they continued down Milsom Street at a leisurely pace.

Alexander was certain that it wasn't his turn to…well, what his sister called "acting like a nanny to the eldest-child *baby* in the family," but he actually thought was a mite offensive to babies. Babies didn't whack you with what felt like a brick just because they felt like it.

"What is in there, anyway?" he asked, still rubbing his chest as they passed a gaggle of giggling women that looked most interesting.

"Books."

Alexander whirled his head around to stare at his sister. "'Books'?"

"Yes," said Maude tartly. "They are these little rectangular things."

"I know that. You were never that big a reader, that's all," Alexander protested, gaze flickering over the gaggle of women and finding—much to his surprise—that his spirits sank when he realized there wasn't a single one of them with a rosebud mouth.

A rosebud mouth that had been remarkably close to his own a few nights ago.

He shouldn't dwell on it. He shouldn't dwell on her, except that he did not appear to be able to do anything else *but* think of her.

Lady Marjorie Dalton. She was utterly intoxicating, all the more so because she seemed utterly immune to his charms.

Which was damned rude of her.

"I'll have you know I read *plenty* when you're not around," his sister said, swinging her reticule on her arm. "I have to do something to stave off the boredom since I'm not allowed to go wherever I please *whenever* I please, like my gaggle of brothers." She paused. "That's where we're going. The library."

Alexander groaned.

"The circulating library is very interesting."

"I don't want *interesting*, I want *exciting*," Alexander said with a sigh, wishing to goodness he had managed to sneak away that morning without their mother seeing. "I want—"

"I think we all have a clear idea of what you want," Maude said severely, giving him a look that would have impressed their father to no end. "Do you not think it's time to stop chasing after skirts and…I don't know. Do something with your life?"

Alexander tried not to gape, but it was a hard-won battle. "Now you sound like Papa!"

"I'm just saying, Thomas has the orphanage; he and Victoria have done wonders there," pointed out his sister as they carefully crossed the street, just missing a rattling dog cart that came rumbling around the corner at breakneck speed. "Leopold has been doing a great deal of charity work at the London Archery Club—"

Alexander snorted. "I still think he's only doing that so that he can take his wife of his there and—"

"I don't want to hear it—honestly, *brothers*!" Maude threw up a hand, though she was grinning all the while. "I should have left you all out for the wolves."

Only his sister could insult him in such a manner but make him feel so cared for. "There are no wolves in England, you idiot."

"I should have taken you to Norway, then, and left you there," shot back his sister. "Ah, here we are. The circulating library."

Alexander groaned as he held open the door and resigned himself to the fact that he would now have to spend at least the next half an hour in almost silence, wandering around the bookstacks with nothing to do and no one to talk to.

"Shush!" berated Maude as she stepped inside.

Well, he supposed it wasn't all bad. There was something almost church-like about a library—in fact, it was almost like a cathedral. It wasn't just the high ceilings, although that helped, or the muffled silence, which always made him think of prayer. There was something in the very air, the sense that something important was happening. Something holy.

Alexander shook his head as though attempting to rid water from his ears. What on earth had gotten into him?

"Shush!" his sister hissed.

His jaw dropped. "But I didn't say anything!"

"If you say another word, I'll do worse than whack you with my reticule," Maude said grimly. "Now go and stand over there while I speak to this nice man about ordering some books."

Alexander glanced in the direction his sister had pointed. It was a dark, dingy corner, surrounded on two sides by bookcases packed full of books that appeared to have seen better days.

"Fine." He sighed.

"Hush!" scolded Maude with a grin before wandering over to the bookseller and bringing out a list from her reticule that she started to murmur over.

Alexander could not help but smile in return. There was no one like his sister; his half-sister, he supposed, though Maudey had always been a part of his life and he could not imagine his family without her. Their fathers might have been different, but the Duke of Cothrom had considered Maudey his very own from—almost—the first moment they had met.

That was how the family story went, anyway.

A pair of ladies spotted him and immediately flushed, a most pleasing stroke to his ego—until they turned away and almost *ran* from his presence.

Alexander's smile frowned. *Damn Gascoyne and Sir Percival.* Their exploits with even unwed ladies had tainted his reputation too far. One of these days, he was going to have to do something about that.

His eyes meandered up the tall bookcases as he obediently moved to stand in the corner his sister had gestured toward. There had to be hundreds of books in here—no, thousands. Books that perhaps would never be read, which was a strange thought, indeed.

Alexander brushed his fingertips along a few spines. The heroes in these books probably had no idea, in chapter one, what their tale would...well, entail. They marched into their stories with no knowing what the outcome would be, and each time the pages were opened, along they would go on their merry way, thinking they had any sort of control, when really they had none at all.

His throat was inexplicably dry.

Here he was, surely living a much similar life. Each Season the same, each day the same. Flirting with ladies, attempting to take a widow to his bed and rarely succeeding—not that he had ever permitted his family to discover that his success rate was so low.

He had a tale to tell about himself, after all.

And no income.

That was the rub, the sting in the tale. With no income, he was at the beck and call of his mother and father and now even his eldest brother, and that only made a man feel a child his whole life. And nothing stretched out before him, no opportunity, no change—

The bell of the circulating library jangled and in walked a severe-looking woman with a frown and a pair of spectacles low on her nose. Alexander sighed. She did not look like a merry widow who would flirt with him in a corner.

The bell jangled again, and this time, a pair of young ladies—almost girls, really—rushed into the place and hurriedly hushed their excited chatter.

Alexander smiled. They reminded him of his younger cousins, Teddy and Gwen, all eager exhilaration and delight at entering into Society properly, now that their elder sisters were wed.

The bell jangled again, and in stepped—

Alexander's pulse skipped a beat.

He clutched his chest. Had it really done that? By God, such a thing was only supposed to happen on the stage, wasn't it?

There stood Lady Marjorie Dalton.

She did not have a severe look on her face, but neither was she giggling away. A woman who had to be her mother pointed to a row of bookshelves on the other side of the shop, but Lady Marjorie shook her head slightly, gesturing in the opposite direction. The older woman hesitated, clearly torn, but then nodded and pointed to the door as she murmured something low that Alexander could not catch. Then the mother walked off in the opposite direction, and her daughter took a long, deep breath.

Lady Marjorie did not look dismayed to find herself in the circulating library. No, there was a look of almost reverence on her face, of expectant joy, as though she knew she would find precisely what she wished to here.

Alexander's lips curled into a wicked smile.

And so she would.

"Ah, Lady Marjorie, well met," he said pleasantly in the smoothest and most debonair tone he could manage.

Utterly forgetting where he was.

"Hush!"

"Shhhh!"

"Who said that?"

"Alexander Montague Arthur Chance, if you cannot be quiet, I shall have you decapitated or at the very least, removed!" hissed his sister, her cheeks scarlet as she turned to glare at him from the counter.

Alexander hardly noticed. His attention was entirely fixed on the woman who was now flushing, eyes averted, right before him.

She had halted at the end of his bookshelf row and was staring at him, perfect rosebud mouth agape, in…well, not in horror, Alexander decided awkwardly. At least, it did not appear to be horror.

Why on earth would she be horrified to see him?

"Lady Marjorie—"

But before he could say more, she had bolted.

Not out of the circulating library, for which Alexander was grateful. She had darted to her left, and so he turned right and followed along the seemingly unending lines of bookshelves until…

"Well met, Lady Marjorie," Alexander said in his very best seductive undertone. "And what a delight it is to—oh."

She had gone.

Well, not gone, but she had not remained to hear his winning and wooing ways. Instead, Lady Marjorie had turned on her heels and resolutely started marching away.

Away from *him*? Ladies did not walk away from Lord Alexander Chance!

"Lady Marjorie, I wondered—"

"Go away," hissed the woman with the rosebud mouth.

Go away? Something dark and delicious rebelled against that very edict in his chest, and Alexander quickened his pace. "I only wanted to ask if you might—"

"I had no expectation of seeing you here, and if you even attempt to *pretend* it was arranged by prior meeting—"

"—help my sister," Alexander said desperately.

For some reason, the phrase worked. Lady Marjorie halted, her breathing quick as she turned to stare at him, and Alexander did all he could not to notice how the frantic little inhales were lifting her décolletage most beautifully.

Well. He couldn't *not* notice unreservedly.

"Your sister?" Lady Marjorie said warily. "She is over there, by the counter, is she not? Go and help her over there yourself."

"It is only that I have come here in the hope of purchasing a book to her taste," Alexander said in an undertone, inventing wildly and delighting in the thrill of the chase. Yes, this was what he had missed. This was how the Lady Marjorie could entertain him while he was suffered to chaperone his elder sister. "And I was hoping—"

"She is *your* sister, not mine," said Lady Marjorie stiffly. Her gaze flickered over Alexander's shoulder once again before returning to his face. There was no warmth there.

But there was curiosity. And curiosity he could use.

"It is just, I am not sure what the genteel and respectable lady about town is reading these days," Alexander said, almost apologetically, as though it had been his sacred duty to keep track of these things. "And I was hoping, as you are so refined—"

"How?"

Alexander blinked. That had not been the response he had expected. "I… I beg your pardon?"

Lady Marjorie crossed her arms, drawing even further attention to her bosom. "How do you know I am so refined?"

Ah. Right. Well.

In any other situation, Alexander would have simply opened his mouth and waited for the charm to pour out.

It never usually failed him, after all.

But for some reason, this time, nothing happened. Oh, his mouth opened, his jaw primed, and his lips readied…but no words came. No witty repartee, no clever non sequitur, no jesting tease that would bring both a smile to the lady's lips and a flush to her cheek.

Nothing. Absolutely nothing. Silence.

"I see," said Lady Marjorie darkly.

"How can you?! I haven't said anything!" Alexander protested.

"Hush!"

"Quiet there!"

"This is a *library*!"

Alexander tried to smile through the awkwardness as the barrage of hushing and shushing erupted over him from all directions. Thankfully, his sister was otherwise engaged in what appeared to be a vicious negotiation with the bookshop owner and so had not gifted him with a particularly sharp rebuke, silent or otherwise.

Lady Marjorie was still glaring at him.

"I cannot understand what I have done to offend you," Alexander said helplessly, attempting to use a tool in his skillset on which he rarely had to rely: the truth. "All I have done—"

"All you have done is send me at least one, perhaps two, unequivocally outrageous letters and *attempt to seduce me* in the moonlight!" hissed Lady Marjorie, her cheeks really pinking now. "I am not impressed, and I am not amused, and I am not your— your plaything!"

Alexander swallowed. *Well, when she puts it like that, it's not exactly my most impressive moment.*

Still. No one else had ever complained.

"All I wish—"

"I know precisely what it is you *wish*, and I can tell you now, absolutely not!" Lady Marjorie spoke warningly in an undertone, glancing about her as though worried a curious bystander had silently crept up behind her to eavesdrop.

Which, knowing Bath, was not completely impossible.

"But I—"

"And you are not as charming as you think, or as clever as you think, or as handsome as you think," continued Lady Marjorie, evidently warming to her theme now even as Alexander's throat tightened in something akin to embarrassment. "I am not spending my days sighing at my window hoping that you'll call, I don't look for you in a crowded ballroom hoping you will ask me to dance, and when we were first introduced—"

"'First introduced'? That again?"

Alexander had no intended to interrupt her, but he could not help himself.

He'd made a mistake in not recognizing her at the Pump Room. He could admit that. But would she blame him for that forever? She had changed since he'd first noticed her years before. Changed from lovely—a catch for the unadventurous man seeking a bride, an heiress somewhere at the back of his thoughts—to incomparable. At the Pump Room, he had been captivated by a rosebud mouth and a pair of beautiful eyes that had refused to meet his own.

Lady Marjorie had no such issue now. Her stare was firmly locked on his own, and Alexander found much to his chagrin that it was he who was finding it a challenge to maintain the connection.

"Yes, *that again*," she said quietly as a rustle of silks suggested that a lady was walking slowly down the line of bookcases to their right. "You are so accustomed to ladies falling at your feet that you have forgotten, my lord, that we have minds and brains and choices."

"Now hang on there!" protested Alexander sharply.

Well, he may have been a cad, and a rake, and sometimes a rogue—but he was hardly the sort of man to ignore a woman's consent.

"Have a heart, woman," he continued sharply. "I have never forced a lady into anything she didn't want."

"Oh, I am sure you have not," answered Lady Marjorie, her eyes gleaming. "But you have never had to persuade her, either."

Alexander blinked. "I… I beg your pardon?"

Lady Marjorie lifted her eyes to the heavens, and a prickle of discomfort skimmed down his spine.

Was he truly so awful a conversationalist that a lady had to reach to the skies for the very patience with which to speak with him?

And for the first time in his life—yes, the first time he could ever remember—something like uncertainty trickled into Alexander's heart.

It was not working.

He had smiled, and flattered, and charmed in the best tradition of the roguish gentleman—and it had not worked.

Lady Marjorie was not simpering. She was not sighing. She was not even smiling.

It was most irregular.

"You know, Lady Marjorie, I…I believe we have got off on the wrong foot," said Alexander awkwardly, delicately feeling his way through a type of conversation he had never had with a woman before. An honest one. "I… Well, dash it all, I never intended to offend you."

"And yet here we are," said Lady Marjorie, her nose tilted upward. "I do not pretend to be an important lady about town, my lord. My father has a title, yes, but I would not say I am from a fashionable family, despite our wealth—"

"Lady Marjorie—"

"—yet I know my worth."

It was the way she said it: so utterly certain, even in the softness of her tone, that it made something in Alexander's stomach lurch.

"You do," he said quietly. It was not a question. It was not really even a statement. No, it was a response to what she had said and how she had said it, the inaudible inevitability, the knowledge that what she'd said was not only incontrovertibly true, but that there was absolutely nothing he could say to dissuade her.

It was intoxicating.

"And now you are going to attempt to flirt with me in some awful manner that I am sure works on most ladies in Society,"

Lady Marjorie said in a hiss, grabbing a book without looking at it from the shelf beside her and marching past him. "And I have no interest in engaging in such affectations."

"Lady Marjorie." Alexander had spoken without thought, moved without thought—the very idea of her departing from his presence was painful somehow, and so he did the only thing he could think of to prevent it.

He reached out.

Lady Marjorie flinched as though he had burned her, the very slight contact between them—his gloved hand grazing her arm— somehow enough to force a ricochet throughout Alexander's entire body.

He staggered back, the bookcase behind him the only thing preventing his fall to the ground.

"Good day, my lord," Lady Marjorie said quietly, something intangible in her eyes that he greatly wished to study.

There was no time. She had turned, marched away, ex-changed a few hurried words with the bookseller—Maude glancing over her shoulder with arched brows and a tilted head as this had occurred—and then had swept out of the circulating library and, presumably, out of his life.

Alexander stood in absolute shock.

What... What just happened?

This had never happened before. Ladies did not march from him—at least not twice, and by his count that was the third time Lady Marjorie Dalton had done so.

What had she heard of him that was so distasteful? Alexander racked his brains but could think of nothing. Did not ladies like experienced gentlemen? Were they not intriguing, enticing, beguiling, exactly what a young lady would wish for? It was why he had accepted Gascoyne's and Percival's requests to use his name in their seductions, an attempt to impress.

Though admittedly, they may have targeted an unmarried lady of Society a time or two in these games. He could not have his name associated with that, and he'd told them so. Whether they kept to their promises or not, he could not be certain. Was that, then, what Lady Marjorie feared? That he would seduce her and leave her, ruin her reputation and ability to ever make a match?

He would never. Not least of which because his parents would never allow him to drag down the Chance name that way.

True, he had accosted her late at night in the garden without a chaperone present, but that was the point, wasn't it? Don't get caught, and no one would ever know. Her reputation had not suffered, as there had been no witnesses. How was he to properly seduce a lady with an old biddy or the like watching over him like a jailer?

His friends' games had led Lord Alexander Chance to become the most notorious lover in England. Which was ironic, considering he'd only bedded—

This wasn't helpful.

"You weren't very helpful."

Alexander blinked. His sister was standing before him with her arms full of books. "I—I wasn't?"

Maude rolled her eyes. "Come on. We're leaving," she said in an undertone, grabbing his arm and marching him toward the door.

He followed her in a complete daze. How had this happened? Had his flirting technique really suffered that dramatically in the three days since he had first met the transformed, goddess-like version of Lady Marjorie—had it been three days? Three years? He could hardly tell.

Alexander blinked in the bright sunlight as he stepped onto the pavement. Lady Marjorie was nowhere to be seen; she had either darted down a side street, jumped into a carriage, or run so quickly that her skirts would have been flying.

All on her own. She'd arrived with her mother and yet had left without a chaperone. Scandalous behavior from this woman so keen to avoid a scandal with him.

So keen, she'd *run away* from him. It was madness! It was

nonsensical. It was certainly far more frustrating a situation than Alexander had ever experienced.

"Oh, dear," said a voice lightly, utterly unconcerned. "You appear to have mislaid your conquest."

Alexander whirled around, glaring at his older sister. "If you don't have anything nice to say…"

"It did not appear that you had anything nice to say to that pleasant Lady Marjorie." Maude sniffed, stuffing what appeared to be several books into a reticule far too small. The thing wouldn't close, and she glared at it just as she'd glared at him. "Honestly, Alexander, why must you push your attentions where they are not wanted?"

Not wanted?

Alexander swallowed. But they had been, for a moment. When Marjorie—when *Lady* Marjorie had forgotten herself, and her duty, and her reputation, when it had just been the two of them, a moment between them in which the whole of Society had faded…

Then she had permitted herself to realize that she wanted him.

Something dark stirred within him, and he knew it was something he should probably not pursue.

It appeared that Lady Marjorie was not going to be the sort of woman who eagerly accepted his advances, allowed his kisses, then pined after him as he disappeared.

Alexander had never worried about such encounters. He was careful about not being caught—as he knew even just being *alone* with an unwed woman of Society could lead her father to demand marriage. Alexander would not be obliged to follow through, but he was not such a cad that he would lead a lady to suffer and walk away in such a position. His father certainly wouldn't let him do that, either. He never promised more than he gave, and matrimony was certainly never a topic of conversation. If young ladies were to infer far more than that, well, that was their affair.

And so it was most discomforting for something unpleasant and previously unknown to twist in his gut.

Guilt.

Had he been…well, a tad lackadaisical with his attentions in the past?

Worse, was he forcing his attentions onto Lady Marjorie Dalton when they were truly unwanted?

He had never considered it before. A woman of Society, unwilling to be flirted with—flirted with by him? It was unthinkable. It was unconscionable.

It was most unpleasant.

"I…" Alexander swallowed. No words came. How could he articulate the rush of heady emotions, both pleasant and unpleasant, that had roared through his mind?

His sister glanced at him with a grin, but the grin faded as she took in his expression. She halted right outside the circulating library and took his arm, saying quietly. "Zander? Zander, are you quite well?"

No, he wanted to say. *No, I feel most unwell.*

And I have absolutely no idea what to do about it.

Chapter Five

March 11, 1841

I T WAS AN unquestionably beautiful day. Such a shame that she hated it, and everything in it.

"Smile, Marjorie!" trilled her mother desperately. "Smile!"

She was not going to smile. What was there to smile about?

Another dull invitation to another dull party—a garden party in March, honestly!—hosted by one of her mother's innumerable friends, none of whom had ever bothered to remember Marjorie's name. Or her mother's, though at least they could remember the marchioness's title. Well, sometimes. As she had been lately a countess instead of a marchioness, there were a few who forgot about the new title.

It was all so…so false. Society was just this strange façade of manners that no one liked to follow and followers whom no one really liked, and Marjorie was sick of it. Sick of it, sick of him—

Do not think of him.

But it was too late. As the carriage carrying the Daltons rumbled and rattled across Bath, Marjorie was unable to stem the tide of memories of the man she had offended so harshly but three days ago.

"You are so accustomed to ladies falling at your feet that you have forgotten, my lord, that we have minds and brains and choices."

Marjorie cringed against the carriage seat. Oh, dear Lord, what on earth had possessed her to speak in such a manner?!

Well. She knew what. The absolute indignity of the man attempting to seduce her without even bothering to get to know her.

Wait—that wasn't right. It wasn't as though she would have permitted him to seduce her if he *had* bothered to get to know her.

Would she?

"There it is," Lady Dalton said genially as Marjorie's lips turned up at the corners at the very thought of Lord Alexander Chance bothering to have a conversation with her that was actually about her. "There's the smile."

Marjorie immediately quelled the smile. "And whose garden party is this, Mama?"

"One of your father's friends," her mother said with a nonchalant wave of her hand. "Some viscount or some other. I think."

Some viscount or some other. Excellent. That was helpful.

"Whose garden party is this, Father?" Marjorie asked politely, her gaze shifting to her other parent.

Her other parent was asleep.

"Father!"

"What?" Lord Dalton grunted, opening one beady eye and examining his daughter vaguely. "What?"

"Whose garden—never mind," said Marjorie with a sigh as she turned her head to watch Bath speed by them.

Never mind, indeed. Neither of her parents seemed to mind very much how their days progressed, one after the other. Each day was mostly the same, each week mostly like the one before that. Were they not bored? Did they not tire of the same mindless, endless repetition of events?

"I wonder if this garden party will a repetition of last year's garden party," said her mother brightly. "I hope it is!"

Marjorie sank lower in her seat.

It was not that she did not love her parents. She did love them, and in many ways, she was grateful to them for all that they had done and continued to do for her. A roof over her head, sufficient pin money for a set of new gowns and accoutrement every year, delicious food and a pianoforte and visits to the opera... All the things she had thought, when she had been young, that she wanted.

Marjorie bit her lip. And yet none of them truly satisfied.

Besides, she could never truly forget the way they'd treated her sister, no matter what Marjorie thought of her elder sister's wild ways, nor the great harm they had done Marjorie herself eight years ago. Oh, nearly a decade had passed and she had learned to live with it, to live with them. But the trust had gone.

She could not trust someone who lied when it really mattered.

"Ah, here we are," said her mother warmly as the carriage slowed and halted before a townhouse that was just as splendid as theirs.

Almost identically as splendid as theirs.

They had returned to their original street.

"I think there may have been a mistake," said Marjorie slowly, exiting the carriage on her father's hand and looking, befuddled, up and down the street. "Is that not our home?"

It was. It was also three doors down from the townhouse where their carriage had deposited them.

"Yes, it is," said her mother lightly, fussing over her gown and attempting to smooth out a crease Marjorie could not see.

"So...we got into the carriage, drove about Bath for twenty minutes, then...returned home," Marjorie said slowly, looking between her parents and hoping there would be at least some sense to be found in the conversation.

Her father nodded. "Precisely."

Marjorie gave up. "And why, exactly?"

"We could hardly arrive at a garden party on foot, could we?" the marchioness said in an undertone, as though to even think of such a thing was mortifying, indeed. "Absolutely not!"

"We must think of our reputation," the marquess said seriously, as though someone had attempted to besmirch said reputation. "Is it not obvious?"

Marjorie sighed.

Perhaps it was obvious, when her father put it like that. But could neither of her parents see the sheer ridiculousness of what they had just done?

Her eyes darted over to their home, three doors to the right.

Well. What was done was done. All she had to do now was enjoy the garden party, whosever it was.

"Now remember, try not to enjoy the garden party too much," her father warned in an undertone as they were welcomed into the townhouse, had their pelisses and coats removed, then followed the portly butler and a lanky footman down a corridor with twists and turns until it opened out into the garden...which they did not step out into until the footman had replaced their pelisses and coats around their shoulders.

Marjorie could scream. It was all so preposterous! Did no one else see it? Was she the only person in the entirety of Society who realized that half of the nonsense they all did was just that: nonsense?

Going through all the pomp of having her pelisse removed, only to have it returned to her less than a minute later?

Oh, it made her want to scream!

"Marjorie?"

Marjorie blinked. Her mother had evidently said something, for she was looking at her daughter expectantly.

"Marjorie?" Lady Dalton said, a tad more sharply this time, inclining her head to the woman who had joined them with a slight widening of her eyes. "Are you not delighted to be here?"

Marjorie focused. It was Lady Romeril. This was not the time to be screaming into the abyss, then. "Very delighted," she said quietly.

Lady Romeril sniffed, a coil of her white hair bouncing over her rouged cheek. "I wish I could believe you, Lady Marjorie, but there we are."

Oh, dear. If she had known that it was Lady Romeril who was hosting this particular garden party, and not "a viscount or some other," she most certainly would have paid attention.

Marjorie tried again. "And it is so gracious of you to invite us, Lady Romeril, I am most pleased to—"

"Yes, yes, I think we gained the truth the first time around." Lady Romeril sniffed again, but there was a twinkle in her eye this time. "The young people are gathered about over there in the grove, Lady Marjorie. I am sure you would like to join them."

It was not exactly a dismissal, but Marjorie was not foolish enough to loiter where she was evidently not wanted.

The garden was large, as was her own. Marjorie tried not to smile as she meandered slowly along the gravel path that ambled past some pretty flowerbeds—or at least, they would be pretty once spring had properly sprung—toward the grove of silver birch trees, where indeed there were some younger people. Most of the older generation—her parents' generation, that was—was chattering on the terrace, standing close to the braziers that Lady Romeril's footmen occasionally stirred with long pokers.

Genteel laughter and chatter emanated from the group within the silver birches, but as Marjorie grew closer to them, she found her feet dragging.

"—and she actually wore it a second time?"

"—so embarrassed, I hardly knew where to look—"

"—the same gown for the opera and the theater!"

Marjorie halted, distaste stirring within her.

She herself was not the most fashionable of women. She knew that. Not even spending the past year at finishing school could change her mind on that point. It did not delight her to read through pages and pages of catalogs from London's and Paris's greatest modistes. She had never bothered to properly learn the difference between a blind hem and an overlocked hem, and when she thought of scallops, it was not hems, but delicious food that her mind conjured. If she wore the same gown to the opera and then another night to the theater, she was almost sure she would not have noticed.

But others did.

The discomfort stirring in her blossomed into downright

distaste. Marjorie could hardly retreat from a conversation that she had not even yet joined, but her interest in talking with such people was dampened.

After all, what might they say about her once she departed from their company?

Unease twisted in Marjorie's stomach. She also did not wish to return to her parents. The conversational topics there would be matrimonial, mostly, she was certain. The older generation would be looking over at the younger generation, wondering who would pair up with whom…

So. Neither it was, then.

Thankfully, as they were still on the same street as her own home, Marjorie considered wryly, she could approximate the rough layout of Lady Romeril's garden almost exactly. If it were anything like her own, there would be a path behind a hedge where the gardeners…*yes, here we go*, and it would lead to…

In Marjorie's own garden, it led to a shed that was double width and provided a space for their gardener both to store the copious gardening equipment apparently necessary to keep a garden happy and to pot up small plants into bigger pots to keep them happy.

In Lady Romeril's garden…

"Goodness," whispered Marjorie, her eyes lighting up.

It was beautiful. A gazebo, in the latest fashion—goodness, it could not have been long since Lady Romeril had had the thing built. Roses had already trailed up one side, a rambling rose species of currently indeterminate color, and what appeared to be a wisteria stump was mostly dormant on the other side. Inside the gazebo was seating, encircling the interior, covered in cushions and throws, and all the comfort that could be provided.

The tension drained from Marjorie as she strode forward, eager to sit and rest and wait out the rest of the—

Another figure had barreled toward the gazebo from another path that Marjorie had not noticed, and the resulting crash between them knocked her head, causing it to spin, but it was not merely the physical impact responsible. The person's scent was—oh, it was delicious. Warm and spiced and sparking something within her that had only happened on a few occasions.

A few, very specific occasions.

Marjorie groaned as she straightened up and the apologizing figure spluttered into silence. "Not you!"

"So sorry, I didn't see—Lady Marjorie?"

Of course it had to be Lord Alexander Chance.

All the wind had been knocked out of her when he had knocked into her in turn; at least, that was what Marjorie was telling herself. There surely could have been no other reason for this tightness in her lungs, this shock of need—wait a moment. *Need?*

"Are you going to follow me everywhere around Bath?" she hissed, allowing her anger to vent through her mouth as she tried not to think about the fact that she was alone with him.

Alone with Lord Alexander Chance.

The gentleman blinked, seemingly just as dazed as she was. "'Follow' you?"

"My garden, the circulating library, Lady Romeril's garden party—"

"The circulating library—I was there with my sister!" Lord Alexander protested, with what sounded like a particularly innocent voice.

"—and—oh. Yes. You were." Marjorie bit her lip. She had momentarily forgotten that fact, faced as she was with the impressive stature of the man, as well as the irritatingly enticingness of the man.

Enticingness? Was that even a word?

"And it is not my fault that I was invited to Lady Romeril's garden party," pointed out the handsome—the *irritating*, Marjorie internally corrected—lord. "Half of Bath appears to be invited, and it would have been rude of me not to attend after my mother accepted on my behalf."

"Yours does that too?" The words had slipped from Marjorie's mouth before she had even thought them.

Lord Alexander's eyes twinkled. "Look, I am sorry for rushing into you. I was just trying to escape—I mean, find a place to sit. In quiet."

Marjorie swallowed.

There was such an aura of goodness about the man when he looked at her like that. As though butter wouldn't melt.

Though now that she came to think about it, hadn't there been that rumor about a year ago, about him and Lady Quintrell, and a stick of butter that would almost certainly have melted—

Marjorie shook her head. "I...I..."

"I have no demands to make upon your time," Lord Alexander said with a bow, gesturing to the gazebo. "I merely wish to repose. Good afternoon, Lady Marjorie."

The gentleman straightened from his bow and walked away and up onto the steps into the gazebo.

Away from her.

Strange flutterings were stirring within Marjorie's stomach, and it took her several heartbeats to understand precisely what they were.

Anger.

Not that he had walked into her. Marjorie could accept, just about, that she had not been looking where she was going, and so she was at least equally to blame for such an encounter.

No, what was infuriating her was that Lord Alexander was now walking away.

From her!

Wasn't he supposed to be violently in love with her? Had he not spouted utter nonsense to gain her attention? Had he not been eager for her company only the last time they had seen each other?

And now—what, he could just walk away as though her presence were nothing more than—

Marjorie just about managed to catch herself before she'd permitted that train of thought to entirely lose her senses.

You do not care about Lord Alexander, she reminded herself sternly, not quite able to draw her eyes away from the nonchalant man who was now seated in the gazebo and looking about him, as though he had seen nothing so interesting in his life before. She did not like the man. She was not enamored with him, she did not crave his touch, and she was glad—*glad* that he clearly had no wish to speak with her.

Right. Good.

But in that case, Marjorie considered rapidly, if he did not wish to speak to her, then to leave would be to give him exactly what he wanted. And she'd be damned if she gave Lord Alexander Chance what he wanted…which meant the correct thing to do would be to sit in the gazebo with him.

Yes—that was right, wasn't it?

Lord Alexander's eyes gleamed as Marjorie haughtily stepped up into the gazebo and sat about a foot from him. "My lady."

Marjorie smiled, despite herself, heat rising in her as she looked at him.

Wait a moment. Has my logic gotten away from me somewhere?

"I did not take you as someone who would hide away from a crowd," Marjorie said quietly. Or stiffly. *Had* she said that stiffly? Aloofly?

Aloof, that was probably what she should aim for, but all she seemed to have managed was cold.

The slight smile that had danced across Lord Alexander's lips disappeared. "Tempting as it is to lie to you, Lady Marjorie, I now know your feelings on that score. It was my sister who wished to attend and my mother volunteered me as her chaperone."

For some reason, a frown appeared, creasing the handsome man's forehead, before it disappeared. But it had definitely been there.

A frown, and connected to his sister, too. Now *that* was most interesting. Marjorie had always been very careful not to inquire too closely about the Chance family—her father had paled quite dreadfully the one time she had spoken of them, a family beset with outrageous behavior now surprisingly connected to their own through Rose—but she had never heard anything about the Lady Maude.

Nothing at all, now that she came to think about it. And was that not odd in and of itself? That a lady of the family should have no gossip, no snippets of stories that had made it into Society?

The fact that he had paid attention to what she had said in her garden was neither here nor there. She did not care. Not at all.

"Your sister is more sociable than you?"

The question was inane, and so Marjorie was a tad surprised to see Lord Alexander smile again—this time, far more warmly.

"Maude has always been more sociable than I am. When she came to live with my father—"

"'Came to live with' him?" Marjorie had not intended to interrupt, but she'd needed to ask the question immediately. It was an odd turn of phrase.

Lord Alexander's eyes danced with mischief. "You never heard of the scandal?"

"No," Marjorie said instantly.

Not quite. That should have been the accurate answer, for now he'd said such a thing, something deep in her whispered about something she had once heard. The Duke and Duchess of Cothrom—the older couple, now that the dowager duke had officially handed his title to his son—had there not been something interesting when they had wed? It had been before her time, before she had even been born...but hadn't Miss Harding once whispered something?

"Well, 'tis no great scandal, really," Lord Alexander was saying brightly, clearly no shame in his countenance. "My mother was married before she met my father, and Maude was the result."

"Oh." That indeed did not sound much like a scandal at all. "So she is not your full sister, then."

"Maude is my sister. Parentage has naught to do with such a thing," Lord Alexander said, his voice not exactly aggressive, but with a certainty and grounding that made it clear there was not only no argument to be made, but no possible thought of disagreeing. "Maude has always been my sister, and she always will be."

In that moment, that brief moment of frankness, Marjorie could not help but smile. There was a protective brotherly quality about him then, something glittering in the eyes and firm in the jaw, that made the man almost…kind.

"My mother always jested that she was always destined for two great loves," her youngest son said, tilting his knees toward her and fixing Marjorie with a brief smile. "Two love lines, she said."

"'Two—Two love lines'?"

She was not talking of love, not really, Marjorie told herself determinedly. It was just…just polite conversation.

With a rogue.

"Yes, in her palm." As though to demonstrate precisely what a palm was, Lord Alexander removed his glove and leaned his hand forward. "See?"

Marjorie acted before she could think, leaning forward to examine his hand.

It was a nice hand. As gentlemen's hands went. Now that she came to think of it, she had not spent a great deal of time examining a man's hand. As she peered at Lord Alexander's hand, she saw that it was large, larger than hers, with a softness to the palm she had not expected, and a strength in his thumb and digits she had. Dark-brown hair grazed the backs of his fingers, and as he widened them, he pointed out two lines etched onto his palm.

"There," Lord Alexander said quietly. "I have but the one love line. My mother has two."

Marjorie could not help herself. Before she truly knew what she was doing, she had pulled off her own glove and was holding it out to the man who, only days ago, she had impugned greatly—and in public.

"And what about me?" she asked softly, the quiet of the garden suddenly deafening in her ears. "How many great loves will I have?"

Lord Alexander shifted along the gazebo seat until his hip bumped up against hers, but her gasp was lost in his words. "Let's have a look, shall we?"

And Marjorie had gasped again, for he had taken her hand, her actual hand, and had lifted it up with a close examination that absolutely should *not* have made her pulse quicken and her arm warm.

His… His attention. That was all it took for her body to heat, and Marjorie had never known the complete focus of another person upon her in quite such a way.

It was intoxicating. It was too much. It was everything she wanted.

"Hmmm," said Lord Alexander, seemingly utterly unaffected by their sudden intimate proximity. "I can see but one love line here."

"Oh?" Marjorie leaned forward to attempt to see what he was seeing, bringing her forehead so close to his, she had to be incredibly careful not to touch him.

She *must not* touch him.

"Yes, see here? One love line, but a deep one. One that lasts almost all your life. A love… A love that is uninterrupted," murmured Lord Alexander, his voice a low thrum that was absolutely not causing her to melt inside. "Oh, and Lady Marjorie?"

"Yes?" whispered Marjorie, looking up.

This gasp was not heard, but swallowed—swallowed up into the kiss that Lord Alexander pressed upon her astonished lips.

She did not remain astonished for long. Though Marjorie knew she should have been outraged, offended, insulted, knew she should have pulled away, knew she should have marched back to her parents and refuse to ever see him again…

How could she, when the man was rippling such sweetness through her?

Just a kiss. Just his lips on hers. Just the knowledge that the gazebo was flying into the air, that the Earth had stopped spinning, that nothing in the world would ever be the same again.

The pressure of his lips, the certainty of the man, the way Lord Alexander knew precisely how she wanted to be kissed—Marjorie clung to him, her hands somehow around his neck and his hands inexplicably cupping her face. She never wanted this moment to end, never wanted this soaring to—

"Marjorie?"

The kiss ended.

"Marjorie, are you behind this infernal hedge?"

"Th-That…" Marjorie attempted to breathe again. How was breathing such a challenge? "That is my father."

"Marjorie?"

"Then you should go," whispered Lord Alexander, looking deep into her eyes.

He did not move. He did not retreat, removing his presence from her. He did not lean back. He did not release her face.

And Marjorie did not want him to.

"Alexander—"

"Marjorie, we're leaving!"

With a groan that escaped her lungs like a cry for help, Marjorie dragged herself away from the man who should absolutely not have been kissing her, and half ran, half tripped down the steps back to the garden.

"There you are," her father said sourly as she turned a corner around a hedge and saw him pulling his greatcoat closer to him. "We're leaving."

"We are?"

"Your mother has a megrim," Lord Dalton snapped. "Have you said goodbye to everyone you wish to?"

Quite against her wishes, Marjorie refused to permit herself to turn around. Either Lord Alexander Chance had followed her out of the gazebo, or he hadn't. And she didn't wish to know either way.

"Y-Yes," she said quietly. "Yes. I think so."

Chapter Six

March 14, 1841

ALEXANDER'S OLDER BROTHER sighed. "I'm not sure what more you could have done."

Alexander groaned. "Don't give me that."

"Well, unless there's something you're not telling me—and I know you, so there is almost certainly something you're not telling me—you have done nothing to harm nor offend the woman," Leopold said, his brows puckered in either worry or concentration as he looked down his cue. "But it's you. So."

It was supposed to be a calming game of billiards. That was what Alexander had hoped for; his brother had called by, supposedly to speak to their other brother, Thomas, about some sort of financial thing—Alexander hadn't really paid attention; no one ever talked money to him because he had none—and he'd thought, *Well. Billiards. That's relaxing.*

It didn't feel relaxing now. It felt like an interrogation.

"And what, precisely, is that supposed to mean? *It's me?*" Alexander asked as icily as he could manage as he watched his older brother take the shot and perfectly pot the ball.

When Leopold straightened, it was with a wry look on his face. "You know precisely what that is supposed to mean, Zander. You're a rake and a cad, utterly untrustworthy—"

"Steady on there!" protested Alexander sharply.

"—and you still owe me twenty pounds, which by the way, I have utterly given up hope of seeing," continued his brother doggedly, grinning as he leaned back against the wall and gestured to the table between them. "Your shot."

It was most unpleasant of his brother to mention that small debt. For it *was* small—what was twenty pounds between family, after all?

Something stirred, uncomfortably, in Alexander's stomach. *Or had it been forty pounds? Were both he and Leopold forgetting some wager or another?*

"Lady Marjorie Dalton is from a good family," Leopold continued, as though Alexander had invited him to continue offending him. "Why on earth would she wish to associate with the likes of you?"

"Hang on—"

"Your reputation is shot, man, you must know that. No lady is ever likely to accept your advances or proposals of marriage."

Heat was pouring through Alexander's bones. "I had no intention of proposing marriage to her. Or any other lady!"

"And why not?" Leopold's look was steady, drilling into Alexander's skull in a manner most unlike him. "What is wrong with Lady Marjorie Dalton as a bride?"

Alexander bit down the obvious answer.

Nothing.

There was absolutely nothing wrong with Lady Marjorie Dalton—in fact, there was a great deal right. The woman was beautiful, in that style that was getting ignored at the moment. Rosebud lips, not fashionable? It was a disgrace.

She was bright. She had certainly seen through him within half a minute every time they conversed. Not a skill Alexander wished to encourage in young ladies throughout Society, but certainly one which was tantalizingly intriguing.

And she had kissed like…like she had never kissed a man before.

Alexander's stomach lurched. And perhaps she had not. Perhaps he had been the first to taste of that fruit.

A snap, a roll of balls, a thunk as two of his targets dropped into pockets.

"I'll tell you what is wrong with Lady Marjorie," Leopold continued, as though Alexander's thoughts had not rushed across town and lingered on the delightful form of the woman in question. "She did not immediately simper, lie down, and lift her skirts for you to—"

"*Leopold!*"

"Well, you know what I mean," shot back his older brother.

For some inexplicable reason, Alexander found his cheeks were burning.

Am I…embarrassed? Surely not.

Perhaps he was mortified at the thought of Lady Marjorie hearing the two of them speak in such a way. Yes, that had to be it.

Or perhaps it was—and this was rather more likely—that he had tired, finally, of his family thinking the worst of him.

Oh, they had plenty of reason to think so. He had hardly been perfect in his youth, but it had been when he had started to permit others to utilize his name as part of their amorous adventures that things had truly gone wrong.

Honestly, Alexander had been quite offended that people had so swiftly believed it. Seducing Lady Axwick and the Dowager Duchess of Gilroyd in one night? When the two lived on utterly different ends of London?

Ridiculous.

But people had believed it. They had always been prepared to believe the worst of him, even his family. Now he had a reputation for bedding widows and stealing kisses from debutantes, and although he had done a little of the latter, he had rarely enjoyed the former.

Not that he was ever going to admit to that.

Drawing himself up as sternly as possible—a spot challenging, when one hardly had the moral high ground—Alexander tried to look down his nose at his brother. This was difficult, considering that it was his, Alexander's, turn at the billiards table. "You must think me more than a rake, a scoundrel!"

Why he had allowed this to continue for so long, he hardly knew. It had seemed like nothing more than a game at first, a favor to a couple of friends—and who would not help their friends?

Now that his reputation had been utterly soiled, even with his own siblings, Alexander was starting to wonder what he had gained from the entire experience.

To be sure, there were certain ladies who sought out supposedly dangerous flirtations—even if momentary—with a rake. There were even some widows, Alexander had discovered, who found the company of a supposed rascal like himself far more interesting than that of anyone else.

And then...then there were those who ignored him. Eschewed him. Downright avoided him, which was never a fun experience and one that had only seemed to be increasing, these days.

It was mortifying. It was frustrating. It was precisely what he should have expected.

"It's not that I think you a scoundrel, per se," pointed out Leopold, unhelpfully reasonably. "It just that any gentleman carrying on the way you do has earned that name three times over. Why would you be any different?"

"Any different to what?" came a voice that made Alexander's spirits sink.

It was not that he did not like the man who had just entered the billiards room. He liked him fine enough; it was just that sometimes, he wondered whether the gentleman in question liked *him*.

William Chance, the Dowager Duke of Cothrom, respected nobleman and Alexander's father, entered the room. He did so with a frown. "Any different to what?" he repeated.

Alexander looked immediately at his brother, who had colored and was babbling something wholly indistinct.

"Oh, you know, you've seen how it is, and obviously, it's never, I mean, not often—"

"We are discussing my moral character, Father," Alexander said stiffly, holding the billiards cue like a pike by his side.

His father caught his eye, then looked away immediately. "I see."

So he did. And so did Alexander.

Oh, there had been no point attempting to be as good and as beloved as Thomas when they had been children. Thomas was the heir—though it had scandalized most of Society when their father had given up the title a little over a year ago—and moreover, other than a short spurt of well-intentioned poor choices regarding the family fortune, Thomas was the one who got these sorts of things right. It was though he had been born just knowing what to do and why to do it, Alexander had always thought. Even his mistakes with the family's wealth had been corrected easily enough with his choice of bride. Though that did remind Alexander that Thomas had not exactly known *whom* to marry at first.

Then there was Leopold. He was a good egg—that was what everyone said about him. Leopold might not get it right, not straight away, but you could always see the heart of the man and it was pure.

As for Maudey—well, she was the darling of her father's eye. Alexander had never been in any doubt of that.

And then there was Alexander…

The Dowager Duke of Cothrom looked between his two younger sons. He cleared his throat. "Billiards, eh?"

Alexander's hopes sank. Oh, hell—was the real reason for his coming here so awkward that his father was going to have to make *small talk*?

"Yes. Billiards," Leopold replied—unnecessarily, in Alexander's opinion.

Well, they *were* in a billiards room…

"May I cut in?" the dowager duke said quietly, reaching for a cue of his own.

It had happened before Alexander was truly conscious of how

to avoid it. If he had been swift, he might have put down his cue, muttered something cheerful about how he had been just about to head out, anyway, then slipped out without any real debate.

As it was…

"Ah, whatanexcellent idea; I was justabout to leavemyself," said his brother Leopold in a stream that made half the words he spoke hardly distinguishable. "Herehavemychalk—"

"Leopold," muttered Alexander, pulse suddenly racing as he realized what was about to happen.

"—and I'll send your love to Kathleen," Leopold was yelling over his shoulder as he half walked, half bolted to the door. "Bye, Zander!"

The door slammed behind him, leaving naught but a billiards table, his father, and an awkward silence.

As Alexander slowly released the air that had become taut in his lungs, the awkward silence somehow managed to remain.

Well, excellent. This had to mean he was about to be treated to one of their father's famous lectures. What was it to be this time? *The family name is being besoiled by your actions? Your sister's reputation is being damaged by your outrage? Your spending is bleeding us dry?*

Alexander had heard all of them. He could almost recite most of them.

His father sighed and stepped around the billiards table with his gaze fixed upon it, as though he were utterly unaware that his youngest son was in the room. When he spoke, however, it was very much to his opponent. "Would you like to rerack and start again with a fresh slate?"

Alexander's stomach lurched.

There could not be too much read into that statement, could there?

Oh, yes, there were moments when he wished he could go back and change his mind about allowing others to use his name in their seductive exploits. It had certainly not helped him, hindering him at times with his own potential conquests, and the way his mother had flushed when she read his name in the scandal sheets…

But it was too late for that, wasn't it? Too late to change his past, too late to change his reputation—*too late*, Alexander thought with a lurch of his stomach, *to go back and make a different first impression with Lady Marjorie Dalton.*

Which was a shame. Because he would rather like to—

"Zander?" said his father softly.

Alexander almost tripped over his own foot. Dear God, he could not recall the last time his father used his childhood name. It had to have been—what, a decade?

"Papa," Alexander said, slipping into the childhood title, "I promise, I am not nearly so bad as you might think I am."

He cringed even as he said it; Christ, could he sound more childlike?

But that was the trouble was speaking with your father when you still lived at home at five and twenty, wasn't it? It was all too easy to slip into the habits of childhood.

His father looked stern. "It is not my fault how I think of you, Zander."

No, it was his own fault, that was true enough. But still… "I have committed no crime, Father."

"None against the law, certainly," William said dryly, leaning down to sedately pocket a billiards ball. "Crimes against decency, however…"

"Father!"

"You think I don't read the newspapers? You think I don't hear the gossip? You think I don't have to hold my head high when I hear others chat about your latest exploits?" his father said flatly.

It was far worse than shouting. That was what Alexander had expected. But then, since his father had relinquished the title and Thomas had gotten married, their father had—now that he came to think about it—grown a little more sedate.

Oh, the fires still burned brightly in the moral center of William Chance, the Dowager Duke of Cothrom. But it was unusual of him to speak angrily about such a thing. In fact, it was far more common for him to let Thomas worry about all that.

Alexander's stomach twisted. For his father to return to his position of familial moral arbitrator... Well, that had to mean something terrible had happened.

His father sighed, placed his cue on the table, and looked directly at his youngest son. "Lord Dalton has been to see me."

Alexander swallowed, though he managed to force a smile to his lips. "Well, you don't have to fear in that quarter, Father. I'm unlikely to attempt to seduce him. Bit too hirsute for my tastes."

"*Alexander!*"

"What?" he protested immediately, shrugging even as heat blossomed over his cheeks. "I'm just saying—"

"Everything you say is a jest. Do you take nothing seriously?" His father was glaring at him now. "Honestly, I spend *years* attempting to get you onto the straight and narrow—"

"But there is no fun on the straight and narrow, Father," pointed out Alexander, adequately fairly, in his mind.

His father's glare did not diminish. "Is that all this is? Fun? Is that all you wish your life to accomplish, the seeking of pleasure and nothing else?"

Alexander swallowed. Beyond the fact that he had managed to bed only three widows in his entire life and managed to steal kisses from four debutantes—including Lady Marjorie, who had been by far the most exhilarating—he was not sure that he had managed to find a great deal of fun in the first place.

It was galling, in truth, to be punished for enjoyments that he had not tasted.

Besides, what else did his father expect of him? No money, no profession—the only avenues for a duke's son were the Church, the law, and the army, and Alexander had neither taste for nor money to buy his way into any of the three. What did his father expect him to do? How was he supposed to fill his time?

"You take nothing seriously, not your responsibility to me, to your brother, to your mother and sister—"

"'The very name of Chance,'" Alexander muttered, turning away to the window.

"—the very name of—what did you say?"

"Nothing." Alexander sighed, leaning his head against the window frame as his conscience warred within him.

Perhaps it was time to give it up. Not just to cease permitting others to use his name in that way, but to give up the truth to his father, to explain he had almost never acted against the family's good name, and in fact had spent a great deal of his time…not doing anything much at all.

But how to begin? *Where* to start—how to get anyone to believe him, after so many years of people presuming, *knowing* the opposite?

"Lord Dalton wished to inquire of me just what your intentions are regarding his daughter."

Alexander whirled around and really did trip over his own feet this time. Managing to use his billiards cue to prevent himself from toppling to the carpet in an undignified heap, he managed to ask, "Why? What has she told him?"

The dowager duke fixed his youngest son with a beady eye. "Just what is there for her to tell him?"

"Well…" *Not much*, was what Alexander could have said.

And that was what made it all the more strange, didn't it? He and Lady Marjorie had barely spent more than twenty minutes in each other's company, and yet he was enamored with her.

He could no longer deny it to himself. The woman transfixed him, and the more she attempted to rebuff him, the more intrigued he became.

She was beautiful, yes, but there was a sparking and angry intelligence in those delicate brows and fine eyes that he could never have predicted. And now that he knew the spirit within the delectable body was perhaps even more alluring, how could he leave her alone?

"Yes, see here? One love line, but a deep one. One that lasts almost

all your life. A love... A love that is uninterrupted."

When Alexander blinked, it was to find his father's brow had darkened.

"Dear God, boy, there was that nonsense with the Lymington girl, but you insisted you were innocent in that affair and I believed you, since she also testified you had been chaste. Entirely innocent, you insisted, despite the fact that you had inspired such strong feelings in the girl that she had shown up at our town-home uninvited in the middle of the night in hopes that you would elope with her. But I had never *really* thought you so reckless as to bed an innocent—"

"I haven't!" Alexander protested quickly, stepping forward with a hand outstretched, as though that could convince his father of his—relative—innocence. The Lymington lady in question had taken a single kiss rather extremely to heart. "Father, I have not—"

"And to think that I encouraged the man to think well of you!"

"I have not bedded Lady Marjorie Dalton—nothing even close to it," said Alexander firmly, though he could not help but add, with a grin, "not that I wouldn't mind it."

He did not exactly wither under his father's eye, but it was difficult to stand before him.

"And what do you mean by that?" his father asked icily.

Alexander opened his mouth, and quite by accident, the truth slipped out. "I like her."

For a moment, there was naught but silence in the billiards room.

Then William Chance, the Dowager Duke of Cothrom, cleared his throat. "You... You *like* her."

Why on earth was it was embarrassing—so mortifying to admit to such a thing? Still, he could hardly avoid it now. "Yes. I like her."

His father examined him closely, and though Alexander's stomach twisted at the unwanted attention, he managed to hold the man's eyes.

William nodded his head. His forehead smoothed, frown leaving…and a wry smile slipped across his lips. "You like her. Good. That is a start, my boy. That is a start."

Oh, dear God, what does that mean?

"I am trusting you to court her properly."

"Father," said Alexander unyieldingly. "What Lady Marjorie Dalton and I get up to is *private.*"

"Alexander!"

"I meant—I would like you to trust me," he said desperately, the truth now sounding more false, even if it was just as true. "I want you to be able to trust me, Papa."

"You do?" His father sounded surprised, which Alexander supposed he should not be too offended by, even if it was a bit disheartening to hear the man so utterly astonished. "Well. Right. Good."

"Yes. Good," said Alexander awkwardly.

Was it good? The whole thing felt rather dreamlike. His father had never acted in such a manner—at least, not with him. Was this what Leopold had to put up with?

"Good," repeated the dowager duke, nodding curtly as he placed his billiards cue on the table before him. "Right. I have some letters to write."

And he said not another word as he stepped around the table, though he did pause for a moment beside his son, clasp his arm, then leave the room without a word.

Alexander could not help but smile, even if it was a wry one. That was the thing with his father; he was not the most effusive man. And besides, he had given his son the most wonderful idea.

It was time to write a letter.

By the time Alexander had returned to his bedchamber, found paper and pen, gone downstairs to swipe some ink from his father's study, returned upstairs, stared at the blank piece of paper for approximately twenty minutes, and cursed all letter writing skills to hell, he had just about managed to think about what to write.

Though needless to say, he thought feverishly as he signed his name at the bottom, he would have to expect now that Lord Dalton could also read his missive. Would the man even allow a letter from a gentleman who was not engaged to his daughter? What had the man seen? Or was it Lady Marjorie herself who had told him something? Despite her clear disdain for Alexander?

Damn it all to hell.

Still, he was proud of what he had created.

My lady,

It was most pleasant to see you at Lady Romeril's garden party. You appeared to be in good health and I hope that continues.

I know my reputation precedes me, and not in the most flattering of lights. I greatly desire you to think differently of me. I would like to formally declare my interest in courting you. Perhaps you might accompany me on a walk in Sydney Gardens? I will of course provide a chaperone if you do not prefer to bring your own.

I remain yours, faithfully,
Alexander Chance

Yes, it was a good letter. He had almost lost control of himself when he had written "I greatly desire you," but all things considered, he rather thought he had managed to rescue himself.

Yes. It was a good letter.

What was even better, however, was the letter that Alexander was to receive the next morning over breakfast.

"Ah, a letter," said his mother cheerfully.

"From a Dalton," his father observed with just a hint of sternness.

"Not Lady Marjorie, surely!" His sister nudged him.

Alexander snatched the letter from the silver platter which Nicholls had so recently brought in and leaned back in his chair to ensure that his curious—fine, *nosy*—sister was unable to read it.

Not that there was much to read. But every line filled him with a strange sort of humming elation.

My lord,

What an interesting proposition. I would be delighted to be courted by you, and I will take you up on your offer to provide an appropriate chaperone.

I remain ever,
Marjorie Dalton

A slow smile crept across Alexander's face.
Ever Marjorie Dalton, eh? Oh, he'd see about that…

Chapter Seven

March 16, 1841

MARJORIE READ THROUGH the latest letter Lord Alexander had sent her one more time.

As though that could reveal anything new. She had perused the small letter—a note, really—at least a dozen times that morning alone, and with each new reading there was no fresh insight.

I remain yours, faithfully…

Surely, that first comma had to be a mistake. A piece of dust. A flick of ink.

Marjorie shivered, even as she sat by the roaring fire in the drawing room.

Alexander Chance remained hers.

It was a nonsense—a complete misunderstanding of her own doing, she was certain. The man was not hers. He was not anyone's. He did not appear to be able to keep to his own company; she had heard enough of the gossip and rumors over the last few years to know that Lord Alexander Chance enjoyed the company of ladies, and a great number of them.

Heat soared through her. Not that she was thinking of what he could have gotten up to with those ladies.

Not that she was hoping he would get to much the same with her…

"You look pink again, Marjorie dear," said an intrusive voice that made her jump. "I'm sorry. Did I startle you?"

Marjorie smiled weakly at her mother, who had wandered

into the drawing room quite without her noticing. "Yes, a little. I…I was lost in my own thoughts."

Lady Dalton might have smiled. There would have been plenty of mothers, Marjorie was certain, who would have smiled at such a statement. It was innocent enough, after all.

Except that both her parents knew whose letter she was holding in her hands.

Why had her father allowed it? It would have been more prudent, after all, for Lord Alexander's mother or sister to write her and set up a meeting, than for a man not yet engaged to her to write. Not that he would *ever* be engaged to her.

Lady Dalton's attention became more focused. "And you are quite sure that he is to be trusted?"

No, Marjorie wanted to say, *and that is the thrill.*

Lord Alexander Chance was a rake, a scoundrel, and an altogether unsettled sort of gentleman.

And that was precisely what she wanted. To be pursued, to be desired, to be known as a woman worth knowing on her own terms and not as the younger sister of a most outrageous woman.

Oh, it was embarrassing enough that Rose had had to disappear off. But to return less than a decade later, not only beautiful and accomplished, but an actress…and a marchioness?

No, her father had never quite forgiven her for it, although he was much better at pretending to have done so, in public.

And that left Marjorie, utterly ignored and kept hemmed in by her parents, who were determined *she* would never run off with a man to get married!

Her stomach lurched. Not that Lord Alexander Chance was likely to ask her to do such a thing…

"Well, I have an appointment with Mrs. Lymington," her mother was saying from inexplicably a long way away. "Do look after yourself today, Marjorie. You know how delicate you are."

"Yes, Mama," Marjorie said faintly, without really considering to what she was agreeing.

After spending a delightful ten minutes thinking about precisely what she would do if the handsome and charming Lord Alexander Chance did ask her to run away with him—and no matter what Marjorie did, she could not make imaginary Marjorie respond in any other way except the affirmative—it was the ringing of the front door bell that interrupted her thoughts.

He was here.

Trying to walk sedately and calmly, and almost certainly not managing it, she reached the door to the hall and opened it just a fraction.

Just enough to hear what was being said on the other side…

"—expecting you?" the Dalton family butler was asking politely.

"Indeed," came the certain and charming voice of Lord Alexander.

Goodness, it was most unfair. Here she was, attempting to keep her good reputation, and the man could make her go weak at the knees through a door.

Blast the man.

"I shall seek out Lady Marjorie and inquire as to whether you are telling the truth," came the stern statement from Sackville, who evidently was most unimpressed.

Marjorie's smile was broad—but it froze when she realized precisely what this statement meant. Launching herself across the room and falling haphazardly into the chair that she had only just vacated, she just about managed to look up curiously—and she hoped, innocently—as the servant entered the room.

It was a shame she was a little out of breath.

Sackville bowed. "There is a visitor for you, my lady. A Lord Alexander Chance, he says."

Marjorie worked hard not to allow herself to smile. *He says.* Clearly, their butler had heard tell of the many outrageous exploits that Lord Alexander had gotten up to over the years, and he was not very impressed by the man turning up at his, Sackville's, door.

"Yes, I was expecting him," she said aloud.

Her butler frowned. "I see. And shall I show him in?"

"Absolutely not," Marjorie said hastily, rising to her feet.

Lord Alexander and herself, alone in the drawing room? Most definitely not. That was where scandal started!

Started, and finished, if Lord Alexander were to have any say in the matter, she was certain.

Heat flushing through her, and trying not to catch the eye of the servant who looked most put out by her hurried statement, Marjorie attempted to say lightly, "No, the Lord Alexander and I will be going out. There is no point in showing him in here. Would you please get a footman to bring me my pelisse and bonnet, Sackville?"

The man arched a brow and pursed his lips, but he could not exactly refuse a direct request. He bowed curtly, muttered something about, "Right away," and stepped into the hallway.

And after a long, slow inhale, so did Marjorie.

It was a good thing she had done so, for the instant that her gaze fell upon the tall, handsome man loitering in her hallway, all the breath in her body appeared to vanish.

Lord Alexander Chance.

Oh, it was most unfair that a man should look so entirely at home in every place he found himself. Why, he was standing with his top hat in his hands and his great coat buttoned, seeming for all the world that he had just returned home.

Marjorie swallowed. Which he had not. Obviously.

"Ah, Lady Marjorie," Lord Alexander said brightly. "I hope you are ready for our walk?"

Our walk. Yes. Yes, she had agreed to that, hadn't she?

That had been before she had remembered that whenever in this man's presence, it was surprisingly hard to walk. The knees, they went wobbly, and one's ankles, they became weak.

"I am greatly looking forward to it," Lord Alexander said earnestly, his smile slight but his eyes round.

And he did appear to be earnest, now that she came to examine him. It was a most unusual attitude in the man, and Marjorie was quite wrong footed by it.

Charming, yes, alluring, yes. Utterly overpowering in his seductive attractiveness, yes, she had expected all that.

But earnest?

"Here is your pelisse and bonnet, my lady," came the quiet tones of Sackville from behind her. One of the footmen, a cherub-faced young man, stood beside him.

Marjorie turned and smiled, hoping to goodness that the servant saw nothing more in her smile than the pleasant attitude of a person about to relish a walk. "Thank you."

Lord Alexander stepped forward, his hand out. "Here, let me."

"No, Joseph can dress the lady," the servant said gruffly, tugging the bonnet away from the eager hands of Lord Alexander, to whom the footman had been about to hand it.

Heat cascaded through Marjorie as the three men stood close to her. One was almost a member of the family, a part of the household—almost a part of the house. Sackville was more grandfather to her than servant. Joseph was new to the household, quiet, and eager to blend into the background.

And the other…

Marjorie tried hard not to catch Lord Alexander's eye as she allowed the older gentleman to nudge Joseph aside and carefully adjust her bonnet so that it was balanced on both sides.

"There," said Sackville quietly. "And you can come home anytime you like, even if you've only been gone for a few minutes. You know that."

It was not a question. Marjorie smiled and took the man's hand, squeezing it for just a moment before releasing it. "I know."

And then she turned, pulse hammering, to the gentleman who was…courting her.

Courting her! No man had ever courted her before! No man had ever wished to, and as far as she knew, no man had ever applied to her father for permission to do such a thing. Quite surprising, considering her connection to a title and her rather tempting dowry. Then again, her mother had sent her abroad for a year after her several Seasons in London, tired of keeping men solely after Marjorie's money away from even *approaching* her, so Marjorie hadn't had many opportunities to get to know any of the unattached gentlemen outside of a dance or two.

And there was the fact that her parents were regarded as somewhat boorish. Relatively new title and all.

Now that she came to think about it, *had* Lord Alexander inquired to her father? Was that why her parents had allowed the letter? Her parents hadn't *known* about the first two Lord Alexander had sent, but they knew about this one. Were they satisfied he didn't want her for her dowry, considering the Chances were plenty rich, even if Lord Alexander was a third son and not an heir himself?

Did it any of that matter?

Oh, all these thoughts swirling around her head, it made it completely impossible to think.

"Shall we, Lady Marjorie?" Lord Alexander said quietly, not waiting for her answer but instead taking her hand and placing it in the crook of his arm.

It was not supposed to be such a sensory experience, standing this close to him. Marjorie cleared her throat in the desperate hope that it would clear her mind, but all she could think of was the heat of his arm and the warmth of his side and the scent of his cologne and the way his smile—

"Oh, there you are! I was worried I had missed you, I know I'm running late and it's all my own fault, but I couldn't find my reticule, the one that matched this pelisse, and so of course I couldn't leave without either finding it or changing my pelisse, and goodness, you look lovely!" said Miss Harding in a rush as she stood in the doorway.

Marjorie smiled. Lord Alexander froze.

"And I'm not too late, I can see that," continued Miss Harding happily, standing there in matching pelisse and reticule. "Mother only just now dropped me off in the carriage and had to go. An appointment for tea. I was worried I would miss you, naturally, but here we all are. Are you ready, Marjorie?"

"Miss…Harding?" Lord Alexander said, mouth agape and a vein pulsing at his temple. "What are you doing here?"

"That is my doing, actually," Marjorie said quietly.

Well, she had to say something. She could not allow her friend to bear the brunt of Lord Alexander's obvious outrage.

Though precisely *why* he was outraged, she was not certain. Well, she could guess—she *had* guessed. That was why Miss Harding was here. But really, Marjorie had the right of things here, not Lord Alexander Chance.

The man in question turned his head to look down at her. "*Your* doing?"

"Well, I presumed your sister might be previously engaged and therefore unable to act as our chaperone this afternoon," Marjorie said slowly, awkwardly checking each word for anything particularly inflammatory.

As she had rather suspected, Lord Alexander's eyes widened. "'Chaperone'?"

So, it was just as I had suspected, Marjorie thought as her heart sank. He had never truly intended to organize a chaperone for the two of them. That had to mean that he had nefarious intentions toward her, did it not?

No respectable gentleman would expect to go on a walk with a young lady, even in public, without a chaperone.

"Yes, chaperone, and I must say how delighted I am that you are courting my friend, Lord Alexander," said Miss Harding, with only a slight hint of envy in her voice. "Very delighted. So glad."

The hint grew stronger.

"Right, well, shall we go?" Marjorie said brightly, trying to ignore both the shock of the gentleman beside her and the clear jealousy of her friend. "We shall not be long, Sackville," she called over her shoulder.

"We won't?" murmured Lord Alexander beside her, in a tone so low that surely, only she could hear it.

When Marjorie looked up and met his gaze, it was to find all air forced from her lungs once again. It was most unfair. "We won't."

It could only have been about five seconds. That was all it was, but in that time, there appeared to be an eon of meaning, of connection, as Lord Alexander's eyes stared into hers and Marjorie did her best to stare back.

Oh, this man. He made her want to do extraordinary and outlandish things, like declare her affection and ask a mail coach to take them to Gretna Green so Lord Alexander could take all her clothes off.

Perhaps not even in that order.

"—terrible weather lately, but we've been lucky with it today."

Marjorie swallowed. Her friend was still chattering away as she descended the steps to the street, and it was now beholden upon herself and Lord Alexander to follow her.

But the man did not appear to wish to take a single step.

"A chaperone," he repeated, his voice still low.

Marjorie allowed her smile to slip from her expression. "You had no honorable intensions toward me, then? You mentioned a chaperone in your letter and I then requested you bring one—did you forget? What, you hoped to solicit further kisses behind a tree, beyond prying eyes?"

The man did not need to reply. His face communicated far more than his mouth ever could.

Marjorie carefully removed her hand from the crook of his arm, hating how painful it was to remove herself from his presence by even an inch. "Right. I see."

Lord Alexander swallowed, his features softening. "No, you don't. I just thought—"

"Come on," Marjorie said brusquely in a loud voice that was intended to carry. She was no fool; she knew her father was undoubtedly listening from somewhere. "Miss Harding is right. The weather is marvelous."

Marvelous it might have been, but the warmth of the sun was almost negligible as she stepped out onto the street and started to follow her friend down it. The wintery sun had not quite made any impact on the freezing Bath streets, and Marjorie pulled her pelisse tighter around her and wished she had thought to bring a scarf.

However, all was not lost. Within five seconds, Lord Alexander was walking beside her, step in step, and the heat pouring through her now as a result of his response was more than enough to keep her half boiled.

"You misunderstand me," he said in a low voice.

"You confuse me," Marjorie shot back, though in as pleasant a tone as she could manage. They were, after all, in public. "You wrote of a chaperone."

"I know, but I—"

"Never actually intended to bring one?" She could not help but raise an eyebrow at Miss Harding ahead of them as the pair of them turned a corner onto Sydney Place, where the gate to Sydney Gardens could be found. "I told you before—I hate liars. I had expected better of you, Lord Alexander."

That, for some reason, made his eyebrows shoot up. "You did?"

Was it so strange to hope that the man who was now officially courting her—at least, she was almost certain he was—could be trusted?

"You do not have to be so suspicious of me, you know," Lord Alexander said quietly as the trio reached the Sydney Gardens gates.

"Oh, and there's hardly anyone about, how lovely," chattered on Miss Harding ahead of them.

Marjorie's stomach lurched. "I-I am not suspicious of you."

"I know it does not look particularly good, that I forgot the chaperone—"

"'Forgot'?" Now that was a very different proposition, indeed. Marjorie stared up at him, half forgetting that she should keep a respectable distance between them, and saw to her astonishment that he appeared to be telling the truth.

There it was; the fine lines of discomfort and regret around the gentleman's eyes.

"It's just..." Lord Alexander swallowed, his throat bobbing and his focus remarkably warm as he glanced at her before looking firmly away. "I would prefer to be alone with you."

Get a hold of yourself, Marjorie. Do not fall for it. "Alone? With me?"

His furrowed brow smoothed out, and the corner of his mouth pulled upward. "You are astonished by such a confession?"

"I... No, I... Yes," Marjorie admitted.

Because it *was* astonishing. For any man to say such a thing, in truth, to her—no man ever had.

Oh, Marjorie knew it was a complicated matter. Her missing sister, whom everyone had been told had been living in the country, only now that had been proven untrue; her overprotective parents; her family's relatively new title; her year abroad last year; the fact that few people ever seemed to remember her name even after being introduced copious times...

It did not exactly result in a recipe for a gentleman looking for an uncomplicated bride.

And that was what made it so unbelievable that a gentleman would wish to be with her. Be with her alone. And not for her dowry.

And that it was Lord Alexander Chance, rake and scoundrel and seducer of ladies...

"I would rather be anywhere, the wilderness of the desert, the chill of a mountain top, the burn of an island, if..." Lord Alexander swallowed, and Marjorie's pulse skipped a beat. *Was that...nervousness, in his eyes?* "If I could be alone with you."

Marjorie swallowed as well.

Oh, it was heady stuff. It would have been far too easy to be mollified by such a statement, and yet he did appear to be speaking the truth.

"What a delightful path! This way, do you think?" Miss Harding called out ahead of them.

Clearing her voice and hoping to goodness it would hold, Marjorie managed, "Y-Yes. What a good idea."

She and Lord Alexander followed her friend for a few minutes in silence, Marjorie desperately racking her brains to try to think of something to say.

Something. Anything!

In the end, it was he who broke the silence. "So, Lady Marjorie. Tell me about yourself."

Marjorie tripped over her own skirts.

"Whoops! Careful now," Lord Alexander said, smoothly grabbing her arm and simultaneously preventing her from falling, and looping her hand into the crook of his own arm. "These paths can be treacherous."

Not nearly as treacherous as you, was what Marjorie wanted to say. Instead, she managed to stammer. "Y-Yes. Thank you. For catching me."

"I'll always catch you," he said quietly, the teasing air gone from his face and nothing but seriousness now in his eyes. "I'll always catch you, Marjorie."

Marjorie swallowed. *Do not lose your head. Do not lose your head!* "Lady Marjorie."

"Do you not think that we are beyond such formalities?" came his low, husky voice.

Warmth shot down to between her thighs. "No," Marjorie said decidedly. If she started to call him Alexander, she may as well ruin herself immediately. "You—You were asking me about myself. I am the younger daughter of the Marquess of Dalton, recently the Earl of Burnell, and I am two and twenty."

There. That should do it. Nice and biographical.

There was also a twinkle in Lord Alexander's eye. "And?"

"And…what else is there?" Marjorie asked, despite herself as they turned a corner with Miss Harding still ahead of them, just out of earshot—thank goodness, for the man was about to say something ridiculous.

"Why, everything else," he said lightly. "Not a single soul in the world knows Lady Marjorie Dalton beyond the fact that she has a rather large dowry—which means nothing to me, I assure you," he added before she could protest, "and I would like to be the first to really know you. What are you reading at the moment? What think you of women gaining the vote? Have you ever been to France? What did you last dream of?"

Marjorie stiffened.

What did she last dream of?

A tall, handsome man, wearing very little shirt. A smile that made her go weak at the knees and yet had given her strength to launch herself into his arms. Whispered murmurs of sweet praise and compliments that made it impossible to think...

Lord Alexander's smile widened. "Lady Marjorie, I do declare—you last dreamt of something *erotic*, did you not?"

"I did not!" Perhaps it would have been a little more believable if she had not shrieked the three words across Sydney Gardens.

Marjorie cringed as Miss Harding glanced over her shoulder at them with narrowed eyes, and a promenading elderly couple glanced over at them with tilted heads.

When Marjorie looked back at Lord Alexander, his grin was even wider. "Was your dream about me?"

"No!" Marjorie lied hastily.

"So it was an erotic dream, but just not about me? I admit myself disappointed," teased Lord Alexander, eyes sparkling. "Still, I suppose I can hardly fault you. It is good, indeed, for a lady to know what she wants."

This is not happening. This is not happening!

"I want to travel," Marjorie said firmly. That was it, get the conversation back onto a neutral topic. "See the world—parts of it."

"Some of its...parts," Lord Alexander repeated.

How on earth did the blaggard somehow make anything

suggestive?

"Yes," she said, wondering to goodness how she would ever sleep that night. "And… And that's it."

For some reason, there was a flicker of disappointment in Lord Alexander's face as he chewed his lip a moment. "That is it? That is all you wish to tell me about yourself?"

"What else is there to tell?" The question had slipped out before she could stop it, and Marjorie felt the need to further explain. "I mean… No one ever asks about me. No one has ever inquired… I am not that interesting a person. Beyond that *rather large dowry*, as you called it, and that is simply a product of my birth that has nothing at all to do with *me*."

It was galling indeed to have to admit to it, but then, Marjorie could hardly hide the truth.

She was not a very interesting person. She never had been.

Rose had always been the far more interesting sister, and then she'd gone and eloped with some man, and her name had faded from the Dalton halls, and Marjorie… She was just the younger sister. Just a pale imitation of what Rose could have been.

"You are the most interesting and curiosity-inducing woman—nay, person, I have ever met," said Lord Alexander quietly.

Marjorie could not help but huff a laugh. "Yes, because you want to get under my skirts!"

"I would not say *no*," came the gentle reply. "But it is what is in your heart, not your drawers, that interests me."

Could it be true?

Oh, how desperately she wanted it to be true. Marjorie knew full well that a gentleman almost never wished to know what was in a lady's heart, as long as she was beholden to him.

But as she examined Lord Alexander's face closely, it was to find—much to her surprise—that the man appeared to be…in earnest.

Goodness. It was a miracle. It was astonishing. It was…

Enticing.

"Oh," said Marjorie helplessly. "You… You truly wish to

know?"

Lord Alexander nodded, naught but honesty in his gaze. "I truly wish to know."

Right. Well. Let's start with the easy things, Marjorie told herself sternly, and perhaps over time, she would feel strong enough, brave enough, to speak of what was truly in her heart.

Eventually.

"I am reading a most fascinating book called *Frankenstein*," she began hesitantly, strength and certainty growing as she saw the genuine interest in Lord Alexander's eye. "Have you read it?"

"I have not," Lord Alexander said lightly as they turned another corner in the gardens. "Tell me about it."

"Well, it starts off with a man who—"

"Don't tell me the story," he interrupted, his focus causing pops of heat to erupt all over Marjorie's body. "I want to know what you think."

Oh, dear God. She was going to fall in love with this man, no matter how desperately she tried not to.

Chapter Eight

March 21, 1841

"—AND I READ about the speeches, none of them sounded particularly inspiring to my mind," continued Lady Marjorie with a grin. "Though I will admit, the thought of being able to enter the galleries to listen to the Parliamentary debates... What is it?"

Alexander blinked. "What is what?"

"Do I—Do I have something on my nose?" Lady Marjorie attempted to examine her own nose, which only made Alexander smile all the more. "You are staring at me. Is there something there?"

"You are perfect. You look perfect, I mean," he amended hastily as they reached the gates of what Alexander had swiftly started to consider *their* garden. To the rest of Bath Society, it was Sydney Gardens. "You look fine. Tell me more about this Parliamentary debate."

For a moment, Lady Marjorie did not appear convinced—but as Alexander opened the gate and gestured that her ladies should enter first, Marjorie watched him with pinking cheeks and downcast eyes.

Which made it all the more easy for Alexander to admire the delicious derriere and the smooth cup of her breasts.

Which was why his own face was pink by the time he had followed her into the garden and retook her arm.

"I'm going to sit on that bench and keep an eye on you," declared the diminutive lady's maid that Lady Marjorie had insisted on bringing—in far too loud a voice, to Alexander's mind.

"And don't do anything—"

"Yes, thank you, Tilly," said Lady Marjorie swiftly, her cheeks now pink for entirely different reasons. For some reason, Alexander found himself admiring that Lady Marjorie didn't refer to her lady's name by the maid's surname. It denoted a bit of familiarity between them. "We'll ensure to stay in sight."

Shame.

The trouble with attempting to become a better man, Alexander thought furiously, *is that it is impossible to do in the company of a pretty woman.* Which was not often enough, but there it was.

He could not monopolize Lady Marjorie Dalton's company without a great deal of gossip…

"I have read about it as much as I can from the newspapers, although clearly all of them are entirely biased," Lady Marjorie continued conversationally, slipping her hand into Alexander's arm without seemingly a thought.

"They are?" Challenging as it was to keep his attention focused on the conversation before him, Alexander managed to speak two whole words.

Which he thought impressive. Especially when one considered that Lady Marjorie was pressed up against him as they leaned to the side to let another promenading couple past them.

Lady Marjorie, pressed up against him. The warmth of her, the heat, the need in him that responded to her…

"Oh, yes, the editors of almost every newspaper without exception have their own political views," Lady Marjorie was saying cheerily, as though Alexander were not covertly attempting to see if there were any convenient trees nearby that he could press her up against out of sight of her maid. "You must have noticed."

Must he have? Alexander could hardly remember the last time that he had bothered to read a newspaper, let alone consider whether or not there was a particular political leaning in the articles, one way or the other.

Now that he came to think about it, he wasn't sure what the

two main parties were at the moment. Didn't one of them wear wigs?

And who *was* the Prime Minister, anyway?

"Don't you think?"

Alexander blinked. Lady Marjorie was looking up at him brightly, her obvious appreciation of their conversation perhaps only marred by the fact that it had slowed.

"I… Honestly, I didn't know," he said aloud, almost embarrassed at having to admit to the fact. "I don't tend to pay much attention to these sorts of things."

"But your own father—I mean, your brother now, he is a member of the House of Lords, isn't he?" Lady Marjorie asked curiously.

Alexander opened his mouth as they meandered down the path. "Yes. Yes, I suppose he is."

It was not something he had ever given much thought to. What his brother Thomas got up to… Why, that was his affair. He had a child now, and another on the way, and there was the orphanage that he and his wife financially supported…and Alexander was certain that Thomas probably found other things to fill his day. Precisely what they were, of course, he wasn't sure.

"And what does your brother, the new Duke of Cothrom, think of it?" Lady Marjorie persisted, gesturing toward a bench, which they started to make for.

Think of it? Alexander wasn't sure. What did Thomas think of *it*? Had they ever discussed *it*, or had he ever heard his brother discuss *it* at all with anyone else?

What was *it*, anyway?

Floundering silently in the private recesses of his own mind, Alexander desperately tried to remember which political point or bill or debate or something they had been discussing.

They had been talking about France, yes, and the rise of the Germanic states…and then the sun had come out from behind the clouds and lit up Lady Marjorie's hair so beautifully, and he had become transfixed by the contour of her curls, the way they bounced when she walked, the delicate way they…

Blast. Alexander could not for the life of him remember what it was they had been speaking of.

"You have forgotten, haven't you?" Lady Marjorie said lightly as they reached a bench.

She slowly lowered herself onto it as Alexander blustered, "No, no, not at all. I was merely considering—"

"You have forgotten, and so you may as well admit to it," said his companion with a wry smile. "I am sorry. I did not mean to bore you."

And it was perhaps that statement that tore the most at Alexander's conscience.

She thought she was *dull?* Hell's bells, it was his utter fascination with her that was the problem. The more he learned about her, her mind, the way she thought, the more he realized Lady Marjorie Dalton was perhaps the most underestimated woman in the whole of Society. Far more than just a tremendously large dowry. He truly had meant it when he'd said that hadn't interested him at all.

He was interested in *her.*

And she was smiling at him.

"Come, sit," she said lightly, patting the bench beside her. "I am not offended."

"It is not—I was distracted by—"

"It does not matter," Lady Marjorie said brightly.

But Alexander knew that it did. He could see it in the taut pull around her eyes, in the wistfulness of her expression. And it would make him vulnerable, to admit that it was her form, the lilt of her voice, the way she tilted her head when she was emphasizing a point, that had made him so utterly dazzled by her.

"It was you," he said quietly, sitting beside her and doing so most carefully so his hip was absolutely pressing against hers. "I was distracted by you."

There it was, the pink in her cheeks that Alexander had known would emerge after saying such a thing. It had been easy, but what was not easy was keeping control of himself as he sat here beside her.

Their chaperone, Lady Marjorie's lady's maid, who had scowled at him the moment they had left the Dalton house, was now loitering by a tree about ten feet from them. She was conversing hurriedly with a young man with large ears and a fervent expression, and Alexander was only now realizing that this had surely been the plan all along.

Lady Marjorie's plan.

When he turned to her, it was to see her smile. "Yes, I rather thought that Tilly's young man might just happen to be walking here in Sydney Gardens at around this time."

Alexander stifled a laugh. "You minx. You 'rather thought so'?"

"Yes, well, after I instructed him to be here, I rather thought so," said Lady Marjorie blithely. "Do—Do you think I acted wrongly?"

Absolutely not.

What he did think, Alexander could not help but muse, was that Lady Marjorie Dalton was quite unlike any lady he had ever known. She was certainly most unlike the Lady Marjorie Dalton he had thought he would get to know.

She was brilliantly smart and wonderfully kind. If the expressions of the two across the path from them were anything to go by, she understood the pain of lovers kept apart. And so she had orchestrated this, had she?

A chance for her lady's maid and her lady's maid's lover to converse…and an opportunity for the two of them to be alone.

Well. Mostly alone.

"—never heard of such a thing, but then Mozart's piece was played just as badly—"

"—heard back from my accountant and the investment is a solid one, assuming of course that I move swiftly—"

"—don't you think? I mean, I heard Lord Alexander Chance seduced fourteen widows last Season alone!"

Alexander stiffened.

Sydney Gardens was fuller than normal, the warmer weather drawing out even those who would scarce consider walking outside without a pelisse and gloves and hat and three scarves. That made it quite a challenge to decipher who, precisely, it was who had spoken that disgraceful gossip about him.

Well. About his name.

Alexander may have stolen a few kisses last Season, but he had not actually bedded anyone in that time.

His friends under his name, however…

"—scoundrel of the first degree, and I wouldn't allow a single woman in my acquaintance anywhere near that Lord Alexander Chance—"

Alexander cleared his throat, and when he looked at Lady Marjorie by his side, it was to discover three most unpleasant things.

Firstly, that she had shifted from him. A whole six inches, leaving a painful gap between them on the bench.

Secondly, that her cheeks were a dark scarlet, and not because he had flattered or charmed her. Quite to the contrary.

And thirdly, that she was resolutely looking away.

Blast it all to hell.

"I suppose you are more than accustomed to hearing such things," Lady Marjorie said, her voice tight and her head fixed determinedly in the opposite direction. "But I am not."

"Marjorie—"

"I have said before, it is *Lady* Marjorie," she said sternly.

Alexander nodded. *Yes, well, I probably deserved that.* "I wish you had not heard that."

Her laughter was dry. "Yes, of that, I do not doubt."

"No, I mean—"

"Is it true?" And now Lady Marjorie was looking at him, and it was the look of a person who was determined to be given the truth, even if it killed them. "What they said, that you…you befriended so many widows?"

Even in this moment of frustration, Alexander had to fight hard not to smile.

Well, really. Befriended? Surely, Lady Marjorie understood the delicate dance that could occur between a man and a woman, when neither of them were wearing many clothes and neither of them cared much for the consequences?

Or perhaps not. He had never satisfactorily dug down into the meaning of her flushes when he had asked her about erotic dreams. Was it possible that, innocent as she was, she did not know quite what amorous congress could consist of?

Surely not...

"Alexander," Lady Marjorie said quietly.

"I thought you wanted to keep a formality between us," he shot back before he could help himself.

Alexander flinched at the pain that scattered across Lady Marjorie's face at his words.

Damn it. He was better than this. Or at least, he had always *hoped* that he was better than this.

"I apologize," he said stiffly.

"Did you... Did you befriend that many widows last Season?" Lady Marjorie said coldly, drawing her hands together in her lap, as though preventing herself from giving in to the temptation of reaching for his own.

It was a temptation Alexander greatly wished she would indulge in—but as it was, he could at least tell her the truth. "No."

"'No'?" She looked almost relieved, the tension in her shoulders immediately lessening, but then Lady Marjorie stiffened. "It was more?"

"No!" Alexander tried not to smile as his mind worked hard to try to extricate himself from such a tangle.

Well, what on earth was he supposed to say? He had not bedded a single widow last Season, but his friends depended on being able to use his name. How else would they be able to get up to so many shenanigans without consequences? Though he had to wonder, nondescript younger Chance that he was, how soon it would be before they ran out of women who wouldn't recognize him and immediately know the truth of the game his friends played.

Though now that he came to think, it was only now Alexander was starting to see that there were consequences even beyond the idea of his friends getting caught.

It was just that it was *he* who was paying for them.

"I want to know the truth, Alexander," Lady Marjorie said, slipping into the informal use of his name seemingly without realizing she had done so. "Do I not deserve that?"

Alexander's stomach lurched.

She did deserve that. She deserved so much more than he could give her, and it was painful to realize such a thing. To know that the woman beside you whom you were swiftly realizing you adored—most inconvenient—was leagues ahead of you in morals and so far ahead, indeed, that you would never catch up.

Lady Marjorie Dalton, however, did not want the truth, no matter how much she said that she did. Besides, it was not as though Alexander could reveal to her what had really been happening with the supposed Lord Alexander Chances who were roaming about Society.

That would take far more explaining than he had breath for.

So: a lie, but a lie that was closer to the truth than the lies currently circulating the upper circles of Society.

That shouldn't be too hard.

"The truth is that I did not seduce—I mean, befriend," Alexander adjusted hastily as the corners of Lady Marjorie's lips twitched. "I did not befriend a single widow last Season."

Goodness. Why did stating the truth like that feel so…so good?

A weight Alexander had not even realized had been pressed upon his shoulders had somehow been lifted. He felt light, freer than he had done in weeks.

In months.

In years.

Was this what it was like to exist in the world without any judgment? Judgment of self?

Was this what it was to know that the truth had been spoken and no one could accuse him of dishonesty?

"Are you being dishonest?" Lady Marjorie accused, her brows furrowed.

Alexander tried to smile. "Why would you not believe me?"

"Lord Alexander... Alexander," she said softly, and just the soft tone of his name on her lips was almost enough to undo him, "you must know... Surely, you must be aware of your reputation. How it precedes you."

Yes, he was—and it had never bothered him until now. Why, quite the opposite: For a few years, Alexander had been rather glad that the whole world thought him a skilled and experienced lover.

It had impressed his friends who had not been in on the secret, it had impressed new acquaintances to no end, and it had made the ladies admire him from a distance.

Or, as it happened sometimes, not at a distance.

But never before had he realized just how much damage it had done to his reputation. Only seated here, with Lady Marjorie's curious and slightly censorious eye, did Alexander see just how damaging such a report could become.

But how to unpick it?

"Because I know that to be a lie," Lady Marjorie said softly. "And I wish you had not lied."

Alexander twisted on the bench, desperate to face her head on. "It is not a lie. But it is not who I am. Not really."

"My own mother told me of two of her friends who had been...been bedded by you last spring," Lady Marjorie continued, her cheeks scarlet now even as her gaze looked away. "I wish you had just told me the truth. Even if it would be hard to hear."

It was all Alexander could do not to curse.

Now, this was where things got tricky. It was not true that he had bedded those widows, whoever they were…but someone had, and in his name.

He could not call Lady Marjorie a liar. He certainly did not wish to call Lady Dalton a liar.

But it was not true. And to explain precisely the scheme that he and his friends had concocted all those years ago… It seemed almost foolish now.

And if there was one thing he did not want Lady Marjorie to think him, it was foolish.

Even if he was.

"I… I do not know what to say," Alexander said aloud, perhaps more truthful in that moment than in any other during his acquaintance with the beauty seated beside him.

A smile twisted Lady Marjorie's lips. "Yes. I see that."

"You will have to trust me when I tell you that I did not do… do them. Do that. What you said," he continued quietly, knowing that the whole truth was impossible to explain, even if he wanted to. "I promise you, Marjorie. I have not bedded a woman in…oh, over three years."

When she lifted her eyes to his, it was filled with hope—a hope that made Alexander's chest tight.

"I… Oh, I so desperately want to believe you, Alexander," she said, and once again, his stomach stirred as she addressed him without his title. "But you must see, surely, that it is your word against the world's."

"I have always felt at odds with the world," Alexander admitted before he could stop himself. "Lying is not in my nature, Marjorie," and his hopes leapt as she did not correct him, "though there have been lies in my past. But as I sit here with you, I can promise you this. I am not lying to you. There has been no one else in my bed for over six and thirty months—and that is not for lack of offers."

All too late, Alexander realized he had said the wrong thing.

"I see." She looked down at the ground.

"No, you don't. I'm sorry, I—"

"I think Tilly and I should be going," Marjorie said distantly as she rose, somehow slipping out of Alexander's grasp as he lunged for her. "The hour is late and the sun draws toward the horizon."

"No, wait, Marjorie—"

"Why?"

Alexander had lurched up to his feet and now stood before Marjorie, so close, her very breath blossomed against his skin. She was looking up at him with an earnest expression, her pelisse hiding most of her body, but her chin jutted upward toward him.

Oh, she was so close to him. So close that his mind was being stirred to long for things he could not long for, to ask for things he could not ask for.

And he was going to lose her company completely if he did not repair the damage he had just done.

"Marjorie," Alexander said quietly, reaching out and taking her hands in his. She resisted, tugging her arms toward her body, but not so strongly that she actually freed herself. He had to take some heart from that. "Marjorie, I… I spoke hastily."

Her raised eyebrow did not brook much hope. "'Hastily'?"

"I… It's just…" Alexander brew out an exhale and realized that only the truth—the full truth—could save him now.

God help him.

"I am a youngest son of a duke and I…I have been known to exaggerate in the past," he said quietly, each word pulled from him like poison from a vein. "Telling the truth…it has not always benefited me. Or shown me in the best light—and when one's brothers are so admired—"

"You are saying that you have lied in the past to look…impressive?" Marjorie said quietly.

Well, when she said it like that, it sounded ridiculous.

"Yes," Alexander admitted, his shoulders sagging. "And yes, I am fully aware of how pathetic that is."

Marjorie's brilliant eyes flickered across his face. Then her hands stopped being tugged away. "It is a little."

"Lying is not my nature, I can promise you that—but I will

admit there have been times when allowing others to misunderstand the truth, or stretching the truth here and there… It has allowed me to feel impressive, and that is something that I have craved in the past," Alexander admitted, his voice low so that only Marjorie could hear him.

So that only the person who mattered most in the world could hear him.

"And…now?" she asked quietly.

Alexander inhaled slowly. "I lied, or allowed others to misunderstand, misinterpret, because I wanted to keep doing what I wanted."

Marjorie stepped closer, or perhaps he had; he couldn't tell. "And now? You are telling the truth now?"

He nodded, hardly willing to speak for fear of breaking this spell between them.

She believes me. At least, it appeared that she believed him. She saw him as a man who was speaking the truth, perhaps even a man who was worthy of her.

"Why?" asked the beautiful woman before him, her question almost a whisper.

Alexander blinked. "Why…what?"

If he were not wrong, there had been a hint of an eye roll in Marjorie's expression as she said, "Why tell the truth now?"

Ah, now *that* was an easy one. "Because I am already doing what I want," Alexander said simply. "I am with you."

Perhaps he should have said something far more impressive. He had thought his honesty would mesmerize, yet Marjorie merely looked up at him with her wide, sparkling eyes, her lips just parted as her astonishment grew.

And then so did her smile. "Charmer."

"I certainly hope so," Alexander said lightly, allowing a laugh to break the tension. "But it just so happens to be the truth."

"Does it, indeed?" And though Marjorie arched an eyebrow, she did not pull away. No, indeed, she leaned forward and turned to loop her arm into his. "Well, in that case, I think we should walk some more around the gardens."

Despite all his instincts, despite his greatest wish to remain alone with her, Alexander glanced over his shoulder at the rapidly conversing couple. "Shall I tell Tilly we're moving?"

"Oh, I think we should leave Tilly alone there for a minute or two, don't you?" said Marjorie with a lighthearted shrug he could hardly believe. "I'd hate to disturb her during an important conversation, wouldn't you?"

Oh, this woman. A wide smile crept across Alexander's face. "Yes, most rude. Shall we?"

Chapter Nine

March 25, 1841

MARJORIE WAS NOT suspicious.

Mostly not suspicious.

Fine, she was a *little* suspicious.

"And a curricle was the only carriage you could find?" she said, arms crossed as she stood outside her home with Tilly beside her, evidently trying to stifle her giggles. "Well, Lord Alexander?

She should not have said that. Marjorie knew that even uttering his name was enough to shoot bolts of lightning through her body, tingling at the most inconvenient of places, and if she were going to prevent her cheeks from burning, then the least she could do was not say his name.

Which was a shame because she had just done so.

"What can I say? The family carriage is being used by my mother. I could hardly demand it from her." Alexander shrugged as he stepped down from the curricle that he had halted right before the Dalton residence. "My brother, as the new Duke of Cothrom, has the chaise and four, and that left me with—"

"A curricle," Marjorie said dismally.

Well, it was hardly the most scandalous thing to have ever occurred to a person. They would be in full view of the public, after all, and they had only intended to drive around the Bath streets for half an hour or so.

But still. A curricle! A carriage that seated only two people, making it impossible for Tilly to accompany them!

"I do hope you do not mind, Tilly, that you will not be able to enjoy a carriage ride with us," Alexander was saying in a most sorrowful voice. "I can only hope that you can find a more…*entertaining* use of your time."

And it was then that Marjorie noted the tall, gangly youth who was loitering on the pavement on the other side of the street. He kept glancing over at them, and when he caught Marjorie's eye, he quickly looked down, shuffling his feet.

Oh. So it's like that, is it?

Marjorie turned to Tilly, who had appeared to have exchanged her head for a beetroot. "Tilly."

"Yes, m'lady?"

Forcing herself not to smile, Marjorie attempted to look stern. "You know what my mother says about gentleman callers, don't you?"

Her lady's maid's smile immediately vanished, though the scarlet cheeks remained. "Yes, m'lady."

"She would certainly not like to hear that you had spent your afternoon with a young man when you were supposed to be chaperoning me," Marjorie said sternly.

Tilly's head dropped. "No, m'lady."

It was all Marjorie could do to keep her lips from lilting into a grin. "So we will just have to make sure she doesn't hear about it, won't we?"

Her lady's maid's head lurched up. "Really, m'lady? Oh, m'lady—"

"Yes, yes, I suppose it is for the best," Marjorie said suspiciously, glancing at Alexander, who looked altogether far too pleased with himself. "And as my mother will be busy not knowing about your little…your little escapade, I hope she will also not be hearing about any *other* escapade, will she?"

All too late, Marjorie realized that she should have been a tad less circumspect when it came to speaking to her lady's maid— who, after all, had once proudly told her mistress that she knew her alphabet, but only to sing it, not to read it. Marjorie knew most lady's maids were more refined than Tilly, but after a year abroad at that overly prim finishing school, she'd had enough of refinement and begged her mother to give a former housemaid the chance at promotion after her previous lady's maid, a rigid old woman, had retired.

She hadn't known at the time how well that would work out in her favor when it came to having a chaperone who might look the other way.

Tilly looked worried. "M'lady?"

"Don't tell my mother I have gone off with Lord Alexander Chance in a curricle," hissed Marjorie, as though there were anyone around them who could hear such a scandalous thing.

There wasn't. Other than the gentleman himself, obviously, and he merely grinned in a way Marjorie was almost certain should have been illegal.

Gentlemen that handsome should not look so pleased with themselves. It suggested mischief.

It certainly felt mischievous to allow him to settle her down in the curricle, tucking her skirts around her in a way that made Marjorie wiggle in the seat. Honestly, Alexander's fingers were— well, they were touching her hips!

But there was nothing she could say to stop him, even if she had wanted him to, and by the time Alexander had cheerfully waved goodbye to Tilly and her gentleman friend then launched the horses forward, there was nothing in Marjorie's mind but this.

I am alone with Lord Alexander Chance.

Which was ridiculous, Marjorie told herself as the carriage rattled along the Bath streets at a steady pace. She had been alone with the man before. It had led to nothing untoward save…

Well. Save for a passionate kiss.

A kiss that Marjorie could not stop thinking about.

A kiss that had awakened something in her that had not since rested.

A kiss that had made it impossible to consider him as just a mere man.

A kiss that Marjorie desperately wished to be repeated…

"What is on your mind, Marjorie?" Alexander asked lightly as he deftly turned the curricle around a corner.

"Nothing—what? Strawberries!" Marjorie almost yelled.

Which was perhaps not the most elegant of speeches. The cad obviously knew her mind was not, strictly speaking, focused on strawberries, but there was nothing he could do to prove it.

That had to be her comfort.

"'Strawberries'? Indeed," Alexander said lightly as the curricle picked up pace on the almost-empty street before them. "I would greatly like to see you eat a strawberry, Marjorie."

Precisely when they had descended into first names and first names only, she was not sure. What Marjorie did know was that whenever the man spoke to her in such a fashion, she wanted to launch herself into his arms and be kissed senseless.

Not entirely suitable when one was rattling down country lanes in a curricle that her gentleman should never have—

Wait a moment. Country lanes?

"Alexander Chance," Marjorie said, not even bothering to take the accusatory tone from her voice. "Where on earth have you brought me?"

They certainly weren't in Bath any longer. Streets and houses had fallen by the wayside and it was hedges and fields now, and a skylark fluttering in the sky, and a blackbird singing somewhere, but its song was swept away as the curricle raced forward.

"Alexander!"

"Well, I have found Bath to be a mite stuffy these last few days, haven't you?" opined the man who was grinning—*grinning*!

"Alexander!" Marjorie almost laughed, which would have been an outrageous thing to do.

She should not have been laughing. *I should be outraged!*

Bad enough that they were in a curricle, no chaperone to be seen…but now they were beyond the reaches of polite Society, out from the eyes and watchful gazes of…of everyone.

And oh, goodness, how wonderful it felt.

"You are not angry with me?"

Marjorie tried to appear severe as she turned to look at the man beside her who brought the horses to a steady and slow walk. "I should be most angry with you."

"But you're not?" Alexander said hopefully.

Honestly, it was near criminal the way he was so charming. How did he do it? Was it something all the Chances had bred into them, Marjorie considered wildly, or was it something they learned as they grew older?

"I... I may have to answer some very difficult questions later," Marjorie admitted, attempting to ignore the frantic pattering of her pulse.

"Who from?"

"My parents, of course!"

"Oh, parents," Alexander said with a shrug, as though he had managed to parse a thousand questions from a thousand concerned parents—*which*, Marjorie thought with a painful jolt, *he probably had*. "And why should they ask such questions? We went on a carriage ride in Bath today—"

"Alexander!"

"Well, we did travel down at least three streets in Bath, didn't we?" he pointed out, far too reasonably for Marjorie's liking. "And it is not as though Tilly is going to say anything, is she?"

For one brief moment, the expression on her lady's maid's face as she'd seen her gentleman friend on the other side of the street flashed through Marjorie's mind.

No. Probably not.

"Still, it is most scandalous of you, to have planned such a thing," she retorted as the sun crept out from the clouds and burst forth with glorious warmth.

There was a sparkle of mischief in Alexander's eye. "'Planned'? I think you will find I became utterly turned around in the busy streets of the town and found myself at a loss to understand where I was going, and before I knew it, here we were."

"Are you always this charming?" Laughing, Marjorie leaned

close to him and slipped her hand into his.

The movement had been so instinctive, she had hardly thought about it until it was done. And now she *was* thinking about it—and could hardly believe she had done it.

Before she could pull her hand away, however, Alexander had lifted it to his lips and pressed a scalding kiss upon it.

"Always," Alexander said quietly, "when I am with you."

The moment sparkled, shifting gravity around them as they continued in the curricle. Marjorie hardly knew what to say, what to do, save to leave her hand in Alexander's keeping, where she was fairly sure it would be cared for.

The worst of it all was that she was jealous—jealous, of her own hand!

It had received another kiss from Alexander, but her lips...

Alexander glanced at her, smiled, and leaned forward closer, and closer, and Marjorie found her eyelashes fluttering as he was about to—

"Now tell me." Alexander's voice came, loud and clear. "Why is it that you hate liars?"

Marjorie opened her eyes, and she was certainly not disappointed. Mostly. "Because I do."

That was a sufficient response, was it not? Did not every civilized person hate the idea that a person could be lying to them? Was it not abhorrent?

"Not everyone cares about such things." Alexander shrugged. "I do, obviously," he added hastily. "But you seem to have a particular anger against such a kind of person. Why?"

She was not going to think about it. The tears she had wept, the sleepless nights, the agony, the certainty that she had been alone in the world...and it had all been a lie.

Well, she would just have to use a distraction technique. That was all. Marjorie smiled. "Would you like to kiss me, Alexander?"

He definitely stiffened beside her. "Kiss you?"

"Yes. You may kiss me, if you wish," she said lightly, closing her eyes and ignoring the thrumming of her pulse in her fingertips.

Surely, he was approaching her mouth this time. Surely, he would avail himself of such an opportunity. Surely, he would—

"Isn't the countryside marvelous?" came Alexander's voice.

Marjorie froze. Then she opened her eyes.

Alexander was staring about the place as though he had never seen a sight more engaging than the barren fields around them.

It was not disappointment that flooded through her, not exactly. It was more…despondency.

Well. He was Lord Alexander Chance. Whether or not she chose to believe him when he said he had not bedded any widows last Season—and she was tempted to believe him; there had been such honesty in his eyes—he had certainly bedded sufficient women to be an expert in the art of amorous congress.

And she was not saying that she wanted to be ruined! That was not it at all!

Just… Well. A little ruination, Marjorie could not help but think wistfully. *A little ruination would not go amiss.*

Perhaps another kiss.

"I must say, it gives me a hankering for Stanphrey Lacey," Alexander was saying.

Marjorie blinked. She had become distracted, and she really must pay attention. "'Stanphrey Lacey'?"

It was not a place she had ever heard of.

Alexander was nodding as he encouraged the horses to keep at their gentle pace. "Yes, the seat of the Chance family—it's my brother Thomas's now, I suppose, though out of deference and respect, he allows my parents to come and go as they please."

"Oh. Your country estate." The Daltons had one of their own, a small Jacobean manor with towering spiraling chimneys and dampness in all the wrong places.

"Not mine," Alexander said shortly. "I don't own property."

"And that bothers you," Marjorie said before she could stop herself. "Doesn't it?"

She had not been wrong; she had examined the man's face

too often in search of affection for her to misunderstand its meaning now.

But perhaps she should not have been so forthright, for Alexander released her hand then shrugged his shoulders. "No. No, it doesn't bother me."

Liar, Marjorie thought, but she did not have the bravery to say it. It was that kind of lie, the protective type, that she was not so stubborn against. Still, she would have liked to have earned his candid honesty about such a thing by now.

They continued on for a few minutes in awkward silence before Alexander sighed, leaned back in his seat, and said, "Fine!"

Marjorie pressed her lips together. "'Fine'?"

"Fine, it bothers me," said Alexander with a sigh. "I come from a large family, you know. Of course you know. Who couldn't know the Chances?"

"And my sister did marry your cousin, the new Marquess of Aylesbury," Marjorie pointed out, wincing slightly at the mention of her sister. The woman she barely knew.

"Yes, yes." Alexander waved her words away airily. "Four branches of the Chances family, and many, many cousins on each branch."

"Yes, I suppose so."

"Yet it is only the Cothrom branch that has three sons. Did you know that?"

In all honesty, Marjorie did not know that. There were, as he said, a great number of Chances, and it was often a challenge to tell to whom they all belonged. What was worse—not worse, per se, but perhaps even more confusing—was that about half of the younger generation was married now, adding several more Chances to the fold, and making it even more complicated. Who precisely had been born a Chance and who had become one upon marriage was something she rarely untangled.

And then Marjorie's gaze flickered to Alexander, understanding finally dawning. "You are one of the only Chance sons without property."

"Without property and without fortune," he said with a brisk smile that did not quite hide his frustration. "And I may not be the only younger son, but I am the only one with nothing to show for his name."

Marjorie winced. Her dowry. Her *rather large* dowry. Was that why the rake had claimed an interest in her, after all?

"Marjorie, please. I can read your panic on your face. I don't need to marry for money because I will always have family who can provide. It's just... I wanted something of my own. Something from *them*, a birthright that I didn't have to beg for. My eldest brother is the Duke of Cothrom and the other has his own townhouse and income from the Stanphrey Lacey estate. My cousin Samuel is now a marquess and the eldest son of my Uncle John, but his younger brother, Benjamin, has a small apartment and comfortable income, and my Uncles George and Frederick have but one son each who will inherit the lot."

It was astonishing, really, to see the lack of personal anger within the man's eyes. Marjorie could see that Alexander was frustrated by the situation, but nonetheless, he clearly bore no ill will toward his cousins.

"It is only I who must survive in the world with no income save that of what my father or brother offers me," Alexander said with a wry smile. "No home, safe for the roof they put over my heads. It is...emasculating."

"I had never considered that," Marjorie said quietly, not sure what she should say. It was different for women in Society. Even with her considerable dowry, she'd never be allowed to buy a home for herself or even touch more than her pin money's worth of money.

"I did not think of it much until this year," he replied, the horses slowly walking around the corner in the lane before Alexander brought them to a stop, the curricle rocking slightly as it came to a halt. "My life was full of joy and laughter and I spent where and when I wanted...until my brother Leopold married."

There did not seem to be much of a link here, but Marjorie

waited for the man to continue.

When Alexander did, it was in heavy tones. "All my life, I have felt an equal to my cousins, but now? Now I see I cannot offer a lady much beyond my name."

Beyond his name? Is the man out of his wits? "Alexander," Marjorie said resolutely, turning in her seat as best she could to face him. "You have so much to offer."

"Oh, you are very kind, and I am sure that in some ways, you are right," came the smiling response—the smile that did not quite reach Alexander's eyes. "But I am hardly a good match for anyone, Marjorie. Even… Even if I wanted to make an offer to a lady, I could not."

Marjorie's heart stilled. "Even… Even *if* you wanted—"

"Where would we live? What would we live off? No." Alexander shook his head. "No, matrimony is not something on the cards for me."

"But your wife! She might have a dowry!" Marjorie could not believe how ridiculous he was being. She'd spent her entire time out as a debutante avoiding fortune hunters, only for the one gentleman to actually get her hopes up to decide *he* was the one who needed to bring a fortune into the marriage?

It was not as if he were a pauper, with family so near to clothe and feed him for life! If he were, she might have thought this some sort of scheme to get her to *think* he would never marry her for her money, only to then turn around and accept the fortune gladly once she'd convinced him of the silliness of his notions.

Except he wasn't turning around and accepting her fortune.

He stared her in the eye. "I promised you I would not marry a woman for her money, and I meant it. I can tell that was important to you, too." Sighing, he looked down at the reins in his hand. "God, I was so foolish to suppose that—and your father, he asked about… No, I don't fancy my chance of ever finding a woman who would happily live off my brother's charity."

And that was perhaps what made her do it.

There was no rational thought involved, not really. Just the instinct to lean forward and try to convince the man seated beside her that she would be honored to receive such overtures.

Not that she was. Obviously.

Marjorie froze, stuck halfway between leaning forward and showing the man exactly just how much she would greatly welcome his attentions and realizing that she was about to throw herself into the arms of a man who would not marry.

Who would not marry.

Not a man who did not wish to marry but who was too prideful to do so. Alexander Chance was a flirt, yes, and a rake—but he had never offered marriage to a lady before because he'd believed he could not. He wouldn't marry for the promise of a large dowry—she was sure of that now. He likely could have long ago if that were true.

And that made him a very different man, indeed.

Alexander blew out an exhale as he shook his head and directed the horses to the side of the empty lane. The carriage rolled to a stop, the horses grazing at the grass. He let go of the reins. "And now you will wish to be taken back to your parents, and our courtship will come to an end, and you will never wish to spend time with me again."

"And what do you know about my wishes?" Marjorie interjected, knowing full well she could never articulate to this man precisely what she wanted.

Not while being able to look him in the eye, that was.

"I... I..." When he swallowed, Marjorie did her best not to stare at his throat.

She failed, but the attempt had been made.

"I wish you had kissed me on the lips just now," she said instead, which was hardly an improvement because it made her cheeks flush and her hands quiver. "That's... That's what I wish."

Alexander's brow furrowed. "But... But I have just told you, I cannot marry a woman for her money. I would want to provide for my wife. I won't be the only Chance who can't do that."

"Did I just ask you to marry me?" Marjorie was absolutely going to regret this; she knew she would. She would lie awake tonight and wish she had not said it. She would wake up in the morning and groan over the fact that she had said it. She would probably have this memory resurface every few weeks for the rest of her life, and every time, she would wish she had not—

Alexander's kiss was strong, and passionate, and yet gentle and slow. He had pulled her somehow into his arms and Marjorie melted into them, her fingers tangling around his neck and pulling him closer as his lips parted hers, delving into their warm sweetness and trailing pleasure through her mouth.

Oh, this was too much.

And yet not enough. Even as Alexander's hands slipped to her waist, holding her tightly as though he never wanted her to leave his embrace, Marjorie moaned as hot, molten need dripped down her body and collected between her thighs. Pressing them together did not help and yet nothing would, nothing could—

"Marjorie," Alexander exhaled in a ragged voice, as though she had taken all his self-control.

That could not have been true, for Marjorie had no self-control at all, none of her own, none of Alexander's—in fact she had never had self-control in her life, from what she could recall.

She could recall nothing: nothing save the fact that Alexander was nibbling on her lips and his right hand was now cupping her buttock and if she were not careful, Marjorie was going to find herself actually in the man's lap—

And that sounded wonderful.

Marjorie whimpered with the overwhelming sensation of it all, and for some reason, that broke the kiss.

Alexander leaned away from her, and it was all Marjorie could do not to crawl toward him and mount him right here in the curricle—

"I should not have done that," he said quietly.

All the spark and fire disappeared from Marjorie. "You... You should not have?"

As he turned from her, Alexander's jaw tightened, as though he had wished to say something but had forced himself not to.

What on earth was this man up to? Telling her he could never propose marriage to anyone, then kissing her like that…as though she were the only woman on the planet, and he wanted to start repopulation immediately?

"You wanted to kiss me," Marjorie said quietly.

Alexander's laugh was brief. "I did."

"And I wanted to kiss you."

There it was—the flicker of tension in his jaw. "You did."

"So why—"

"I am attempting to…to get back on the straight and narrow, as my father would say," Alexander said, his voice both harsh and rueful at the same time. "I am trying to be a gentleman. I am trying not to tempt you to—"

"To what? Wish to kiss you?" Marjorie interjected, *need* thrumming through her and causing her to throw caution to the wind. "*Need* to kiss you?"

"*Marjorie!*"

She almost laughed at how scandalized the man beside her looked. "You are a fine one to look mortified. Have you not done far more?"

"Yes. But not with you, and however much I might wish—"

Hope leapt within her. "So you *do* wish to bed me?"

Alexander muttered a curse that was most inventive, one Marjorie had never heard before. "Woman, you are most tempting!"

Then be tempted.

That was what she wanted to say. But even as they sat there, in the bright spring sunshine with a cuckoo calling out the beginning of the season, Marjorie was not so enamored with the man beside her that she had lost all reason.

Not completely.

"You… You are trying to be respectable," she said slowly, understanding—and disappointment—dawning in equal measure.

When Alexander glanced at her, his expression was conflicted. "And failing, yes. But trying."

And though Marjorie knew she should be impressed, that she should applaud a rake attempting to restore his reputation, that she should be grateful the man who was courting her was trying to be respectable, and even more honored that it was she who had prompted such a change of heart...

Well. She could not help but be disappointed.

"Does this mean that you are not going to seduce me?" Marjorie asked before she could stop herself.

Alexander repeated the curse she had only recently learned and did not turn to look at her as he picked up the reins. "No, Lady Marjorie. I will not lie to you."

Lady Marjorie. It's like that, is it?

I am insufficient to tempt him, Marjorie thought dully as Alexander turned the curricle around in the lane and steered the topic to the weather as he drove them toward Bath again. Other ladies had managed to break down those walls, but not her.

So what was the point, then, of all this courting? If he were not going to bed her, and he was not going to marry her...what, precisely, were they doing?

And why was she so pathetic as to greedily accept any iota of attention he gave her?

Chapter Ten

March 27, 1841

"**A**ND YOU ARE absolutely sure I cannot—"

"When I asked you to accompany me, Alexander Montague Arthur Chance," said the Dowager Duchess of Cothrom severely, "I meant *accompany me.*"

Alexander sighed as the carriage pulled to a slow stop outside the large townhouse from which light, music, and general noise were already emanating. "Yes, Mother."

It was not so difficult a task, he supposed. Had circumstances been different, he would naturally have been delighted to accompany his mother to one of her balls. It was always amusing, dancing with pretty, young things, smoking and drinking with whichever of his friends were in town, and there was always the possibility of a kiss…

But now the circumstances were different.

Now the only kiss he wanted was with a woman he was almost certain had not been invited to such a prestigious gathering.

Alexander swallowed. Considering the relative newness of her father's title and the bores the marquess and marchioness were, Lady Marjorie Dalton was not always part of the refined set, despite her large dowry—though her sister's recent marriage and restored reputation had slightly changed that. Still, she had not mentioned attending tonight, and that meant one thing.

He was not going to enjoy it.

"I'm sure you'll enjoy it," his mother said soothingly as the carriage door opened and a footman's hand extended. "I heard Lord Gascoyne will be here. Won't that be nice?"

Alexander's smile did not falter. Not exactly. "Oh, Lord Gascoyne. That will be nice."

And in a way, he was not fibbing. It would be nice to have the chance to speak to the old boy, see how he was doing…and perhaps run by him an idea which had been percolating in his mind since they had last met at the Pump Room, what felt like an age ago. He had wished to rebel once, long ago now, but the intrigue had faded, and all he wanted was his reputation back.

Or he could leave now, hightail it across town, climb up to a window, creep into Marjorie's bedchamber—

"Alexander!"

"Bedchamber," he blurted out—then froze as he caught himself saying probably one of the few words that would directly spark his mother's ire.

The dowager duchess glared from where she stood on the pavement, leaning back into the carriage. "Alexander Montague Arthur Chase, if I hear you have been sneaking into ladies' bedchambers again…"

"You won't," Alexander said hastily.

What he did not say, of course, was that it was impossible for her to hear it again because he had never done it. No, the few times that he had entered a lady's bedchamber, he had been invited and stepped through the doorway. No need for sneaking.

That was, however, beside the point.

His mother was still glaring. "If you can't behave yourself—"

"Yes, yes, I will behave myself. Anything for you, Mama." Alexander offered her a brief smile as he stepped forward and exited the carriage to stand beside her.

It was a wide pavement, but that did not preclude it from being incredibly busy. Evidently, the Sharnwick ball was a refined affair, but that did not ensure that it was refined all the way from out here. Pie sellers and hawkers had gathered around the front door, where there was a great deal of movement, a pair of singers had put down their caps in the hope of a few coppers, there were other guests and their servants attempting to push through, and a few drivers who had already deposited their charges trying to reach the braziers.

"Oh, we'll never get in at this rate." The dowager duchess sighed. "Well, there's nothing for it."

Alexander offered his arm. "Do not concern yourself, Mama. I will—*Mama!*"

If he had not seen it with his own eyes, he would not have believed it. He was still not sure if he did believe it.

The lovely yet distinctly middle-aged woman carefully removed a hairpin, steadied herself, and then began jabbing.

"Mama!"

It appeared all Alexander could do was follow in the woman's wake as individuals jumped and started, rubbing their behinds or scratching their backs as they twisted to see what they had inadvertently walked into. Serenely, and most worryingly, as though she had done this countless times before, the Dowager Duchess of Cothrom sailed through the crowd without a care in the world.

"Mama!" exclaimed Alexander in a hiss as they reached the front door and sailed through it. "I could have helped you through. You did not need to do *that.*"

"Oh, I am sure you would have done an admirable job," his mother said placidly, returning the hairpin into her delicate coiffure. "But I saw Lady Marjorie Dalton out there, and presuming you would be distracted—"

"Marjorie—Marjorie, here?" Alexander pained his neck by twisting around so hurriedly. "I have to go back. I have to see her."

"I can't believe it. You *do* care for her."

Alexander froze. *Oh, dear.*

When he turned slowly back to his mother, there was a knowing smile on the woman's face and he could have kicked himself for so easily falling into her trap.

Alice Chance, the Dowager Duchess of Cothrom, was not a meddling woman. She rarely forced her way into her children's lives, preferring to observe from a distance.

But not all the time.

"That was unfair of you, Mama," Alexander pointed out sharply—though admittedly, not as sharply as the previously wielded hairpin—as footmen stepped forward to relieve them of their outer garments.

"Perhaps it was, and perhaps it wasn't," said his mother cheerfully. "Are you going to tell me about her, Zander?"

Goodness, if she was using his childhood pet name, she must truly wish to know all about her.

And though the need to discuss the woman who was fast capturing his heart was buzzing within him, Alexander hesitated.

Until now, Marjorie had been…his.

Not actually his. Though he did desperately wish to possess her, he had not entirely lost his head and taken her to bed.

But their times together, those had been *his* times. Their conversations were something precious, not to be shared with just anyone. As were the few kisses he had stolen, but there would surely never be any further kisses now he had declared he could not marry her. He'd meant it when he'd told her he wouldn't marry her for her dowry. He could tell the prospect of being someone's payday bothered her. While he'd understood when Thomas had sought a rich wife—why he had even given consideration to Lady Marjorie himself—circumstances weren't so dire for Alexander.

But his circumstances weren't anything to be proud of, either.

"Zander?"

Alexander blinked. He had been standing before his mother, attention lost in the distance, thinking of his own stupidity with Lady Marjorie Dalton, and not moving.

Not a brilliant way to attempt to convince his mother that he had no great feelings for the young woman.

"Lady Marjorie Dalton is a very beautiful woman," he said

hoarsely.

Blast. He hadn't actually intended to speak that way. It just appeared that his throat had been unable to do anything *but* speak that way.

Which was most inconvenient.

His mother beamed. "I knew it! I knew eventually you would find a lady who would be worthy of you!"

"I think it far more likely that *I* am unworthy of *her*, Mama," Alexander said gruffly, keeping his voice low and hoping to goodness no one else in the Sharnwicks' hallway had heard them. "Come on. In we go."

"Yes, yes, we mustn't keep Lady Marjorie waiting…"

It would have been a fine thing, indeed, if they had been keeping Lady Marjorie waiting, Alexander could not help but think as they stepped through the double doors into the large ballroom of the Sharnwicks. But he'd heard nothing to indicate that Lady Marjorie Dalton—and her boorish parents—had been invited.

As it was, the room was packed to the rafters with people who were not the Daltons. The center of the room was full of waltzing couples, barely able to turn in the crush, while the walls were lined with spectators. At least, they were *supposed* to be watching the dancing. As far as Alexander could tell, most of them were chattering loudly, arguing, or drinking as much wine as the Sharnwick cellars could afford.

Hell's bells, but he did not miss this. Why on earth was it that he had agreed to come with his mother to this infernal ball?

Ah, yes. Because she gave me no choice.

"Now, I'm going to go and speak with Lady Romeril and a few other ladies," the dowager duchess said brightly, lightly patting her son's arm.

A wry smile crept across Alexander's face. "But you'll hate that."

"You don't attend a ball for amusement, dear," his mother said placidly, though with a sparkle in her eye. "At least, not at my time of life."

"Woman, you're not yet fifty."

"Oh, hush, do you want the whole world to know?" The dowager duchess tapped him lightly with her fan. "Go and be a nuisance elsewhere."

His mother bustled off into the crowd and Alexander could not help but smile. The woman may not have been born a Chance, but she made a very good effort at scandalizing everyone she came up against.

A Chance trait, if ever there was one.

Right. He was standing in the middle of a ballroom, no longer accompanying his mother, desperately not thinking about Marjorie, wondering if there was any easy way of hailing a footman with a glass of wine, determinedly not thinking about Marjorie, being careful not to catch any lady's eye so he would not have to dance, and most definitely not thinking about Marjorie.

Wait a moment. He had already spent a great deal of time thinking about Marjorie.

Alexander groaned. *Blast it all to hell.*

"Yes, I was thinking just the same thing," said a familiar voice behind him.

Trying not to smile, for he could lay good odds on the fact that his friend had *not* been thinking of Lady Marjorie Dalton, as he'd made comments once years before that despite her large dowry, she was far too unassuming for him, Alexander turned. "Gascoyne!"

"That's *Lord* Gascoyne to you in these circles." Gascoyne grinned as he thrust out a hand.

Alexander shook it. "You found yourself dragged here too?"

"Mother insisted," said his friend, rolling his eyes. "And who am I to deny her?"

"You and I arrived in the same boat, then." Alexander chuckled.

There was always something so comforting about being with

friends…and yet in a strange way, there were tendrils of tension meandering up his spine and across his shoulder blades as Alexander realized precisely what conversation must be had this evening.

Enough was enough. The name of Lord Alexander Chance had been used as a scapegoat for years now, and Gascoyne as well as a few other friends had more than benefited by hiding their true identities as they'd seduced and beguile their way through the widows of Society. It was growing riskier and riskier for them all, as they were no longer cherub-faced, almost indistinguishable dark-haired men fresh out of school and more and more people were sure to recognize them by their true identities.

It was time for this to come to an end. Time for things to change.

A time for Lord Alexander Chance to reclaim his name.

"Gascoyne," he began.

His friend ignored him. "So, which are you taking back with you?"

Alexander blinked. "'Back with me'? Back with me where?"

What on earth was the man talking about?

It took only an additional fraction of a second, however, for his mind to catch up with him. Gascoyne's eyes were roving around the ballroom, lingering on the ladies who were fair, mostly unattached, and below the age of fifty.

Ah.

"I wasn't actually—"

"I will admit, it is much easier to bed a woman under the name of Chance than my own," Gascoyne said blithely, nudging his friend in the arm as he grinned. "It does help, there being so many of you, of course. I don't wonder that you get all the ladies falling into your arms!"

That had never happened. Oh, Alexander had wanted it to in his younger days, but now…now all he wanted was Lady Marjorie Dalton.

Blast. Concentrate, man!

"Yes, on the topic of using my name—"

"So which one are you going to choose for yourself?" asked Gascoyne curiously. "I will admit, it might be a mite challenging for us to both use the name Lord Alexander Chance at the same ball, but Percival and I have managed it before."

"I am not going to take a woman here to bed," Alexander insisted, hoping to goodness his voice was not carrying.

It would not do for his mother to find out that he'd been having such a conversation, and in public, to boot.

"Excellent. Off to meet a lover elsewhere? I'll have it all my own way, then," Gascoyne said cheerfully.

Alexander sighed. "I'm not taking *any* woman to bed."

His friend blinked rapidly. "You're not?"

"No," Alexander said firmly.

"Not even a chambermaid?"

"No," he repeated, even more firmly now—or at least, he hoped he did. "Look—"

"Oh, I see what's happened," and now his friend's lips were curling into a smile that was not actually kind. "You've fallen in love."

Alexander balked before he could stop himself. "No I haven't."

"I thought it might catch you eventually, but I was hoping you wouldn't fall into such a trap, my good man." Gascoyne sighed, rolling his eyes, as though his friend had greatly disappointed him. "Is it her? She's dazzlingly beautiful. Where have I seen her before? You think I would remember a woman with such a...*shape* to her. But it must be her, mustn't it? She can't stop looking your way."

The man gestured with a refined cuff into the distance.

Despite himself, Alexander turned and looked in the direction his friend was pointing, and his stomach lurched.

There, standing in the doorway, having just entered the ballroom...was Lady Marjorie Dalton.

And she looked magnificent. Her gown was sumptuous,

shimmering silk and delicate gold embroidery shaped around a figure that was delicious enough to make every man around her stand to attention. But it wasn't just her figure that was brilliant; it was her face. Her eyes, bright and inquisitive, and yet reluctant somehow to engage in the chatter around her. That graceful neck, those delicate lips, all parts of the woman that Alexander had examined closely and believed he now knew by memory.

And she was alone.

That was, her parents had evidently been delayed in the hall, but right at this moment, she was alone.

"Her?" Alexander croaked.

"Yes, she looks pretty enough to take any man's fancy," said Gascoyne with a shrug. "Or if you don't want her, I might—"

"No." The syllable was sentence enough, and Alexander had to force his hands to stay by his sides rather than grasp his friend by the throat and threaten him to never look at, let alone speak to, the woman in question again. He stepped in front of his wretched friend and blocked his line of sight of the lady in question. If Gascoyne figured out who she was, how she had blossomed during her time abroad, that fact combined with her ample dowry might give the viscount a new perspective on the prospect of matrimony to an "unassuming" bride. "Look, Gascoyne, about the way you use my name when you're seducing—"

"Yes, I suppose one day I shall have to retire it." His friend sighed melodramatically, grabbing a glass of wine from a passing footman. He did not retrieve one for Alexander. "But to be quite frank, my good man, I relish using it. Saves my family name getting dragged into scandal."

"What?" Alexander said blankly. He'd been staring over his shoulder as the viscount had spoken and most unfortunately, as Marjorie had taken a step into the ballroom, a gentleman had approached her, causing Alexander's mind to stop.

"What?" repeated his friend, clearly nonplussed. "I was saying that I'm not so well-known as Viscount Gascoyne yet that I've been recognized. There was one incident where a lady did wonder, but well, just the one. Mamas aren't eager to marry their daughters to a man with a title if he's lacking the fortune to back it up. One day, I'll have to marry a fortune, and I can't have a reputation when I do. So I will keep using the name Alexander Chance for my—"

But Alexander was no longer listening.

How could he, when he had already taken five steps away from the man whose voice was fading into the background of the general ballroom hum? Besides, even if he had stayed close to Gascoyne, the wild buzzing in his ears that had forced the rest of the ballroom to disappear would have made it quite impossible.

His Marjorie was speaking to another man.

Oh, it was ridiculous, how possessive he felt of her, but despite Alexander having absolutely no claim to the woman save his own desires, he felt deeply within himself that it was a crime, almost, for a man to be talking to her like that.

For any man to be speaking to her at all, now that he came to think.

Feet propelling him forward without thought—what did he need thought for, when instincts were so powerful?—Alexander strode up to the woman he now knew had a greater power over him than any other.

And she was giggling.

"Oh, come now, I am sure that is not—"

"Introduce me to your friend," Alexander said gruffly, glaring at the gentleman who had the audacity to speak to his woman.

Ahem. Speak to Lady Marjorie Dalton without being introduced. Obviously.

Only then, once the broad-shouldered rogue turned around, did he realize that in fact, he knew the man in question. "Sammy!"

"Zander, you old dog," said his cousin, the new Marquess of Aylesbury now that his father had decided, much like Alexander's own, to relinquish his title. "You did not tell me you'd kept up an acquaintance with the Daltons after their ball!"

Acquaintance? Oh, he wanted to be far more intimately involved...

Not that Alexander was about to admit to such a thing. In public. To his cousin. In front of Marjorie.

"Ah," Alexander managed, trying his best to smile but realizing at once that he was in fact grimacing. "Yes. Marjorie—Lady Marjorie and I... We... Oh, and you're her brother-in-law."

That fact was only just seeping into his mind, and it was making Alexander feel like a total fool of the first degree.

Not a pleasant feeling.

"I was just about to ask Marjorie to dance the next waltz," Cousin Samuel was said placidly. "But I suppose now that you are here, she will wish to dance with you, rather than her own relative!"

And that was when Alexander's blood froze.

Dance. Dance, in public, with a woman for whom he truly cared? He'd never done such a thing in his life.

Oh, he had danced in public, and with ladies who'd fawned over him and the Chance name. A few of them had even danced with him on a second occasion, even after discovering that he had little to live on and no opportunities for matrimony if they did not already have a sizable dowry themselves.

But there had been no soft feelings, no emotional stirrings, when he had taken those women in his arms.

To dance something as intimate as the waltz, and with Marjorie...

A Marjorie whose breath hitched as she stared at him. "I would be delighted, Lord Alexander."

Alexander opened his mouth, but no sound came out.

He closed it again.

He opened it again, desperately willing his mouth to say something, anything. *Words, man, words! You know words! You can't just stare at a pretty woman and say noth—*

"Pretty," Alexander said thickly.

Marjorie flushed as his cousin smirked and clapped him on the shoulder. "Excellent! That leaves me to dance with Rose and make a true scandal of the whole evening. Good to see you, Zander."

He disappeared. He might have walked off, Alexander wondered wildly, or he might have vanished in a puff of smoke. He wasn't sure.

He hadn't been paying much attention to Samuel.

"You really think so?" Marjorie asked, her cheeks pinking as she held out her hand.

Alexander took it instinctively but had to ask, "Think what?"

Her cheeks darkened. "That I'm pretty?"

Pretty? Had she no concept of what she looked like, how dazzling she was—were there no looking glasses in the marquess's household? Could the woman really not see the effect she was having on all the gentlemen around her—on him?

Alexander smiled weakly as his pulse skipped a beat. "Yes. Very."

The musicians ended their piece and light applause filled the ballroom, causing Alexander's breath to catch in his throat.

A new dance. A dance with Marjorie.

How the hell had he never been nervous before in his life? That had to be what he was feeling in this moment, wasn't it? The fluttery twist in his stomach, the weakness in his knees, the dryness in his throat, the way his gaze could not tear itself away from Marjorie…

That was nerves, wasn't it?

"I think they're about to start," murmured Marjorie quietly, her large eyes peering up at him brightly.

"Start," repeated Alexander, transfixed by the shape of her mouth.

"Alexander?"

"Marjorie," he whispered, delighted to have the excuse to say her name.

Her eyes flickered down to their entwined fingers. "The—the

dance. The waltz."

Waltz?

Oh, yes, right. The waltz.

Alexander stepped forward in a dream, leading the woman of said dreams with him into the center of the ballroom. There was his mother, beaming happily and fluttering her fan as though there were no tomorrow. There was his cousin Samuel, arm in arm with Marjorie's sister and his wife, Rose, and causing a great amount of murmuring at the audacious decision to dance with his own wife, and in public, when unwed ladies were in need of partners. There was his friend Gascoyne, eagerly talking away with a young lady who was fluttering her eyelashes.

None of *that* mattered.

Only she mattered: Marjorie. When Alexander took her in his arms, he wondered why his gloves did not combust with the heat pouring between them. When they waited, arm in arm, for the music to begin, Alexander could not tear his eyes away from hers, from the trust within them, and something more.

And when the music began and Alexander led them to the right, one two three, one two three, the gentle rhythm of the dance swaying them slowly around the ballroom…

Well, there was absolutely no one else in the world except Lady Marjorie Dalton.

Heat was roaring through Alexander's veins, his feet were moving of their own accord, and all he could think to say was, "I didn't want to dance this evening."

A shadow flickered over Marjorie's face. "I-I am sorry. I did not intend to put you into such a position."

"I am glad you did. I am glad you are here." Alexander knew he sounded like an absolute fool, but as it turned out, whenever he was in Marjorie's presence, he was one. "I… I…"

There were words, Alexander was almost sure of it, but they slipped through his mind like melted butter, covering him with the sense of the words but nothing concrete to hold on to.

Oh, this woman. How has she managed to bewitch me so utterly?

Marjorie's smile was light, and her eyes were earnest as she said, "I quite agree. At the very least, I am glad you are here to distract me from the current familial drama."

"That sounds far more like a Chance problem than a Dalton one," Alexander said, chuckling. "What—oh. I see."

His gaze had followed hers, and he saw Lord and Lady Dalton standing stiffly a few feet from his dancing cousin Samuel, and his wife, Rose. Lady Rose Dalton, once upon a time.

It was the way they were very carefully not looking at each other which gave it away.

"Wounds not fully healed, I suppose?" Alexander murmured as he tried to both inhale that delicious scent she was wearing and not trip over his own feet.

Marjorie allowed herself to be effortlessly carried around the dance. "Not quite. I haven't quite forgiven my parents yet, either, I suppose. Not entirely."

Now *that* was interesting. "Why? Forgive for what?"

Was that a flicker of discomfort on her face—no, more, a pulse of uncertainty?

Whatever it was, Marjorie gripped his hand more tightly and said, in almost a whisper, "When my sister... When Rose left home...disappeared, I suppose is more accurate... Well. She had eloped and my parents could not bear the shame so they...my parents told me she had died. I know we told everyone else that she had been sent to live with relatives in the country, how fresh air was better for her frail condition. They told me that at first, too, that her need for air had been so sudden, she'd left when I'd been fast asleep one night. But when I asked to visit her, they said I could never. That she was dead. But that no one else could know the truth." She scoffed. "The *truth*."

Alexander really did trip over his own feet this time. "What the blazes?"

Managing to get a hold of himself and straighten up, smiling at the other dancing couples who stared over at them in curiosity, he looked down at Marjorie and felt, finally, that he was starting to understand her.

"I told you before—I hate liars."

Of course. There had to have been a reason, and now it all made sense.

"They told you that?"

"They only told me that she lived two years ago, when apparently she wrote," Marjorie said, her voice taut and her face expressionless. Purposefully so. "All that time, they had lied to my face. Day in, day out, our whole lives had been a lie. And it had to continue to be so, that I was still to pretend she was off in the country for her health. Not that anyone ever asked after her by that time."

"I am so sorry that they said that to you," he said quietly.

Marjorie did not allow her head to fall as she said brightly, "I was but fourteen, and I suppose they thought it would be easier."

"'Easier'? To inaccurately believe that your own sibling was dead?" Alexander said incredulously. "What cruelty!"

Perhaps too incredulously. Marjorie's expression altered, something between a defiant glare and a repentant awkwardness. "They are my parents. Only *I* get to criticize them."

Which was a fair point. "You amaze me," came the words from Alexander's mouth, most unaccountably.

The dance twisted them around again and his fingers tightened around her waist. Every point of contact between him and this wonderful woman was precious somehow.

"I do?"

"You do. You are a woman who has been lied to about one of the most important things, dragged into a more complicated lie yourself, yet you have not complained nor criticized."

"Or cut them off," added Marjorie helpfully with a wicked smile. "Which I did consider, for a time, though where would I go? Like you, I am dependent on my parents. I cannot just decide to leave them. They will give my dowry to no one but my husband. Certainly not me. But anyone else who lies to me about something so grave...anyone at all. I will not have them in my life."

A shiver ran down Alexander's spine.

I need to tell her. She deserved the truth—and surely, it would a relief, for her to know that the man poorly courting her was nowhere near the renegade she believed him to be?

Alexander bit his lip. Or...was that the attraction? Was Lady Marjorie Dalton the sort of woman to desire a man with a roguish reputation, a man condemned by Society?

The music finished. The dance ended. The applause rang out and all he could do was look at her.

This enigma. This forgiving, unforgiving woman.

When would he be brave enough to tell her the truth?

Chapter Eleven

March 31, 1841

"A ND THEN I realized, I was in the wrong street! And so of course there wasn't a number forty-seven, the street simply wasn't long enough, and naturally, I felt like a dolt, but really, there aren't enough street signs these days."

Marjorie made sure to nod at what she presumed was the right place. She had to presume because she wasn't listening.

Oh, it wasn't Miss Ramsay's fault. The story was surely fascinating, and even in the hands of a more accomplished storytelling, Marjorie would not have been able to pay attention.

Because although the Mrs. Wainright's Teashop and Emporium—one of Marjorie's favorite haunts whenever she was in Bath—was not that busy, there was one table that had gained her notice from the moment that its occupants had entered, five minutes ago.

The Chances.

"Though chocolate is so dear at the moment, I just had to have another slice. The cake was so delicious!"

"Yes," Marjorie said vaguely, her gaze affixed not on her golden-haired, buxom friend, but on the gaggle of people seated just over her shoulder.

The Chances. The Cothrom Chances, to be specific. Each of the four branches of the Chance family had its own foibles, that was what the gossip said, and the Cothrom branch was the most senior and therefore—apparently—the more decorous and conscious of scandal.

Which perhaps explained the stiffness of the people seated before her.

"And each sandwich to be cut into exact quarters," an older gentleman was saying sternly to the poor footman of the establishment who was acting as server. "No more and no less—"

"The man understands how to cut a sandwich, dear," a woman with silvering hair and sparkling eyes said genially. "Now then, as to tea—"

"I really must have Earl Grey. There is no other option," came Lady Maude's voice, bright and brilliant over the mutters of her brothers. "Victoria?"

"Oh, I would much rather have Ceylon," said a woman also seated at the table whom Marjorie vaguely recognized. "Kathleen?"

"You know, I have never tried it," said another woman, this one a little rugged in her beauty, her complexion kissed by sunlight—surely another Chance wife? "What do you think, Leopold?"

"A pot of everything, I say." The second Chance brother grinned. "That is, different pots, not all in one. What say you, Zander?"

And a small part of Marjorie melted within her as she was given permission by the conversation—finally—to look over at the man who had caught her attention in the first place when the crowd of them had entered the tearoom.

Zander. Alexander Chance.

He looked...different.

"But then if I had worn it to the Waldens' card party, there would have been quite the rumpus, for, as you would expect, the hostess was wearing much the same, and I do hate to be twinning especially accidentally..."

Yes, there is something different about him, Marjorie mused as her eyes flickered over the face of the man that she knew so well—or at least, she thought she did.

Perhaps it was because she had never seen him with his family, outside of that brief meeting at the Pump Room. Alexander Chance had always been the wooer, the pursuer, the seducer—not that he had managed to seduce her, of course. Not entirely. Not that she would have said *no* at this point...

The point, Marjorie reminded herself firmly as her cheeks burned, *is that he is always confident*. Always the director of the conversation, always leading the day.

This Alexander was just...sitting there.

Hands folded in his lap, shoulders slumped, eyes downcast, there was nothing about the figure behind Miss Ramsay that said that the man was a great rake and seducer of women.

And it was—well, odd.

Odd, to see him so differently.

He had not looked over at her, which Marjorie was telling herself was a godsend because there was no possibility of her saying anything to such a prestigious family, let alone in public. As though it weren't enough that her sister had caused a scandal by reappearing in Society and aligning herself to one of the most notable families in Society. The last thing she wanted was to cause a scene.

"Ah, Lady Marjorie!"

Marjorie flinched. *Oh, no.*

"Lady Marjorie!" The older woman, who had to be the Dowager Duchess of Cothrom, and Alexander's mother, was waving to her most happily, though a cloud appeared to have descended on her husband's brow as she did so. "Maudey, it's Lady Marjorie!"

"Oh, excellent," came Lord Leopold's voice as he rose from his seat. "Come, Kathleen. Let me introduce you to Lady Marjorie!"

"What is happening?" Miss Ramsay hissed, leaning forward over their half-consumed sandwiches and cooling tea.

Marjorie had absolutely no idea. "I... I..."

But there was no time for her to say anything else before the entire Chance table descended upon them.

"—so lovely to meet you. Leopold has told me all about you—"

"—your sister is working wonders with old Sammy; he's quite a changed man—not that there was anything wrong with him to start with, mostly—"

"—delighted to see you here. Are you a patron of Mrs. Wainright's Teashop and Emporium often? We'll have to arrange luncheon—"

Marjorie was barraged with noise and sound and polite smiles and none of them mattered.

Because none of them had come from the one person to whom she wished to speak.

Crowding her table was William Chance, the Dowager Duke of Cothrom; his wife, Alice Chance; their eldest son and the new Duke of Cothrom, Thomas Chance; his wife, Victoria Chance, the new duchess; then Lord Leopold, the next brother, and his wife, Kathleen Chance, Lady Leopold; and Lady Maude, swiping a sandwich from Marjorie's plate and declaring that it was mightily good. And there was Alexander.

Standing quietly. Saying nothing.

Marjorie's stomach lurched and instead of heat flooding her cheeks, she rather thought she was now made of ice.

Is he...embarrassed by me?

That had to be the only reason, did it not? Why else did he stand there awkwardly, not quite reaching the table, saying nothing?

A sense of desperation poured through her lungs like water and Marjorie was gasping, gasping for air as she drowned in her seat.

"You know, Lady Marjorie, you do not look at all well," Miss Ramsay almost shouted to be heard over the hubbub.

And the hubbub ceased. All eyes turned to Miss Ramsay, giving Marjorie a modicum of relief, before all eyes turned slowly to herself.

Ah. Wonderful.

"She does *not* look well," said the new Duchess of Cothrom, leaning forward and peering at Marjorie, who shrank back.

"Don't crowd her—"

"Don't push me, Leopold—"

"All I said was—"

"I shall escort her home."

The five words were not spoken loudly, nor with any hint of demand or arrogance within them. Quite to the contrary, they were gentle and spoken as though to the air, not to a particular person.

The entire Chance family fell silent as all eyes turned, this time—and to Marjorie's great relief—to the man who had just spoken.

Alexander.

He gave a brief, utterly unwarm smile, and held out his arm. "Come, Lady Marjorie. Let's get you home."

"Oh, but I don't have the carriage, how terribly unfortunate," began Miss Ramsay, her voice a mite sharp now that Marjorie came to think of it. "Besides, I haven't finished my cake."

"I can walk her home, and Maudey can come with us. Besides, fresh air will undoubtedly do her good," Alexander said, his voice still low and quiet, none of the bombastic power in it that Marjorie knew so well. He extended his arm.

Marjorie swallowed. She was not, absolutely not, going to think too much about this. She was not going to consider the meaning of walking home with a gentleman courting her, she was not going to think of precisely what her friend was going to tell absolutely all of their acquaintances the minute she saw them, and she certainly wasn't going to ponder what the Chance family—what Alexander's family was going to presume from this unexpected and totally out of character act of chivalry.

No. Not at all.

She rose from her seat and took Alexander's arm. His sister, Maude, gasped.

"Maudey!" hissed her mother.

"It's just…he didn't *ask* me."

"You will do him this favor. And you will behave yourself!" the dowager duchess said sharply before turning a smile to Marjorie. "And you will remember me to your mother, Lady Marjorie. Give Lady Dalton my—tell her I can't wait to—that is, give her my compliments."

And there it was, Marjorie could not help but think, as she stepped away from her table through the now-silent tearoom on Lord Alexander Chance's arm with Lady Maude trailing behind them. Just when she thought it could not get any more awkward…

"You know, Society's stuffiness notwithstanding, I do actually need to pop into the circulating library to collect my order," Lady Maude said with a brief smile before they'd even made it to the end of the block. "I am certain the two of you can handle a little walk on your own?"

"Maude," her brother said quietly.

Marjorie's breath caught in her lungs. She couldn't be suggesting—surely, she wasn't suggesting… Didn't she require a chaperone herself? Or was Lady Maude actually considered a spinster, now that Marjorie came to think of it?

"And I'll catch up with you!" called Lady Maude, practically over her shoulder as she rushed off. "I won't be long!"

Marjorie swallowed and looked up at the man with whom she was now alone.

Well. As alone as two people could be in the middle of Bath, which was not alone at all.

But unchaperoned.

Alexander had been right. The fresh air was invigorating, the chill of early spring pinching at her cheeks and making her feel more awake than she had done since she'd first sat at the tea table with Miss Ramsay.

Which was perhaps not a kind thing to think, but it was true.

"I apologize."

Marjorie looked up into the handsome and clearly unsettled

face of Alexander as they stood outside the tearoom. "You do?"

What for should have been the question on her lips, but she was momentarily distracted by the fact that the window of the Mrs. Wainright's Teashop and Emporium closest to them was now absolutely packed with faces.

Chance faces.

The dowager duchess, the duke and the duchess, and Lord and Lady Leopold, along with two other patrons Marjorie did not recognize, had all rushed to the nearest window to watch them leave and were now gawping at them. The only member of the Chance family who appeared not to have done so was the dowager duke—undoubtedly because it was so shameful, though Marjorie could still see him, standing on tiptoes in an attempt to catch a glimpse of them.

Oh, Lord...

"My family. They are very direct, you understand, and though that works in a family..." Alexander sighed. "Come on. Let's get you home."

It was not, Marjorie could not help but think, the most encouraging of statements to make, but perhaps that was only because he was unsettled by his family's frankly blatant behavior.

So did they think that she and he were...and that they would marry?

It was a startling thought, particularly given the nature of their last conversation on the subject, Marjorie could not help but think.

She had not brought it up again—why would she? There had been no more to add, and she was not going to presume on intentions that, regardless of whether or not they existed, could never be acted upon if he were to remain stubborn about accepting a wife's dowry.

And so they walked, slowly and in silence, along the pavement.

Marjorie managed to last a whole two streets, which she thought was impressive, before she said impulsively, "Your family seemed very pleasant."

Alexander snorted and did not look at her. "They are *pleasant*, I grant you that."

It did not sound a particularly pleasant statement to her, and Marjorie swallowed as she looked away. *Well, I attempted conversation.*

It was only when they had crossed over the next street that Alexander said suddenly, "I have had an argument with my father."

Marjorie's stomach twisted. "I am sorry to hear that."

"It was my own fault, as usual," came the bitter reply. "I wanted to ask him for—I mean, it did not seem like much. And it would greatly change my life. Change the life of another, too."

I am not going to look too deeply into that, was what Marjorie told herself sternly.

Her next thought was, *Could he mean me?*

"And… And the conversation did not go well?" was her audible reply.

Alexander sighed as they passed a row of shops packed with people, a haberdasher, a jeweler, a bakery emanating delicious scents.

"It did not," Alexander said curtly.

Marjorie hesitated, then decided not to say anything. What was there to say? It was evident that the man was conflicted— why did he bring up the argument if he did not wish to discuss it? But she was hardly going to press a gentleman to speak on such a delicate and clearly painful topic.

No, if Alexander did not wish to accept her dowry to support them, there was no point on hoping for it.

In fact, the mere idea that he hinted that he'd need to ask his father for money to "change the life of another," as if his wife wouldn't come with one of the largest dowries in all of England, probably meant it could not *possibly* have been about her.

"It was about you."

"M-Me?" Marjorie tripped over her own skirts. "Aarrghh!"

It was fortunate, indeed, that Alexander had such a strong grip of her arm, for without it she would surely have flown across the pavement and smashed both nose and head—but his sturdy grasp of her merely meant that Marjorie twisted and flung herself...

Right into Alexander's arms.

He held her there, breathless, her head whirling and her mind unable to take in what had just happened. All she could think about was Alexander's strong hands grasping her waist and arm, his warmth, his scent, the sense of power and yet comfort, the way she wanted to spend the rest of her life standing right here.

Right here, in the middle of Milsom Street...in public.

"Ah," Marjorie said helplessly, as the sound of people whispering rose in the background. "Oh, dear."

"You almost fell there, Lady Marjorie," Alexander said loudly—far too loudly for the statement to be for her benefit. "It's a good thing I caught you. Are you quite well?"

And she knew the appropriate response. Lady Marjorie slipped from his embrace, made a great show of dusting down her skirts, and replied in an equally loud voice, "Goodness me. That fall could have greatly injured me, but thankfully, I am quite well. Thank you for your assistance, Lord Alexander."

It was a little pantomime, even she had to admit—what her sister, Rose, would have said, she dreaded to think.

But the careful politeness and pointed remarks that absolutely nothing untoward had occurred here had done their work. Gawpers were now passing by, the gaggle of people whispering had now wandered off, and no one appeared to be staring at the clearly accident-prone, clearly chaperone-less Lady Marjorie at all.

Which left her. And Alexander.

A small smile was lilting the man's lips. "I am glad you are not injured."

Marjorie nodded. "Yes."

"I am even more glad that I could catch you."

Simple words like that, she thought furiously, *should not, repeat* not, *inflame my body*. They shouldn't have made molten lava and need ache through her bones. She shouldn't have wanted to taste that mouth again. And she should absolutely not throw herself into his arms and beg him to take her.

Absolutely not.

It was a good thing we're on Milsom Street, then, she thought wryly, *as otherwise, temptation might be too good to resist.*

"I am sorry. I am all at odds at the moment, and my natural charm is somewhat diminished," Alexander said, his easy calm manner returning as Marjorie slipped her hand into the crook of his elbow. "When I say my conversation with my father was about you—"

"You do not need to tell me, if you don't want to."

"But I *do* want, Marjorie. Blast it all. That is rather the problem," Alexander said with a sigh.

They resumed walking, each step taking Marjorie closer to her home and closer to the end of this conversation, which had just gotten very interesting, indeed. The trouble was, if they kept along Milsom Street then took a left, they would be but five minutes from her home.

But if they turned right…

"Let's go this way," she suggested softly as they reached the crossroads, tugging Alexander to the right.

His eyes met hers, and Marjorie hoped all he could read within them was warmth and friendship.

Besides, she did want to be Lord Alexander Chance's friend. And she certainly felt warm about him.

"When I spoke to my father, it was about whether the estate could afford an income for me," Alexander said quietly as they turned to the right down a much quieter street with almost no other pedestrians. "An income that would afford me the opportunity to marry, I mean. Without relying on a wife's dowry."

Yes, Marjorie had not needed that additional clarification, though it was more than welcome. After all, her head was now spinning and her pulse was thumping so wildly within her that she would not have been surprised if the whole world could hear it.

An income—to marry?

Why, that was surely a pointed remark, was it not? Did he mean…? Surely, he had to mean that he wished to marry her. Who else had the dowry he'd mentioned he'd rather avoid relying on?

"But my father pointed out three large impediments to such a decision," Alexander said, his jaw tightening as he spoke.

All the hope Marjorie had permitted to enter her heart started to fade. "Three?"

"Firstly, that he is technically no longer the Duke of Cothrom, and so no longer makes decisions about the estate," Alexander said with a laugh that was genuine now. "I should have remembered. It was my brother Thomas I should have spoken to."

"Oh. I see." *Well,* thought Marjorie, spirits lifting, *that is not an insurmountable problem, is it?*

"Secondly," and here Alexander's tone darkened, "my reputation has so sullied the Chance name over the last few years that to give me an independent income would be to, in a sense, reward poor character."

Ah. Now that was a little more difficult to overcome.

"And thirdly," Alexander said brightly, though there was a tension in his eyes, "the estate is not made of money, and Maudy's dowry is still unpaid and so no decisions could be made until that was sorted. And now her engagement has ended—"

"Lady Maude is—*was* engaged?" Marjorie had not intended to speak so swiftly, nor to halt her footsteps at the shocking news, but she could not help herself.

She had never heard of any engagement. Surely, such a thing would have been all over the town, all over England; it would have been announced in newspapers, mentioned in the scandal sheets. The news would have been everywhere.

Alexander swallowed and cleared his throat. "Oh, blast— forget I said that."

"'Forget'?"

"It is not supposed to be spoken of," he said hastily, his voice low and his gaze darting about the deserted street as though in fear he had been overheard. "Please, Marjorie. Please don't speak of this to anyone."

Alexander could have asked her to do anything with that voice—anything. It resonated deep within her, thrumming through her very core, such a potent tone that Marjorie would have obeyed him no matter the instruction.

The fact he had used it to protect his sister only made the blaggard even more attractive.

"I assume your father brought up the prospect of your wife coming with money of her own?" she asked.

"He did. But I told him I would not be the only Chance man to offer his bride nothing."

"I see. It sounds to me," she said, as lightly as she could manage, "that if you are so insistent you cannot accept a bride's dowry, you need your sister to be wed, and your reputation to be cleaned up, and then you could speak to your brother Thomas about...about such things."

About marrying me, she wanted to say, staring up into those dark eyes and losing herself in them.

Marry Lord Alexander Chance. The rake, the rascal, the man whom fathers warned their daughters about. Yet she had seen all the charm and none of the cheat, all the wit and none of the womanizing.

Why, sometimes it was hard to reconcile the man before her with his reputation.

"I thought the conversation might end differently," Alexander said ruefully, his mouth a grim line. "And I have no right to ask anything of you, Marjorie, not when I can offer you nothing, but...but if I were to be bold..."

His voice trailed away, his attention dropping to her mouth.

Marjorie stepped forward, knowing she was standing far too close and absolutely not going to do anything to change that. Unless, of course, she stepped an inch farther and pressed herself bodily up against the man.

"Be bold," she whispered.

Alexander's throat bobbed and she reveled in the power she inexplicably had over him. Him! Alexander Chance! The man could have any woman in the world and he was standing here with her.

"I would ask, if I were to be bold, that…that you do not accept any attentions from any other gentleman," Alexander said softly, lifting a hand to brush her cheek with his knuckles. "You are… You are precious to me, Lady Marjorie Dalton. And though I cannot offer you anything, I ask that you wait. Wait for me."

"Wait for me."

He didn't have to wait. Marjorie was almost certain she was ready for the taking, ripe for the plucking, absolutely gasping to be kissed so thoroughly, she didn't know which way was up. It was painful, being so close to the man and not be kissing him.

"Wait for me."

"You are a good man, Alexander Chance," she whispered. If only she could convince him there was no shame in accepting her dowry. What did he plan to do with it should they marry? Leave it untouched? Give it entirely to her? And yet not let her pay a cent for their home, their home's upkeep?

His low chuckle whispered across her skin. "You wouldn't say that if you knew what I was thinking in this moment."

Oh, yes. "You wouldn't worry," Marjorie said quietly, never letting her gaze leave his eyes, "if you knew what I was thinking."

Alexander groaned, leaning forward to press his forehead against hers, the kiss they were not sharing so close, Marjorie could almost taste it. "Damn it, Marjorie, I'm trying to be good."

"You are good," Marjorie returned, thinking of that heady kiss, the way he had made her very bones melt. "So *very* good."

"Not good enough. I'm never good enough," he shot back,

still pressing his forehead against her own. "But I will be. One day, I will be good enough for you—"

"You are more than enough already," Marjorie said, hardly able to believe what she was saying, how forward she was acting. "You are enough for me, Alexander. And I have a dowry. Please stop ignoring that fact."

They stood there for what felt like an age. He was too stubborn about the dowry issue. But maybe he was right. Maybe that stubbornness—that determination not to take from her, to *give* to her—was part of what drew her to him. All Marjorie wanted to do was stay in this moment, rest in this moment of joy, of closeness, of togetherness…

Even while she knew it could not last.

Footsteps.

Alexander stepped back and his sudden absence was a twisting knife in her gut.

"Come, Lady Marjorie," he said quietly, a warmth in his expression that she had never seen before. "Let's get you home."

Chapter Twelve

April 2, 1841

ALEXANDER HAD KNOWN it was going to be a difficult conversation from the start.

But not *this* difficult.

"I still don't understand," said Lord Gascoyne, his brow furrowed. "You cannot go back in time, Chance, that's ridiculous!"

"I am not suggesting that we go back in time," said Alexander with what he hoped was a smile. "I am saying that from now on, going forward, after today—"

"I'm lost," complained Sir Percival, looking as befuddled as Gascoyne. "You said you did not mind!"

"That was five years ago, man," Alexander pointed out, working hard not to let his temper rise. "A person can change their mind after five years!"

Really, what he wanted was precisely what Gascoyne had pointed out was impossible: to go back in time and prevent his friends from ever using his name in such a disgraceful manner in the first place.

It would have been much easier to clean up his act that way.

But as it was, Gascoyne happened to be correct. He could not go back in time. And so that meant the change had to start from here.

If he could make his friends understand what on earth he was talking about, that was.

"You know, I only arrived back in Bath last night, and already, I am wishing I had just stayed in London," Sir Percival complained loudly, gaining glares from the other inhabitants of the Dulverton Club. "I mean, when I heard this place had a Bath branch, I thought excellent, peace and quiet!"

His last of his words were almost shouted. A mutter from another gentleman on the other side of the Blue Room was just about audible. "Young pups!"

"Well, if it's peace and quiet you want, then that is perfect," Alexander said hastily. "That will make it all the easier to stop using my name in your...your romantic interludes. So we are agreed?"

Perhaps he had hastened through that final part, for both his friends were staring at him from their leather armchairs in absolute astonishment.

"Look, let's be reasonable," said Gascoyne finally, clearly about to be very unreasonable. "I will have to marry for money someday, as not all of us are born Chances. I shall need a clean reputation. Whereas, it hardly hurts you for all the ladies to think you are an impressive lover, does it?"

"Well..." said Alexander awkwardly, deciding it best not to comment on being born a Chance and his own lack of personal fortune.

"And I will also need to impress the Society mamas once I'm ready to settle. I can hardly go about bedding widows and chambermaids and even a few young debutantes as Sir Percival Walters. Be serious," added Sir Percival, a very unserious smile on his face. "So I vote—"

"This is not a voting matter," Alexander snapped.

Blast. He had promised himself that he would not lose his temper; it was hardly going to help his cause.

Lord Gascoyne was looking at him coldly. "There's no need to shout, Chance. You'll notice *we* aren't shouting."

Not at the moment, Alexander wanted to say. Still, he managed to calm his tongue, and instead said, "This is a request, gentlemen, between friends. An honorable request after years. I have promised not to claim you responsible for anything done in the past, just ask that you cease from this moment on. I do not see the problem."

But of course he did. What gentleman did not wish to bed a lady without consequences? It was all too easy to use another person's name, and why should they not continue?

It was a minor miracle that a lady in the family way had not turned up at his family's doorstep, Alexander knew. He'd hardly thought about that when he had agreed to loan out his name.

"Utter rubbish," Gascoyne was muttering.

"Never heard the like," chuntered Sir Percival.

Alexander stood up and tried to channel his father. Aloof, reserved, and absolutely certain in one's moral rightness. "This is not a negotiation, gentlemen. You have been informed that I withdraw my consent, and that's an end to it. If I hear you have been using my name in future—"

"What? You'll hand us over to the Peelers?" Sir Percival leered at him.

"No, he'll tick us off like old Mrs. Forbes, my governess!" Gascoyne giggled.

Alexander drew himself up and hoped to goodness it would never come to this. "No. I shall write to your mothers."

As expected, the smiles were wiped off the two men's faces.

"Good evening, gentlemen," said Alexander with a short bow.

He made absolutely certain not to look back as he exited the Blue Room, but he could not help but smile as he trotted down the staircase two at a time.

He had done it. Finally, and probably at least five and thirty months late, but he had done it. He had reclaimed his name, and with it, his honor. Within weeks, the rumors of Lord Alexander Chance's seducing would diminish and there would be a slow renewal of his reputation.

And then... And then...

He should not have spoken to Marjorie so openly about his hopes, Alexander knew, as he allowed a Dulverton footman to slip his greatcoat around his shoulders. Lord knew it could be another twelvemonth before his father—his *brother*—would even consider his reputation even halfway restored, and there was the small matter of marrying off Maudey, which now Alexander came to think of it, was perhaps the hardest part of the bargain.

But it was a step, he thought as he stepped out into the freezing evening air. A step in the right direction.

A step toward Marjorie.

His footsteps in the here and now echoed in the almost empty streets. A nearby church clock chimed the hour, which was a singular bong—could it really have been that late?

It was certainly that cold. Alexander tugged his greatcoat closer around him as he turned a corner onto a street whereupon a household had obviously been hosting a gathering. Light was spilling onto the pavement along with a gaggle of people, carriages dotted about the street as drivers jostled to retrieve their masters and mistresses. There was some sort of conversation going on taking up much of the pavement, and so Alexander stepped across to the other side of the road to avoid it altogether.

That was why he saw the figures.

He would not have spotted them otherwise, but from this angle, he was gifted a direct view of a lady and a man. He would not call him a gentleman; no gentleman should have been standing that close to a lady, nor tugging at her sleeve in that manner. It was unfortunate, indeed, and he knew he would have to step in. If it had been a woman he cared about accosted somewhere else, he would hope another gentleman would do the same. The poor woman—

Alexander's heart stopped.

Marjorie.

No further thought was needed—no further thought was possible, for Alexander had already launched himself across the busy street, pulse pounding, lungs burning, a voice shouting in his mind—

Mine.

"Jusht a quick kiss. A pretty lady like, like you. I just wanna—arghhh, Christ!"

Alexander wrenched the man away from his woman and threw him to the ground. "Get your hands off her, you dirty—"

"Alexander!"

"I only askeded for a kiss," muttered the man, who, now that Alexander was closer, he realized was clearly drunk. "Jist a quick kissh."

"You stay away from her and all women like her, you rogue!" bellowed Alexander, absolutely unable to moderate his voice in any way. "How dare you?!"

"Alexander, I am quite well."

Alexander turned to Marjorie and saw quite plainly that she was *not* well.

Her sleeve was torn. The lace had been torn from the cuff and its frayed edge left a mark of guilt on the man's soul that Alexander was not certain could ever be repaired. Her pelisse no longer had any buttons, either, he was horrified to see, and there was a mark—a bruise on Lady Marjorie Dalton's collarbone.

A mark on my woman.

Alexander growled as he leapt forward, intent on pummeling the man into such a small square that he would be entirely unidentifiable, but something held him back.

A warm, soft something.

"Leave him," Marjorie said quietly, her hands tugging at his sleeve. "Alexander, please, leave him."

"What's going on over there?"

"Who is that? Can anyone make them out?"

Alexander's chest was heaving, his shoulders rising and falling with desperately contained anger, but even he was starting to realize he was causing a scene.

Or ending it.

"Lady Marjorie?"

"Oh, good, my carriage," came Marjorie's voice, full of relief and a long way off. "Tilly was with me, but I let her go meet up with her beau. I was just waiting for—Alexander, leave him. Honestly, it's not worth—"

"He hurt you." Each word was clipped, painful, as Alexander stared. Marjorie's hair was messed too, as though she had been forced to tug her head away.

Dear God, if he had not been walking down the other side of the street…had the party revelers no awareness of what had been happening?

"Carriage," Marjorie said determinedly. "In."

Perhaps it was being raised by such a forceful mother, but Alexander found his feet obeyed quicker than his mind could disagree. Before he knew it, the pair of them were seated side by side in the Dalton carriage, which was rattling away from the scene of the crime.

And it *was* a crime, he was certain of that. Why, if he had not stopped whatever had been about to happen…

"Thank you," Marjorie said quietly, slipping her hand into his. "For rescuing me."

A lump formed in Alexander's throat. "If anything had happened to you…"

"Oh, I didn't fancy his chances in winning my favor," she said lightly, her laugh a tad forced, but it was good to see her smile. It untied one of the thousand knots within him. "You, on the other hand…"

Alexander was not sure what made him do it.

Fine, that was disingenuous to say. He knew precisely what made him do it. The breathlessness of the woman, her beauty, the fact that she had so recently been in danger… Those were all elements that definitely contributed to the movement.

But in the end, it was Marjorie. That was all Alexander needed.

The kiss was bold, and desperate, and though he tried not to overwhelm her, it was impossible to hold back the aching desire that had flooded his heart long ago—far longer ago than Alexander might care to admit.

His hands cupped her face as his tongue teased along the slit of her mouth, demanding entry in the most respectable of ways, and Marjorie mewed with pleasure as she permitted him deeper.

Oh, deeper. He wanted to be within this woman, and though Alexander knew logically that no carriage ride would be long enough for him to take his fill of her, he also knew that there was absolutely no possibility of doing much more than kissing.

And so kiss he did. His tongue tangled with hers, his hands somehow now lost in her hair, and Marjorie showed no evidence of disliking his amorous attentions.

Quite to the contrary, she had somehow managed to slip onto his lap, her legs straddling him in a way that was most wonderfully pressing against Alexander's swollen manhood, and he groaned into their kiss as she ground against him.

Oh, Lady Marjorie Dalton might be an innocent in body, but the minx was no innocent in mind.

The desperate need for her only increased as their kiss deepened. If Alexander had thought a taste of her would satiate his hunger, he was sorely mistaken. The softness of her thighs made his fingers quiver as they slipped under her skirts, his moan swallowed by her kiss as Alexander trailed his fingers up her outer thighs to reach her buttocks, soft and warm and achingly close.

"Oh, Alexander," murmured Marjorie, breaking the kiss to look deep within his eyes. "I—I want—"

"I know," Alexander said before he could stop himself, and he did know, and it was agony that he could not give it to her. "But we can't…"

Or could we?

It was not as though anyone would know, after all. She would still, as far as all others knew, be an innocent, and he would be able to give her such bliss…bliss the like she had never known.

Alexander looked up into the eyes of the woman he craved and made his decision. "If you want me to stop at any moment, tell me to stop."

Marjorie's eyes widened. "Why would I tell you to stop?"

Groaning into her mouth as he pressed a fervent kiss on her lips, Alexander tried to prevent his pulse from racing as his right hand moved slowly, slowly around her thigh to her inner thigh, stroking up, slowly caressing—

She gasped in his mouth and he swallowed her cry, almost crying out himself at the sweet, warm wetness that met his fingers.

Oh, God, she wants me.

It was almost enough to make him fall apart in his own trousers, but Alexander was controlled. Slowly, slowly, he built a stroking rhythm with his fingertips against her sopping slit, his thumb caressing up to her nub, which he slowly circled.

Marjorie was unable to kiss him anymore, the sensations—he hoped—too overwhelming, and so she rested her head on his shoulder as she panted and mewed and pressed herself against his hand, grinding against him, taking pleasure from him as eagerly as he gave it, and when her whole body stiffened and a desperate moan of ecstasy poured from her lips into his ear, all Alexander could do was wish this moment would never end—

The carriage stopped.

Alexander broke away from the woman he was almost certain he…

No. He could not even permit himself to think it. To think it would be to hope, and he could not afford such a valuable emotion.

Not yet.

"We're… We're here?" Marjorie glanced out of the carriage window with glazed eyes. "We can't be."

"I'm afraid we are," Alexander said in a ragged voice. How did this woman do this to him? "Your parents—oh, dear Lord, were they attending whatever it was tonight? Did we leave them behind?"

"A small party at the Ramsays'." Marjorie stifled a smile as the carriage door opened. "No. No, they left early," she continued as she stepped onto the pavement before her home. "As they'd summoned Tilly to accompany me before they'd departed, they did not think I was in any danger. Not that I think *Tilly* would have been a help with that lout."

Before Alexander knew what he was doing, he had descended from the carriage with her, and her eyes widened in surprise.

"Just want to make sure that you get home safely," he said more than a little pompously. Where on earth had that come from?

It was not that Marjorie was smiling, but more that she was definitely trying not to smile that made Alexander's stomach lurch.

"Home safely," she repeated, glancing to her left and the large building that was but two feet from them. "Well, I think you have managed it."

Alexander nodded, suddenly unable to speak.

This was the moment. The best moment, the right moment to tell her the truth.

That it had not been he who had been gadding about town, bedding women all over the place. No, that had been Gascoyne and old Percival, and from now on, that gadding would cease and the whole world would see that he was indeed a respectable gentleman.

A suitor, suitable for the hand of Lady Marjorie Dalton.

Yes, he should tell her…but something held him back.

Would she believe him? What if she thought he was merely inventing an excuse to explain away his past and did not trust that he spoke honestly? It would be painful, indeed, to own up to the truth, only for one of the most important people in the world to disbelieve him.

Alexander's stomach twisted. Or worse, what if she believed him and hated him for lying about it all previously?

He was not sure what would be worse.

Being disbelieved, certainly, Alexander thought wildly. Or was it being believed? Would she think him an utter fool for allowing them to use his name in such a fashion—so great a fool that she would not marry him? A liar, the type of man she desperately wanted to avoid?

"Alexander?"

"What?" he said distractedly, blinking to find Marjorie standing before him, slowly coming into focus.

The trouble is, I want to impress her.

That was what it came down to, Alexander was painfully starting to realize. That was why he wanted to offer her everything, a fortune of his own. Without that, he had nothing to give her. Nothing but a sordid reputation. But that wasn't what one offered a bride. What had impressed so many ladies in the past was the fact that his exploits, for want of a better word, had always been so highly regarded and much talked about.

But surely, Marjorie had not fallen in love with Alexander the rake.

If she had fallen in love at all.

Oh, damnation.

"Marjorie, is that you? I thought I heard the carriage," came a sleepy voice from a suddenly blinding front door. It had opened. "Marjorie? I—Oh, dear God, Marjorie!"

Alexander turned from the figure outlined in black in the doorway to the woman beside him and suddenly understood the panic in her mother's voice.

Yes, his own mother would surely have responded in such a way if her daughter had emerged from a carriage with a gentleman, only to reveal that her cuff was torn, along with her sleeve, her hair thoroughly mussed, and there was a bruise blossoming across her collarbone…

"You varlet!"

"Mother!"

"Oh, dear," Alexander said weakly as the woman hurried down the steps toward him and started battering him with her fists. "I think there's been some awful misunderstanding!"

"Oh, it *is* awful, what you've done to her!" railed Lady Dalton, punching every inch of Alexander she could reach as he tried helplessly to step back. "You stay away from her, you leave you her alone, you scoundrel! Marjorie, where is Tilly? Why is *he* here?"

"What is going on out there?" came a peevish voice from the doorway.

Marjorie swore under her breath—a curse Alexander had only heard his cousin Frank use, and he had been shocked then.

"Is that Marjorie? What on earth are you doing out there, dear?" called out the waspish voice of Lord Dalton from the doorway as Lady Dalton continued to pummel an unresisting Alexander for all her worth. "Are you—but Marjorie, your cuff!"

"I can explain," Alexander said hastily.

Not hastily enough.

"My daughter, my precious daughter!" Lady Dalton now wept as all the energy went out of her fists, but she still continued to gently prod Alexander with a shaking finger. "Ruined, utterly ruined! After all those greedy fortune hunters I kept away from her, to think we'd let *you* near her and this is how you repay us!"

"I am not ruined, Mama," Marjorie remarked quietly.

She was thoroughly ignored.

"And after Rose—" The marchioness wailed.

"What have you done to my daughter, sir?" snapped Lord Dalton as he too strode down the steps toward them.

This time, Alexander truly did retreat a step, his back hitting the carriage and preventing him from retreating farther. "Now, my lord, I know how this looks—"

"Do you? *Do* you, by God?!" cried Lord Dalton as a dog in a nearby house started to howl and a light appeared in another house's window. "I'll have you before the courts! I'll have you before the king! I'll—"

"We don't have a king anymore, Father," Marjorie pointed out quietly.

She was once again ignored, but it gave Alexander the opportunity to attempt to take control of the conversation.

Mostly. "My lord, when I was returning home from the Dulverton, I happened to espy Lady Marjorie. Her lady's maid had—er, she was ill, so she'd gone home."

"Home? *Home?* She'll have no home once she's no longer under my employ!" Lord Dalton snapped, staring over his shoulder, though Alexander imagined he wouldn't find the missing lady's maid there. "Where is that useless woman?"

"*Papa!*" said Marjorie, swallowing visibly. "She couldn't help it!"

The marquess's mind was not changed. Nor was he long to be deterred from showering his wrath upon Alexander. "So you found my daughter alone and you took advantage of her, by God!"

Lady Dalton was now sobbing with her head laid on Alexander's chest, which did not help matters.

"No, my lord," he said steadily, trying to keep his temper. "I saw her being accosted by a drunkard!"

"It's true, Papa," Marjorie said hastily, stepping forward and gently pulling her mother away from Alexander, who was now damp. "I was waiting for the carriage and…and Alexander—Lord Alexander saved me."

Lord Dalton had lifted his fist as though he were about to punch the younger man, but his arm stayed. "'Saved' you?"

His wife's sobs halted. The night's silence—or as silent as Bath ever got at past one o'clock in the morning—fell upon them like a heavy blanket.

Alexander did his best not to look at Marjorie. No matter how restrained he managed to make it, he was certain one or both of her parents would spot his desire within him, and this was not the time.

Lady Dalton burst into even louder sobs. "Y-You—You saved her!"

"You saved her?" Lord Dalton said suspiciously, glaring at Alexander.

"He saved me." Marjorie nodded sagely.

Alexander cleared his throat. "I… I saved her."

And she saved me, he wanted to say as warmth spread through his limbs.

He had not even realized he had been desperate, and yet she had saved him. He had meandered through the world with no purpose, no true desires, no interest in his own betterment or the world, and she had cut through that nonsense like a knife.

Like a scalpel, cutting away the dead flesh and leaving him whole.

Lady Marjorie Dalton had changed his life, Alexander could see that now; and all he wanted to do was spend the rest of that life with her.

Marjorie was now comforting her mother, who was weeping gently onto her daughter's shoulder, while Lord Dalton was huffing and puffing in a way that was vaguely reminiscent of Alexander's own father.

"I presumed, obviously… And it certainly appeared…but you seem a good sort, and I suppose I must thank you for protecting my daughter…"

He supposes that he must thank me.

Well, Alexander supposed in turn that he should be grateful the man wasn't punching him on the nose or calling for the magistrate.

"I do hope Marjorie—that Lady Marjorie is not too fatigued from her evening," Alexander said aloud, hoping the return to civility would in some way calm the pair of them down.

"Not too fatigued, no," Marjorie said with mischief dancing in her eyes as her mother straightened. "I would not have minded a longer carriage journey, though."

Alexander's jaw dropped.

"To calm my nerves after such an ordeal," she continued, placing her hand in her father's arm. "Good evening, Lord Alexander. Thank you again for your willing hands."

"I… I…" *Dear God, the woman was a minx!*

"Yes, good evening, Lord Alexander," said Lord Dalton curtly. "Goodbye."

Alexander watched as Marjorie walked up to her front door and entered her home. His gaze remained on the closed door for several minutes after.

Perhaps... Perhaps he could count today as a beginning of the restoration of his name. He had been most firm with his friends, he had saved Marjorie from a terrible fate...and even her parents did not appear to be wholly disgusted by him.

A slow smile crept across Alexander's face. It was a start.

Chapter Thirteen

April 3, 1841

"A LEXANDER!"

"Lady Marjorie," said the most handsome, debonair man who had, the last time she had seen him, brought her to such ecstasy with his fingers that she'd had trouble sleeping that night. "You look very well."

She did not *feel* well. At least, she had felt fine before the butler had entered and announced she had a visitor, and in had stepped the most charming, most handsome man she had ever seen.

In her drawing room.

"Alexander!" Marjorie repeated, stunned, rising to her feet and allowing her embroidery—not particularly good—to fall to the floor.

"Marjorie!" scolded her mother, seated beside her on the sofa.

"Lady Dalton." Alexander bowed, as though he had not seen her mother.

"Lord Alexander." The older woman nodded sternly.

"Marjorie," said Marjorie helplessly.

Both her mother and her lover—for what else could she call Alexander, even if only in the privacy of her mind?—turned to her with their heads tilted sideways.

Marjorie gave them both a weak smile. It was as if she'd responded to a roll call. "I do apologize. I got a little carried... Lord Alexander, how pleasant to see you this morning."

So early, she wanted to say. *And looking so...so delicious.*

Do not, Marjorie told herself decisively, *think about what happened in the carriage ride last night.* Or rather, this morning, for it had been nearly two o'clock when her concerned parents had finally allowed her to retreat to her bedchamber. Tilly must have gotten home at some point after that, for she'd been there this morning to wake her mistress. She'd gone green when Marjorie had told her all that had happened, most apologetic, but Marjorie had said she wasn't to blame herself. The two of them shared secrets, after all. Fortunately, her father seemed to have forgotten Tilly's role in the incident entirely.

And Marjorie… Her memories of the worst of it were now completely overwritten by something far more enticing.

Do not think about the way he kissed you.

Do not think about the way you somehow managed to find yourself on his lap.

Definitely do not think about the way you came apart around his fingers and gained your first taste of innocence and goodness. Didn't wickedness taste sweet?

"—don't you think, Marjorie?"

Marjorie blinked. Alexander had obviously been invited to sit down, that or else he was determined to further scandalize, for he was seated in an armchair opposite the two ladies. He was sitting so far on the edge that he was nearly tipping into her lap.

Not that such an occurrence wouldn't be welcome…

"Marjorie!" snapped her mother.

Marjorie jolted this time and wished to goodness she had perfected the art that so many ladies in polite Society appeared to have been born with: that of being able to passably pretend one had been listening to a conversation without actually paying it any heed.

It was most provoking.

"I am sure Lady Marjorie will insist on accompanying her ill lady's maid home next time and not send her off in a hansom cab," said Alexander smoothly, rescuing her from her own debacle. Her own *lie*, she reminded herself, even if in purpose of

Tilly's own good. "Is that not right, Lady Marjorie?"

"Yes? Oh, yes!" agreed Marjorie happily, now that she knew what on earth she was supposed to have been listening to. "Yes, I shall be most circumspect to accompany her home next time, Mama. Goodness yes."

Absolutely not.

Not when such a decision had led to such ecstasy. Oh, the mere memory of the way Alexander had touched her...

Marjorie's cheeks burned and she hastily picked up her embroidery for something to do with her hands. It was scandalous, what she was thinking. Scandalous!

It was all the more scandalous that she had done it in the first place!

And yes, it had not unequivocally been top of mind at the time to request that Alexander not pleasure her within an inch of her life. These things never are.

"And to what do we owe the pleasure of your company, Lord—yes, what is it, Sackville?"

Marjorie looked up from the dandelion that she was inexpertly embroidering to see their butler standing in the doorway looking more than a tad uncomfortable as he swallowed visibly.

"Yes?" Lady Dalton repeated.

"It is her ladyship, the Marchioness of Aylesbury, my lady," said the butler awkwardly, his attention flickering inexplicably to their gentleman guest. "She hopes for, and I am quoting here, 'a quiet word.'"

Try as she might, it was almost impossible for Marjorie not to glance at Alexander. Her sister was here? Why?

"'A quiet word'?" repeated their mother. "Now?"

"I am given to understand she would not like an audience, my lady," continued Sackville, obviously pained at giving such rudeness to the daughter of the house. "I have shown her into the morning room, and I wondered—"

"Yes, yes, right," said Lady Dalton distractedly as she cast a worried look over her daughter, and then her daughter's gentleman caller, and then to the door through which sat her other daughter.

It was a conundrum, even Marjorie could see that. The fact that Rose had turned up unannounced and with no prior engagement was surprising, and her noticeably fragile relationship with their parents could so easily be scuppered if Lady Dalton did not hasten to the morning room.

But still, leaving her younger daughter alone with a gentleman…a gentleman, moreover, who had a rakish personality and a reputation so soiled, it was hardly worth mentioning…

That was another evil. Even if her parents now recognized him as their daughter's hero.

"What pleasant weather we are having lately," Alexander said blithely, cutting into both Marjorie's thoughts and, presumably, her mother's.

Marjorie attempted not to smile. As banal conversational topic went, it was probably the best. "Most pleasant," she said in a monotone, eyes now fixed on her embroidery. "For the time of year."

Seemingly satisfied that no hijinks or escapades could occur when discussing such a dull topic as the weather, Lady Dalton rose to her feet and nodded at Sackville. "In the morning room, you say?"

Marjorie tried not to smile. The fact that the prodigal daughter had returned was shocking, yes, but her parents' tempers had been mollified somewhat by Rose's extremely titled husband, and his extremely great wealth. Why, the rumors were that he had inherited over one hundred thousand pounds from a distant relative, more than twice Marjorie's own dowry—and so he'd asked for not a penny after marrying Rose.

Just as the man's cousin was determined not to ask for any money from his future wife.

Samuel's wealth had naturally made the wayward daughter's new husband far more palatable than the first man to claim the position.

The instant the door had closed behind the marchioness and the butler, Alexander moved swiftly into Lady Dalton's vacated seat on the sofa—right beside Marjorie. "I had to see you. I couldn't wait."

"I am glad you did not. That is, it is I suppose very shocking that you have come before visiting hours," Marjorie said, her cheeks burning. "But I am glad, all the same."

It *was* very shocking; not just because the polite expectation of a visit was only to occur between the hours of twelve and three, but because he had come at all.

Lord Alexander Chance in her drawing room was a creature altogether different from Alexander, excellent kisser and maker of love in the darkness of a carriage.

No, having him here in the brightness of day, bowing to her mother, discussing the weather... It was as though another Alexander had appeared before her to add to her collection.

Alexander, rake and scoundrel, breaking into her garden to attempt to ravish her.

Alexander, heartfelt gentleman attempting to restore his reputation.

Alexander, awkward and shy before his parents and family.

Alexander, seducer and charmer swiftly able to get under her skirts.

And now Alexander, cheerful conversationalist and communicator with mothers.

It was dazzling. It was giddying, making Marjorie's head spin and also making it difficult to understand precisely what on earth she was supposed to do with all these Alexanders. They mystified her, making it impossible to understand.

It was almost, though this was naturally a foolish thing to even contemplate, as though there were two of him.

Two Alexanders: one charming and roguish, and one gentle and shy. One determined to ruin his good name, and the other hopeful of retaining the good opinion of others. Why, the first should *want* to marry a woman with a fortune. The second, she could almost understand his determination to provide for her on his own.

It was most peculiar.

"You are not seriously injured after last night? You are not hurt?" Alexander said in a low voice, his tone hurried, as though he expected Lady Dalton to return at any moment.

Marjorie's hand fluttered to her collarbone, currently hidden by a lace shawl her mother had insisted she wear until the nasty bruise the drunkard had inflicted on her faded. "No, no, I am quite well."

"I… Well, I did not mean that." And Alexander's gaze flickered, just for a moment, to the meeting place of her thighs.

Oh. "Oh," Marjorie said helplessly, unable to think of anything else to say.

Oh.

He was thinking of—and of course he was, for he had altered her body with his touch in a way she would never truly recover from. There was nothing that could be done to alter what had occurred. His mark on her was perhaps not visible to the naked eye—*do not think about naked*, Marjorie thought desperately, *do not think about naked*—but it was there, all the same.

She was altered, irrevocably, by Alexander's touch.

"Yes, I am quite… I mean, there was a little soreness," Marjorie added, unable as usual to lie to him or in any way sugarcoat the truth. "But it was gone this morning and I would not say it should prevent…a repeat."

A repeat.

It was far more than she should have said and yet far less than she wished. With Alexander seated so close to her on the sofa— so, so close—it was a miracle she was able to say anything at all.

He was so…so *potent. That is probably not the correct word,* Marjorie thought hurriedly, *yet there's nothing better.* Everything about this man exuded power—power over himself, power over others—yet it did not seem to be a clout that he used often. Or even used consciously.

Did he know how tantalizing he was, seated so close to her like this? Did he have any idea how desperately she wanted to lean forward and kiss him?

No, more than kiss him. Kiss him and clamber onto his lap and beg, beg with no shame for another touching that would bring her such bliss?

Marjorie swallowed the plea that rose unbidden in her throat and instead managed to say, "I am grateful to you. For your great act last night."

This time, it was Alexander who smiled. "Are you referring to what I did for you in the street, or what I did to you in the carriage?"

"Both," said a furiously flushing Marjorie who could not believe she was saying such a thing. "I… I have never…" She swallowed. *I will be brave.* "I did not know anything could feel like that."

It did not completely pass her by that Alexander crossed his legs at that exact moment. It was pleasing, in a way, to know she had just as much impact on him as the other way around.

"We should not talk so," Alexander said quietly in a voice that might have been husky. "We shouldn't."

"But it's all I want to speak about," Marjorie said, leaning forward just as she had told herself she would not. "Oh, Alexander, how can anyone stop speaking about it—how can anyone stop *doing* it?"

"Marjorie," he hissed, cheeks scarlet now. "We mustn't."

"And I can quite see why you have bedded so many widows," Marjorie continued, the words spilling from her lips now, absolutely nothing she could do to stop them. "I mean, widows and gentlemen, they are able to enjoy all the bedsport they like, are they not, with no consequences? And so it is unwed ladies like myself—"

"Marjorie!"

"If I asked you to do it to me again, would you?"

The question burned in the air between them, hot with

promise and need and desire and absolutely no regrets.

Marjorie tried to still her breathing as she looked deep into Alexander's eyes, but she could not. This was not who she was. She had always been the Dalton daughter who did what she was told and asked no questions.

But that part of her was gone. Gone, in the instant Alexander had looked at her and wanted her.

She knew that now.

She also knew she was in love with him, worse luck.

"I cannot answer that question—no, I cannot," Alexander said ruefully, as though warring with himself in the desperation to give her what she wanted. "And I would be a fool to attempt it here."

Marjorie blinked, looking around her, as though she had only just realized where she was.

The drawing room. The landscape painting on the wall by the door that she knew so well, the delicate brocade wall hangings, the bay window, where over the years she had sat and watched the people of Bath go by whenever they were in town. The cushion on which she had once spilled tea, and the footstool on which Rose had, in their younger years, stood upon and declaimed Shakespeare.

Rather badly, from what Marjorie could recall.

All of it was so familiar, yet none of it seemed habitual at all. As though she had stepped into a world almost exactly a duplicate of her own, but in a way, it was one that could not quite ape the reality.

Perhaps it was more that her real life felt no more real to her now than a shadow, a wisp on the wind.

The only real thing…was Alexander.

Oh, bother. She had fallen in love with him.

"As much as I would like to tempt you into a life of sin," Alexander said, utterly unaware that the very fabric of Marjorie's reality had just reorganized itself around her, "I am afraid I am trying desperately to turn over a new leaf, starting yesterday."

Marjorie blinked. "Why yesterday?"

It was not such a surprising question, considering his statement, yet Alexander colored and looked away for a moment. "No reason."

There was evidently a reason, but if there was one thing Marjorie had learned about the man—other than the fact that his hands were genius—it was that Alexander Chance did not like to be pushed.

"Alexander," she said softly.

When he turned back to her, Marjorie's stomach jolted.

Treacherous thing, she could not help but think knowingly. *At least* attempt *to hold onto some semblance of calm.*

"Marjorie."

Her disobliging stomach lurched again, and so it was with utter calmness that she managed to say, "Where is all this going, Alexander?"

Perhaps it was the wrong question. Instead of answering, Alexander abruptly rose to his feet and walked from her to the window—which, Marjorie could not help but think with sinking spirits, was probably answer enough in and of itself.

"I don't know what you mean."

"Yes, you do," she said unhappily, her gut wrenching as she in turn rose, her embroidery forgotten, her muslin gown swishing as she stepped after him. "And though you cannot or will not tell me, then I'd rather know that than be told a lie!"

Her voice did not exactly ring through the room, but she had hardly spoken in an undertone. The adjoining door to the morning room was close by and in horror, Marjorie realized the low-level voices that had been emanating under that very door had halted.

So had her breath. Marjorie stared at the door, willing her mother and sister to continue whatever passingly interesting conversation they were having in the next room.

Only when the murmur of two voices returned did Marjorie let out the air stuck in her lungs.

"Marjorie."

She turned to the man she had followed across the room and wished to goodness that he did not have such an effect on her. It was painful, how she would simply melt at the way he uttered her name.

Alexander was smiling, though there was tension pulling at the corners of his eyes. "I… I do not know where this is going, if I am honest."

Marjorie laughed dryly. "You could have lied, you know. To spare my feelings." Surely, *that* sort of lie she could handle. She would be arrogant if she could not admit she'd lied before. Just never about anything so serious, so hurtful, as the lie her parents had told her.

He did not respond for a beat. Why was her pulse thrumming so painfully, so powerfully?

"Perhaps I could have done," returned Alexander, stepping forward and cupping her face, staring into her eyes with such intensity, it took her breath away. "But I wouldn't do that. No, not even if it were more convenient to do so. I promise—from this day forward, you will know the true me. I will never lie to you, Marjorie Dalton."

Such words should not have filled her with such utter delight, such abandon, but they did.

Abandoning all hope of decorum, Marjorie launched herself into his arms.

Not for a kiss—the kisses would come, Marjorie was sure, and there was no point in demanding them now when what she wanted most in this moment was to be in his arms.

Alexander's arms. The man who made her feel so joyful—and yet so at home. The man who infuriated and delighted her in turns and at equal measure, whom she could not predict and yet who seemed to know her so well.

Perhaps she did not need to know where this was going. Marriage, yes, surely, but not yet—and that was quite all right. After such weighty expectations on her from the moment Rose had left home—*died*, Marjorie had thought for years—under mysterious circumstances, it was only now, held in Alexander's tight embrace, that Marjorie knew she no longer needed such rigid control over her life.

This was what she wanted. *He* was what she wanted.

And if it was that important to him to procure his own income to provide for them, so be it. She could wait. She'd been waiting for him her whole life.

"—and so what I wanted to say was—Marjorie Dalton, put that boy down!"

Marjorie froze. Her sister's voice had never sounded so sharp.

Alexander released her and the two of them turned to see both Lady Dalton and her eldest daughter, now the Marchioness of Aylesbury and wife to Alexander's cousin, staring at the previously embracing couple.

"Ah," said Alexander weakly.

"Mother," said Marjorie firmly, determined to take control of the conversation this time.

"Marjorie!" said Rose breathlessly, eyes wide.

"Rose," scolded their mother.

"Mother!" gasped Rose, gesturing at her sister.

"Marjorie?" muttered Alexander out of the corner of his mouth.

"Oh, no, we're not getting trapped in that loop again," said Marjorie as calmly as she could manage. "Mother, we were just—"

"Celebrating," prompted Alexander cheerfully.

All eyes turned to him, though they unsurprisingly held different expressions. Marjorie was aware of her mother's scandalized expression, and her sister looked far too pleased with herself. And why on earth was she cupping her stomach like that?

Marjorie fixed Alexander with a stern, *I think you should let me handle this* look, and Alexander nodded.

Marjorie's shoulders relaxed. Right then, all she had to do was come up with an explanation. "You see, we were celebrating. Celebrating—"

Hell, what on earth could they be celebrating that would necessitate…?

"My sister, Maude, has been invited on a day trip to see a stone circle," Alexander supplied confidently, as though he frequently made up stories all the time—which, Marjorie realized with a sinking heart, he probably did. Well, he had promised not to lie to *her*, and that made all the difference, in her opinion. "I wondered if Lady Marjorie would like to accompany the two of us, and she has accepted my invitation."

"Your 'invitation'?" Marjorie hissed.

"Lady Maude?" said her mother quietly, as though considering just what impact it would have on her daughter, for her to be seen publicly as friends with the daughter of a duke. The marchioness had kept gentlemen callers away from Marjorie for so long, always waiting for a man with something more to offer her daughter. A duke's family… That could finally be what she'd waited for, and befriending Alexander's sister could only help her chances of joining the family.

"Marjorie," Rose hissed, quiet enough their mother couldn't hear. "That can't seriously be all this is?"

"What a delightful invitation, to be sure," Lady Dalton said brightly, giving her daughter a warm smile. "And what pleasant day is this adventure to be?"

Chapter Fourteen

April 6, 1841

"**T**HIS IS NOT," Alexander said ominously, "a pleasant day."

The rain poured heavily upon the carriage roof, satisfyingly underlining his point, as Marjorie grinned. "It's your own fault. You would insist that we still go even with the dark clouds gathering. Honestly, a stone circle!"

It had sounded a good idea at the time.

Alexander had been surprised at his sister's interest in a load of rocks—his words, not hers—and had initially grudgingly agreed to accompany her. It had only been when faced with the wrath of Lady Dalton, delicately packaged but weighty nonetheless, that he had desperately used the planned excursion to his benefit.

Of course, it had not worked out as he had hoped.

"I'm not going," Maude had said flatly as the dark clouds had rolled over Bath and the sound of distant thunder echoed across the town. "Absolutely not."

"But I need you to be there to chaperone Marjorie—Lady Marjorie," Alexander had wheedled—sad and pathetically, even he had to admit.

His sister had raised an eyebrow as he'd tugged on his great-coat. "'Chaperone Lady Marjorie'? Since when did you care about chaperones?"

Since I realized that I need to marry the woman, and only by gaining her family's approval can I do such a thing, were the fine words Alexander had not said.

Instead, he'd given his sister a grin. "Come on, Maudey. This was *your* idea. You love a stone circle."

"I also like being warm and dry," his irascible sister had pointed out. "And I seem to recall you not caring about '*a load of rocks*' when I first brought it up. You can make a foolhardy adventure out into the countryside during a storm if you wish, but you won't be so foolish as to get me to step into that blasted carriage. You know it threw a wheel on the way here from London."

It had, and he well remembered it—but Alexander had been certain that their coachman had made the necessary repairs. They were to have a lovely day in the countryside, he decided resolutely, whatever the weather.

The first drops of rain had started to pitter-patter on the roof of the carriage the moment that Marjorie had stepped into it.

"Good day, Lord—where's Lady Maude?"

He was not, Alexander had told himself unyieldingly as he'd tapped on the roof of the carriage and his driver had driven on, going to be upset that her first concerns were about his sister. He was not.

Alexander had shrugged and offered a wink. "I'm afraid my sister—"

"She *was* going to come, wasn't she?" The concern had been written across Marjorie's face, and he'd known exactly why.

She'd thought he had lied.

"I told you before—I hate liars."

His instinct had been to defend himself, to shoot back with his good intentions, but Alexander had managed to hold back those particular instincts.

This is Marjorie, a woman you know you care for deeply.

Think, man.

"The entire excursion was Maudey's idea," Alexander had said quietly as the Chance family carriage had rattled down the Bath streets. "She was the one who suggested it, but she is a little...ah. *Distrustful* of the carriage."

The carriage had lurched to the left and made a strange pinging noise.

The look Marjorie had given him had not been filled with confidence. "Precisely *why* is she distrustful of the carriage?"

Alexander had tried to smile as the pitter-patter of rain had increased in volume on the carriage roof. "It... It doesn't like rain."

Marjorie had put out a hand to steady herself against the wall of the carriage, then removed her hand quickly, as though touching it in such a fashion could inadvertently cause it to collapse. "'It doesn't like rain'?"

Lightning had flashed and thunder had rolled and Alexander had watched helplessly as rain had washed down the carriage windows as they'd left Bath. "It's just—well, it doesn't—"

"I suppose we shall just have to hope that no misadventure befalls us and the rain clears so we can look at this stone circle of yours," Marjorie had said, her eyes sparkling. "Though I am not worried."

Alexander had perked up at that. "You're not?"

"No," she'd said softly, her eyes warm and whispering of things he could not fathom. "I am with you."

After thirty minutes or so of enjoyable conversation, during which Alexander had absolutely not been staring at her breasts when she'd laughed at his inane jokes, and the rain had continued to batter down upon them, he was starting to wonder whether the whole escapade had been a bad idea.

Oh, he adored his time with Marjorie, and snatching it away from a chaperone made it all the sweeter...but this rain. It had not ceased from the moment they had left Bath.

"Do you think the rain will stop?" Marjorie asked hopefully, attempting to look up at the sky to see whether the clouds were scudding across the sky or heavily dormant above them.

It was difficult to tell. Firstly, because the windows were almost entirely translucent now, the rain making it almost impossible to see through them. Secondly, because the lane they were now traversing down was covered over with trees, their bare and budding branches obscuring the sky. Thirdly, because the sky itself was so dark, it felt less like two o'clock in the afternoon and more like seven o'clock in the evening.

None of which boded well.

"Are you interested in history, Marjorie?" Alexander attempted in a light, cheerful tone.

It was perhaps her laughter that made him smile. That, or the sparkle in her eyes. "Are you...making small talk with me, Alexander?"

"No!" he protested swiftly, though his stomach twisted at how easily he had been caught out.

Be civil. Be polite. Be courteous.

Wasn't that what all the gentlemen of polite Society did all the time?

"You don't have to pretend to be someone else when you're with me," said Marjorie with a bob of her head. "I... Well, I like you just the way you are."

Alexander's spirits soared, even as the rain came down heavier, almost deafening on the carriage roof. So Maudey would not come with them. Perhaps that was not the worst thing in the world. So it was raining. Perhaps the rain would clear by the time they reached this stone circle of hers. So there probably wouldn't be a pleasant inn within which to have afternoon tea. The picnic under his seat could be taken out and eaten. It was all going to be a wonderful—

A twisting, a tilting, a wrenching, a cracking, the carriage tipping to its side and Marjorie's screams—

Alexander acted on pure instinct. Grabbing the falling woman and pulling her into his arms, he twisted as he fell and ensured his back hit the carriage door, which was now *the floor*. The carriage had turned on its side and the scream of horses rent the air, the shouts of his driver muffled through the pouring rain.

And then stillness.

And then silence.

Alexander blinked. His head was dazed and his back would be

surely bruised, but the first thing he did was look down at the woman in his arms. "Marjorie?"

She was staring around them, clearly befuddled by the speed at which the accident had occurred.

That there had been an accident was clear enough.

"Alexander," Marjorie exhaled, slowly extricating herself from his embrace, only to lift a hand to her head. "What... What happened?"

The picnic basket had slipped out from underneath the seat and pies, bread, and apples had scattered across the carriage door, which was now on the ground. Alexander looked up at the other carriage door, now playing its part as the roof.

He could get out of here, and if Marjorie was uninjured, he would certainly be able to help her out. But what of Douglas? Was he uninjured? The horses, were they—

"M'lord? M'lord, are you well?"

Relief poured through Alexander. "Douglas!"

With a wrenching sound and a sudden downpour of water, the Chance coachman's ruddy face appeared as he opened the carriage door, letting the rain in. He was grinning. "It's that damned wheel again!"

Alexander muttered a curse he certainly should not have uttered in the presence of a lady.

"I quite agree," said the indominable Lady Marjorie Dalton. "Would you be a dear, Douglas, and help me out?"

This woman was an absolute marvel, Alexander could not help but think as he and the driver managed to half-pull, half-lift Marjorie out of the tipped-over carriage. *She doesn't like being spoken to in a circulating library, but a carriage accident is just par for the course?*

The carriage was a sorry sight, indeed, when Alexander was able to pull himself out of the wreckage. One loose wheel may have caused the incident, but every part was damaged in a small way, and it would not take a small amount of coin to fix. One of the horses had bolted, though Alexander could not blame it, and the other was standing nervously nearby, a clear injury on its hindquarters. The rain was pouring down, the road was barely visible under the six-inch-deep mud that it had become, and lightning flashed above them as though to better illuminate their trouble.

"Not a quick fix, that one," Douglas said quietly at Alexander's side.

Marjorie had stepped off the road and over to the horse, speaking softly and warmly to it. Alexander's affections swelled. Even in a moment like this, she was caring for something other than herself.

"It'll be almost impossible to get back to Bath," Douglas muttered low in Alexander's ear, giving him a serious look. "But we passed an inn half a mile back. You and the lady might make for it. In but a few hours, I can bring a carriage—"

"Lady Marjorie Dalton, spend a few hours alone in a common inn?!" Alexander could not help the outrage seeping into his voice as he stared in horror at the mud-bespattered man, his hair plastered to his face in the rain. "You cannot be serious!"

The driver raised a sopping-wet eyebrow. "But she won't be alone, m'lord. She'll be with you."

She'll be with you.

Perhaps the man had intended it in an encouraging, protective manner, but that was certainly not the instinct that roared through Alexander's veins.

Marjorie. Alone, with him, at an inn.

No one would know. Other than Douglas, and the Chance servants weren't gossips. They were paid too well to anger their employers.

Alexander forced the desire deep down, but that only concentrated the aching need settling within him. This was his opportunity; after living with such a terrible reputation for so long, perhaps it was time to benefit from such a thing?

His focus flickered over to Marjorie. She was wet through, her gown clinging to parts of her a gentleman such as himself should certainly not be able to see, and she looked—

Joyful. Cheerful, even, despite the rain trickling down her face and the nervous horse tapping at the ground beside her.

But she would soon chill, and get sick—and that could not happen.

Alexander drew a slow inhale. "Take the horse. Return to Bath. Come back in a fresh carriage for us."

Yes, that was the right course of action. It was the only reasonable one, after all; one singular horse could not get the three of them back to Bath, certainly not in this weather. He and Marjorie would repose at the inn for—what, an hour or two? Surely, it would not take any longer than that for the man to return.

Douglas winked. "And if that rescue occurs tomorrow morning...?"

"As soon as you are able, thank you, Douglas," said Alexander, trying hard not to sound pompous and absolutely failing. "I'll inform Marjorie—*Lady* Marjorie."

It was all he could do to keep upright as he staggered across the road that could only passably be considered the word, and when he reached Marjorie, she held out an arm to steady him.

"It's a mite wet out," she shouted over the pouring rain.

"I am so sorry—"

"Yes, when I ordered a fine day, I expect one," she said, eyes sparkling. "Come now, Alexander, there is no possibility that you could have expected this."

Alexander considered his sister's words only a few hours before, the consistency by which the Chance carriage threw a wheel, and the pitter-patters of rain that had already started falling as he'd collected Marjorie from her home.

"Maybe not," he conceded, not fully convinced. "I'm sending Douglas back to Bath on the horse."

Marjorie immediately put a concerned hand on the horse's flank. "But she's injured."

"The other's bolted, and she'll get better care when she's

warm and dry in my father's stables," Alexander said, raising his voice over the storm. "He'll return to fetch us a carriage, bring it back here, and we shall depart."

"So we are to stand here in the rain all that time?"

He was not surprised at the way her eyes bulged, so he quickly replied, "There's an inn half a mile down the road. We will wait for rescue there."

Marjorie glanced down at her sopping gown and grimaced as she took a squelching step forward. It sounded as though her shoes were as sodden as his own. "Lead on, then, I suppose."

Alexander attempted to hold her steady as the two of them half walked, half staggered along the lane in the direction that Douglas had pointed before he'd mounted the injured mare, not pushing her to more than a trot. Nevertheless, the pair of them quickly disappeared out of sight behind the sheets of rain, and it was disheartening to say the least.

So was the walk. *Half a mile does not seem like much,* Alexander thought depressingly, *on a dry, sunny day with bright birdsong and a steady path beneath one's feet.*

It was a most different thing altogether when one was hobbling in wet shoes across half-a-foot-deep mud along a track that appeared to be undecided whether it was a track or not, in the pouring rain, in growing darkness.

And yet Marjorie was on his arm, and that propelled him forward until the two of them were staggering into the entrance-way of an inn that looked a little careworn but was, thankfully, watertight.

"Oh, dear God," Marjorie said helplessly, looking at the carpet they were standing on in horror.

It was soaking wet. That was, *they* were soaking it as they dripped onto the fine fabric, mud splattered everywhere.

"Goodness, we expected no more travelers in this weather," said a man as he bustled toward them. "Mr. Plunkett, at your service. Let me take that greatcoat from you, sir, and your pelisse, madam. You'll be wanting a room."

"No," Alexander said firmly, thinking of the damage to Marjorie's reputation.

"Yes," said Marjorie, just as firmly.

The pair of them stared at each other in genuine amazement.

Alexander did not understand it. He had been perfectly clear that Douglas would be returning, hopefully within a few hours, with a carriage. The very idea that they would stay the night here, utterly ruining Marjorie's reputation, scandalizing the entirety of Society… No. It was not to be borne.

Even if he might wish it.

Marjorie was looking at him with just as much confusion. "It may have passed you by," she hissed, cheeks burning crimson, "but I am soaked to the skin, and if I am not to take a chill I will need to get out of these wet clothes and—"

But Alexander's brain had stopped working at *out of these wet clothes*. "It won't be long before Douglas returns."

"And you want me to spend the intervening time seated down here?" Marjorie asked pointedly, raising an eyebrow. "Dressed like *this*?"

Alexander hesitated.

His gaze took in more of the inn, now that they were safely out of the storm. The place was not so much rough around the edges, but rough and ready—ready for a fight. There were only men in the bar area and they looked worse for wear for drink already, and it could not have been past four o'clock. There were no ladies present, and already, quite a few of the patrons were staring at Marjorie in a way that made Alexander want to punch them on the nose.

He turned back to her and opened his mouth, only to realize precisely why they were staring.

He shut his mouth. *Oh, dear God.*

It had probably seemed like a brilliant idea at the time, wearing a delicate white muslin gown. Naturally, she had been wearing her pelisse as they had half walked, half staggered to the inn, so he had not noticed, but now the innkeeper had politely taken Marjorie's pelisse, he had revealed... Well.

A white gown. Except now that she was soaked to the skin, so the fabric had tightened against her flesh and simultaneously disappeared.

Well, not *disappeared*. But become so transparent, it may as well have not been there.

Hastily stepping in between his woman—*the woman*, Alexander corrected mentally—and the numerous men now leering, he said aloud, "Yes, we'll take two of your best rooms, thank you Mr. Plunkett."

He wasn't going to allow the situation to get out of hand, absolutely not. They were trapped—for the time being—at an inn of debatable repute, and they were alone—but at the very least, he could ensure they had different bedchambers to retreat to while help was on the way.

He should have known by the wry look on the innkeeper's face, however, that his carefully laid plan was not going to plan.

"Two rooms?" blinked the man. "Oh, I am sorry to say, sir, that we have only the one—but you and your *lady wife* will be most comfortable there, I assure you."

Alexander almost groaned aloud.

Of course. Of course there was only one bed.

"I'll take anything at the moment," Marjorie shivered, her arms crossed in an attempt to protect her modesty. It was not exactly working. "Please show us upstairs, Mr. Plunkett."

Alexander followed the pair of them in a sort of dream. This... This could not have been happening. After attempting the most aboveboard and socially appropriate day out, everything had conspired against him. His sister, the weather, the carriage, the inn: everything seemed hellbent on constructing the most outrageous series of events.

And he couldn't have been more pleased.

The bedchamber, when they reached it, was not too shabby. *In fact*, Alexander thought as he stepped closer to the blazing fireplace and pulled off a water logged boot, *it is quite perfect.*

It had a bed and a fireplace. Right now, that was all he wanted.

As the door closed behind the smirking innkeeper, Marjorie let out a huge sigh—of relief, he hoped. "Right, then."

Alexander had almost pulled off his second boot but staggered and practically fell to the ground at the sight before him. "Marjorie!"

"If you think I am going to sit in drenched clothing, you are much mistaken," she said resolutely as her fingers continued to unbutton her gown. "Turn around."

"But—"

"Or don't," Marjorie shot back, her eyes glittering with mischief. "I know you planned all this to give us time to ourselves. You may as well make use of it."

Alexander pressed his lips together, turned around hurriedly, and hoped the dampness of his clothes would prevent his loins from burning.

"I did not plan this," he told the wall. "You could have been *hurt*! I would never. It's all a series of coincidences, I promise you."

"You know, a few weeks ago I would not have believed you," came Marjorie's lilting voice from behind him. "But now... Now I believe you."

Alexander's spirits soared. Perhaps all this wasn't the most terrible thing that could have happened, after all.

And they were alone. Alone, and likely to be for the next hour or so. This was perhaps the perfect opportunity to do the one thing that he dreaded and yet that he knew was perhaps absolutely essential if they were to have any kind of future together.

He had to tell her the truth. "Marjorie, I... I need to tell you something."

The sound of very wet fabric hitting the carpet reached his eyes, and Alexander swallowed hard. *Do not think about the woman being mostly naked behind you. Just don't think about it. How hard could it be?*

He took a deep breath. "I… I know you have heard a great deal of gossip about me, over the years."

Marjorie's snort, thankfully, did not sound wet. "'A great deal' is perhaps an understatement."

Alexander winced. He should never have permitted Lord Gascoyne and Sir Percival—but that was in the past.

He was far more interested in his future.

"Well, there have been some misconceptions, some misunderstandings about it in the past," he said quietly. Was that the right way to begin? Christ, he had never considered actually telling someone the truth about this whole debacle.

But Marjorie…she deserved the truth. She deserved so much more.

She deserved everything.

"And I wanted to tell you—"

"Alexander?"

"Yes?" he replied, turning around before he could stop himself.

And he couldn't stop himself from stepping forward.

What man could, when presented with an almost-nude Marjorie, her hair falling in waves past her shoulders and down her back, a look of ardent desire in her eyes.

He was only a man.

Alexander crossed the distance between them in an instant, pulling the woman he adored into his arms and kissing her passionately, breathing her in, almost shaking at the need that threatened to overwhelm him.

Marjorie had clearly hoped for such a reaction, for she tilted her head and immediately parted her lips, welcoming him in, and the needles of prickling pleasure pouring through Alexander's body were more than he could bear.

He needed her. He wanted her.

And yet he was trying to restore his reputation—a man couldn't restore his reputation by bedding innocent ladies!

Even if just being here, just going on the trip without a chaperone, had been enough to ruin her. If anyone ever found out…

Marjorie broke the kiss, and before Alexander could say a word, she said in a low murmur full of promise, "I know you want to bed me, Alexander Chance."

Chapter Fifteen

"*I KNOW YOU want to bed me, Alexander Chance.*"

Perhaps she should not have been so direct.

But perhaps, Marjorie thought as her pulse skipped a beat, *I should have*. Perhaps this was what she should have said days ago, when she had realized this man was the only person she ever wanted to kiss for the rest of her life.

Alexander was standing there, his arms still around her, apparently uncertain precisely what he was supposed to do next.

It was almost enough to make her laugh, except that Marjorie did not feel like laughing.

Not while she stood on this precipice.

Two lives stretched out before her. In one, Alexander Chance would accept her suggestion and ravish her so sweetly yet so wickedly, she would probably not be able to walk down the staircase of the inn to the carriage when it arrived to rescue them.

In the other, Alexander Chance would step back, apologize for putting her in such a scandalous position, and carefully wrap her up in a blanket to protect her modesty.

It was the latter Alexander she had thought she had wanted when she had first been approached by him weeks ago in the Pump Room. That had been the gentleman Marjorie had thought appropriate.

And she could not have been more wrong.

She ached for him, desperate need tingling up and down her thighs, and when she caught his gaze, Marjorie was astonished at how little the man was giving away. It was as though a part of him were closed off to her, impossible to read.

Impossible to know.

"I… You… Bed you?" Alexander said weakly.

Once again, she was forced to push down laughter, but it was tinged with something Marjorie did not initially recognize. It was only when she'd swiftly examined it that she realized it was…disappointment.

Disappointment, that she was clearly not enough.

Disappointment, that the man before her clearly had no real interest in her.

Disappointment, that just when she'd thought she was going to enjoy the heights of a climax once again, it was to discover she may never do such a thing again.

Trying not to let her shoulders slump, Marjorie said quickly, "Forget I said anything."

Something flickered in Alexander's eyes. "But—"

"No, honestly, it was foolish of me to suggest it," she said, embarrassment twisting her gut as she attempted to free herself from the man's clutches.

That became fairly difficult when the man held on to her tightly. "But I have not given my answer."

This time, her laughter was raw. "I think, if you have to *think* about it—"

"Marjorie." Alexander spoke her name like a blessing, and all she could do was halt her struggling and look up into his eyes.

It was in moments like this when she realized just how small she was compared to him. Why, Alexander almost *towered* over her, with those broad shoulders and his taut jaw.

Marjorie swallowed, tasting both desire and uncertainty on her tongue. The man liked her, she knew. There were moments when she almost thought he *adored* her. And yet there was something…something holding him back. Something between them that he had not spoken.

"I did not intend to put you in—I am not demanding," she

began fiercely, her desire to defend herself overcoming any sense or thought.

"I know—I know that," Alexander said quietly, pushing back a curl of hair behind her ear. Marjorie tried not to shiver as he did so. "Marjorie, you do not know what you are asking. What you are offering."

Her mind flickered back to that moment in the carriage when she had come undone on his fingers. "I think I have a relatively good idea."

Perhaps he was thinking about it too, for Alexander's lips lilted into a smile. "Perhaps you do, of the diversion in the moment. But there are consequences to such things, Marjorie, such acts, they… They change a person. They mark them."

It was undoubtedly because she had been soaked through that Marjorie shivered at that moment. Surely, there could be no other reason.

"But I am asking."

"And I am saying, you cannot take back that decision once made," he said softly and irritatingly reasonably. "Marjorie, when a woman gives herself to a man—"

"I don't need a lecture," snapped Marjorie, hurt searing through her as she finally managed to pull away.

"Perhaps you don't want one, but you need one," Alexander said quietly, no anger in his tones. "You know this is different, that Society will treat you differently than it would me if this is discovered."

The thought had not even occurred to Marjorie, and as it did so, a flash of uncertainty sparked through her. If she lost her reputation, her spotless innocence…what would her parents say? What would they do?

Then again, any one of the things that had happened today, if discovered, would be enough to ruin her in Society's eyes. Would requesting to *actually* be ruined make so much of a difference?

Marjorie's eyes flickered back to Alexander, and just seeing him brought all her certainty back. This was the man with whom she wanted to spend the rest of her life, and she was sure he felt the same way. Had he not spoken of matrimony? Had he not asked his father for an income, specifically to marry, talked of refusing a wife's dowry, as if alluding to the fact that it was *her* large dowry he could not accept?

Yes, it would take time for his reputation to be restored...so why wait, if they knew they would one day be man and wife?

Alexander's brow was still furrowed. "I cannot believe I'm saying this, Marjorie, trust me, but... But I think you should reconsider."

"I just thought—I want you, I want this," Marjorie found herself saying, swallowing a knot in her throat that had formed at the intimacy of what she was revealing. "I thought you wanted it too."

There: a twitch in his jaw as he prevented himself from speaking.

So he does want me?

Marjorie could almost throw her hands up in despair. How difficult was it supposed to be to seduce a rake?

Here she was, standing in naught but her underclothes—and they were wet through—with her hair down and her voice telling him, clearly, that she wanted to be carried over to that bed and ravished so thoroughly, she'd never walk again... Fine, she hadn't exactly articulated that part...

But still he resisted? Was there something wrong with her?

"I am not saying I do not want you."

Marjorie whirled around to stare back at the man who was so confounding her. "Yet you resist me?"

"I am trying, may I remind you, to be a better man," Alexander said wryly, tugging his hand through his hair and wincing. "Damn it, woman, I'm trying to be good for you! To deserve you!"

And it was perhaps this that prompted her to hesitate.

Blast it all. The man was right; he had tried to be good since meeting her, which was something to be delighted by and infuriated by, as far as Marjorie was concerned.

After all, one did not permit a scoundrel to court you if you did not wish to be courted by a scoundrel.

So, the answer was clear. *She* would have to seduce *him*.

If only she had absolutely any idea how to do that.

The rain continued to pour past the window and lightning momentarily lit up the room as Marjorie attempted to organize her features into what she presumed was a most seductive smile. "You do deserve me, Alexander."

His smile grew. "You're just saying that so I take you to bed."

Oh, she could stamp her foot in frustration! "I don't understand," Marjorie said helplessly. "Am I not pretty enough, not attractive enough?"

Alexander swore and turned away for a moment, biting his lip as he turned back to face her. "You can ask me that—have I not shown you how desirable I find you?"

"But you never say—"

"I adore you, Marjorie Dalton," he said quietly, gazing deep into her eyes. "What do I have to do to prove that?"

Well, for a start, keep speaking in a voice like that. "And yet *I* am the one asking you to…" Marjorie hesitated.

This was in some ways ridiculous, undeniably, but she could not help but be a little impressed by the man who had bedded so many ladies—*so* many, if the rumors were to be believed—yet when his heart was involved, he was attempting to be honorable.

It was the sort of manners she would have heralded as superior, just a few months ago.

That had been then. This was now.

He was now.

"I know you have been trying to be very good," she said slowly, tilting her hip to one side and smiling in what she hoped was an enchanting manner. "But right now, Alexander? Right now, I want you to be very bad."

The man groaned. "Marjorie, what are you doing to me?!"

"You have a choice. Walk out of that door…or ravish me."

Marjorie was not accustomed to giving ultimatums, but she held her head as high as she could manage and hoped to goodness she did not have mud splattered across her face. "What is your choice, my lord?"

Her words hung in the air, a moment of decision for the gentleman who had decidedly wished to bed her for so long.

Marjorie's breath caught in her throat as she stared into Alexander's eyes. He had frozen, his expression entirely blank, as he stared back without moving.

"Because," she said softly, "I don't fancy your chance staying here and not touching me, with me dressed like this."

With almost-shaking fingers, she plucked at the damp material stretched across her breast.

Alexander swallowed, and when he spoke, it was in a ragged voice. "Marjorie, you know I want you."

Pulse racing, she stepped toward him, her heart increasing its pace with every step. When she was standing mere inches away from the man who made her want to rip off all her clothes, Marjorie tilted her chin up. "Then show me."

Alexander leaned forward slowly, half inch by half inch, retreating once but then continuing to lower his lips to hers, until he finally pressed a gentle, reverential kiss upon her mouth.

Marjorie stood there, accepting the kiss, disappointment cascading through her…until Alexander wended an arm around her waist, pulled her sharply against him, and parted her lips with his oh-so-clever tongue.

Yes.

That was all she could think before the man made thought utterly impossible.

Oh, this man. He knew precisely how to kiss, how to make her toes curl, how to make it near impossible to stand upright. Thankfully, Alexander's strong arm around her waist meant she could sink into the kiss, her hands splayed against his broad chest and her head tilted back to accept all the kisses he could bestow upon her.

The kiss deepened, changed in a manner Marjorie had never known before. It wasn't just that she had parted her lips and accepted his tongue trailing molten need in her mouth, or that the pressure of his lips had changed and made her pulse skip a beat.

No, it was more than that.

This was not seduction, though it was intensely arousing. No, this was connection: a desire to give gratification just as much as to receive.

He was being noble in a completely different way, and Marjorie could not express—even if she had not been kissing Alexander furiously—how much it mattered to her.

He loves me.

Oh, he hadn't said the words, but what need was there for him to do such a thing?

He was showing her his affection. And that was all that mattered.

Well. Almost.

"How on earth is one supposed to escape this sort of thing?" Alexander asked with a laugh as he nuzzled kisses down her neck and his fingers struggled with the ties of her stays. "Is one encased at birth?"

"It's—It's a lot easier once my undershift is removed." Marjorie gasped, hardly able to put two words together as his fingers brushed past her wet, glistening shoulders.

When on earth had the shoulder become such an enticing part of the body?

She gasped at the sudden removal of Alexander's arm around her waist, not only his arm, but all of him. The man was gone, stepping away and toward the door.

Frantic thoughts whirled around Marjorie's mind. Was she truly that bad a kisser? He had never complained before, but then perhaps he had merely put up with her inexperienced technique and was now—

Alexander turned the key in the lock of the bedchamber door, turned around, and gave her a grin of such ardent desire and wickedness that Marjorie was astonished she was still standing.

"There," he said quietly. "We won't be disturbed."

It was a new line they had crossed, to be so hidden away from the world, and Marjorie shivered at the liquid look of ardor Alexander bestowed upon her as he stalked back toward her.

Oh, he wanted her. There was absolutely no denying it.

In a swift movement, Alexander rid her of her undershift, the damp material falling to the floor along with his coat. Marjorie's legs were shaking, not with fear or cold, but with anticipation, and she reached out eagerly for him, desperate for more contact.

"Patience," Alexander whispered, his smile making her knees quiver. "It'll be all the better if you are just patient."

Marjorie wasn't sure what the brigand meant by such a thing. She was burning for need of him, the ache between her thighs so desperate that if he didn't do something about it soon, she would have to take matters into her own hands.

Thankfully, Alexander appeared to understand her bursting need. He turned her around slowly and pressed kisses down her neck and across her shoulders as his fingers now made light work of her corset ties, every fluttering exhale on her skin laying down promises she could only hope he would keep.

"Alexander—"

"You wanted me to ravish you," came his gentle, though slightly teasing voice as he slowly removed her corset over her head, leaving her utterly nude. "So let me."

Let him?

Right now, there was almost nothing Marjorie would not let him do, but it was with slight trepidation that she allowed him to slowly turn her back around so that she was facing him.

Well. So she was naked.

Marjorie looked up into Alexander's eyes as he feasted on her form, his pupils widening as his gaze flickered from her mouth to her nipples, pert and throbbing, to her soft, dimpled stomach, to her secret place now surely dripping between her thighs.

"Very nice," he murmured.

And that was more than enough. "If you do not touch me soon," Marjorie warned, "I shall—"

Precisely how she would punish him—and it would be *him* who was punished, not her—she had not decided, but as it turned out, that particular threat did not matter. Alexander lifted her bodily, threw her onto the bed, and stalked toward her.

Marjorie had yelped in the air, the sudden journey most unexpected, but she swallowed down her cries of surprise as the handsome man before her slowly removed his clothing.

Oh, this was something beyond what she could have ever imagined. This was desire, pure and simple, yet there was something intimate, something profound in the way Alexander was looking at her as he dropped his waistcoat to the floor and then his shirt. Dark, wiry hair spread out across his chest, trailing down to the trousers, which were slowly being unbuttoned and dropped to reveal—

"Oh, my."

Well. She may have been innocent of naked men in reality, but she had seen statues, after all. She had been to finishing school—on the Continent, at that. She knew what a naked man looked like.

But the statues had gotten a few facts wrong. For a start, there was no figleaf beneath his trousers, as so many of the statues suggested. Furthermore, the few statues that had been figleaf-free—of much interest to all the young ladies at her finishing school—had displayed members of an inch or two, lying meekly in a downward position.

Not so here.

No, as Marjorie stared at the resplendent man before her in all his glory, it was to see a jutting manhood of several inches, a girth she had never realized was possible, and its direction was most definitely not down.

Marjorie swallowed. She was no doctor, sure enough, but was that...right?

Alexander grinned. "You look surprised."

"I am," she admitted faintly, her lungs catching as Alexander prowled around the bed and mounted it. Would soon mount her. "I did not expect—I mean, it's rather—"

"The important thing is that you enjoy yourself," Alexander said quietly, pressing her shoulders back onto the bedspread and grinning as he most strangely positioned himself between her knees.

Well, between her knees was to be expected, but she had thought his head would be near her own. From this angle, it almost looked—

"Try not to scream," said Alexander in a low, hungry voice as he lowered his head.

Scream? Marjorie propped herself up on her elbows to see precisely what the strange man was doing. *Why would I—*

She tried not to scream. "Alexander!"

But Alexander could not reply, and in a way, she was glad. After all, his tongue was otherwise engaged.

Oh, dear God, how did anyone get anything done in the world when there were such delights to be had! The man was kissing, licking, lapping at her secret place with seemingly all the delight of a man devouring an ice, and the waves of unrelenting bliss that were storming through Marjorie's body in response were enough to make her weep.

This was too much—*too much*—and yet simply not enough.

"Oh, Alexander," Marjorie murmured, squirming her hips down to do the unthinkable and thrusting herself onto his face. "Yes! Yes, there!"

Somehow, the man's tongue was able to twist and tease every inch of her, but there was a particular nub within her that his fingers had found so cleverly that time in the carriage, and now there were stars popping in the corners of Marjorie's eyes as the pleasure built, higher and higher, harder and harder, and once again, she was about to—

"Alexander!"

It took all her strength within her not to scream his name to the high heavens.

As it was, she uttered it as a whisper, a moan for only the two of them to share as her body burst apart in ecstasy and she bucked wonderfully against the Alexander's merciless tongue.

He gripped her hips, preventing her from escaping as the waves of ecstasy inexplicably increased, something surely impossible and yet Marjorie arched her back into the moment and knew she would never love another man again.

Never again.

When her eyesight returned, it was to see a grinning Alexander leaning over her. "Was that any good?"

"Were there no clues?" she said weakly. "Goodness, Alexander, that was...*my God*."

"Are you sure you want to go further? We can stop here if you want," he whispered, his tight eyes and gasping breaths a mixture of pained restraint and desperate desire. "You decide, Marjorie. You."

It was delicious, to be the one in charge—though she was half-certain she had been in charge from the very moment they had first met.

She licked her lips and wriggled her hips in elation at the way Alexander's breath caught in his throat. "I asked you to ravish me, Alexander, and that is what you shall do."

He groaned in a clearly delighted reply, leaning down and pressing a swift kiss upon her lips as he parted her knees and pressed his hips between hers—

Marjorie gasped in the kiss.

Surely, that had been his intention as Alexander slowly pressed his manhood deeper and deeper within her. Oh, it was like nothing she had ever experienced, more than intrusive, more than intimate, a strange medley of the two with hints of decadence and need and a building need once again, though how she could climax again so soon, she did not know.

"Alexander," she exhaled as he ended the kiss, fully sheathed within her.

He blinked down at her with a dazed look. "Marjorie you feel—damn, you feel incredible."

High praise, coming from a man who had bedded so many women.

Marjorie pushed the thought away and instead arched her back. "I am almost certain there's more to this than just lying here."

Alexander muttered a curse that she was starting to enjoy tugging from his lips. "You minx."

"You rogue," she shot back. "Show me. Show me how much you care."

Perhaps that was the wrong thing to say—or perhaps it was the right thing. Alexander seared another kiss upon her lips as his hips lifted, taking away the delicious manhood that so perfectly filled her, and Marjorie almost broke the kiss to complain—until he thrust himself back into her, deeper this time, and the strings of bliss were once again plucked.

Marjorie shivered. "Again. Again! More! Harder!"

"Marjorie!"

"What, you think ladies don't experience pleasure?" she returned, twisting her hips and relishing the look of momentary ecstasy on the man's face. "I said *ravish me*, Alexander. That's what I want. *You're* what I want."

There was no air for words after that, from either of them. Marjorie held on to his shoulders for dear life as Alexander built a steady but slow rhythm, ploughing into her lightly at first and then deeper, faster, his right hand on her breast teasing her nipple and making her back arch.

The pressure was building, and now that Marjorie knew their destination, she was eager to get there, desperate to feel the overwhelming bliss again, and their pants and whispers and undertones echoed in the small room, their small room, their own little world.

"I'm—close," Marjorie managed to pant as her body tensed

all over, the precursor she now knew for that pinnacle of pleasure.

Alexander pressed a kiss upon her lips as his hand left her breast—a disappointment, until his thumb slowly circled her nub at the place where their bodies met and Marjorie—

"Alexander, oh, God, yes!"

The climax roared through her, somehow even more intense than the last, and it was everything, *he* was everything, and Alexander was crying out her name and pouring himself into her—

He collapsed into her waiting arms and their breathing was ragged, and Marjorie knew in that moment. She knew.

She was going to marry this man.

Chapter Sixteen

April 8, 1841

ALEXANDER WAS NOT exactly walking on air when he entered the Pump Room, but he might as well have been.

"You have a choice. Walk out of that door…or ravish me."

He'd done it. He'd won the trust of arguably the most distrusting woman in all of Bath, and he had done it by entirely losing his heart.

"I adore you, Marjorie Dalton. What do I have to do to prove that?"

Never could he have imagined that he would have bedded Lady Marjorie Dalton in such a manner. Oh, he had hoped, he had initially schemed, but the moment he had started to get to know her, Alexander's plan had swiftly changed.

To matrimony.

Now he had tasted of her delights and had impressed her parents by returning her safely after a carriage accident. An accident for which they'd so carefully neglected to mention his sister had not been present, assuring them Lady Maude had also been fine when they'd asked after her condition. It hadn't been a lie—not the important kind Marjorie disliked, anyway. Alexander was not sure the outing could have gone better.

But that had been days ago. Today, he had been asked by his mother to show his face at the Pump Room as a representative of the Cothrom Chances.

"For after all, the Aylesbury branch is coming to Bath next week, and we cannot have it be said that we only returned to Society because they were here," she'd pointed out, as though that had made any sense.

Alexander had wrinkled his nose. "But we have hardly withdrawn from Society."

"Very few people know about your sister's broken engagement," the Dowager Duchess of Cothrom had said in a whisper, though they were alone in the morning room. "And we have to keep it that way!"

And so he was spending a perfectly good afternoon standing around a room that was far too small for the number of visitors, drinking water that was frankly disgusting, and chattering away niceties with people whose names he had almost certainly not remembered.

Alexander smiled lazily as he wrote his name in the Pump Room book. Because none of that mattered. Because he had his memories to dwell on.

"I know you have been trying to be very good. But right now, Alexander? Right now, I want you to be very bad."

Dear God, to think that bedsport could be so…so intimate. So touching. So connecting, bringing them closer together in a way Alexander could never have predicted.

And he had been right. Marjorie had been changed by the encounter.

Oh, not so that anyone would be able to tell. Douglas had certainly not said anything, when he had arrived at the inn two hours later, full of apologies and explanations that the road had been bad, the other Cothrom carriages had been unavailable, and it had been near impossible to convince a hansom cab to come all this way.

He hadn't remarked on Marjorie's loosely pinned hair, or the fact that one of her stockings was missing. They hadn't been able to find it after their frantic tumble in the bed and eventually had been forced to give it up.

Perhaps Douglas had not noticed.

But all Alexander had been able to do in that carriage ride back to Bath was notice. Notice the pink of her cheeks, the curve of her breasts, the way her lungs kept her décolletage moving, the way she—

"Zander Chance, as I live and breathe!"

Dragged unwillingly from the reminisces that were so delightful, Alexander blinked in the shock of the afternoon sun to see his two friends striding toward him.

Strange. Until recently, the appearance of his two oldest friends would have filled him with joy, even delight.

For some odd reason, his spirits sank.

"Lord Gascoyne, Sir Percival," Alexander said aloud, abiding by the social niceties that were expected, given they were in public. "How pleasant to see you."

Lord Gascoyne rolled his eyes as he slapped Alexander on the back. "You don't have to keep that up, you know, it's only us."

"I am glad you are here," Sir Percival added. "I was just about to congratulate Gascoyne here on his latest conquest!"

Alexander's smile faded somewhat.

Goodness, was this what he had sounded like when he had played the rake? So dull that there was nothing on his mind save for ruining the reputations of ladies?

God, how dreary. No wonder his sister had once thrown a book onto his lap and demanded that he at least *attempt* to be cultured.

His friends, however, did not appear to have any problem with their lack of culture. Sir Percival was tipping his head to Lord Gascoyne, who appeared utterly bemused by the courtesy.

"I am not sure who I am supposed to have conquered," the viscount was saying cheerfully, "but I will take your praise either way!"

"Oh, do not be so coy. I heard the news at the racecourse only last night." Sir Percival chuckled, winking at Alexander as though he were a part of the joke. "And you thought you could keep it a secret!"

Alexander's gaze flickered around the Pump Room. To be sure, they had not agreed to meet here, per se, but then there was always the chance that Lady Marjorie Dalton and her mother might decide to brave the chilly afternoon and socialize here.

"I do not know to whom you are referring," Lord Gascoyne was saying, his curiosity clearly growing. "Who is it I am supposed to have bedded, pray?"

And if she does attend, Alexander's frantic thoughts continued, *why, then, I could have a word with her mother, perhaps.* Emphasize that he was merely waiting for the right situation to propose matrimony, but that it was certainly coming for himself and—

"Lady Marjorie Dalton," said Sir Percival craftly, wiggling his eyebrows.

"Where?" Alexander said hastily, jerking his head around to look in all directions.

But she was not there. Not a single Dalton was to be found, in fact.

It was with a significant amount of disappointment searing through his lungs that he turned back to his friends.

"What are you talking about, Chance?" Sir Percival asked, scoffing and shaking his head. "I was merely congratulating Gascoyne here on bedding Lady Marjorie! She of the forty-thousand-pound dowry. Or was it fifty? Money does sort of lose its meaning at a certain point. Not that *I* would complain of snatching that dowry up."

The entire Pump Room went silent.

That was, *mostly* silent. Alexander could still hear sounds, but from a long way away, as though they were underwater. Or perhaps he was the one underwater. That would explain why his head felt so heavy and his mind was hurting, and he could barely think or move, just stuck here, hearing his friend's words echo and echo…

"I was merely congratulating Gascoyne here on bedding Lady Marjorie!"

No. No, it wasn't possible.

Marjorie wouldn't… She would never…

She had blushed with all the innocence of a virgin, and yet

she had been so desperate to have him, had she not?

Alexander's thoughts spiraled out of control as his friends' conversation continued without him.

"Don't know what you mean, old chap," Gascoyne was saying cheerfully. "I've never touched the woman, worse luck."

"But the rumor was most definite," Sir Percival was saying, a slight frown puckering his brow. "At least two gentlemen had stayed at some inn of some sort—"

Alexander's heart skipped a beat. *Oh, no.*

"—and they said they saw Lady Marjorie Dalton and Lord Alexander Chance—"

Oh, dear God. Please, please, no—

"—and they looked mightily ruffled when they emerged—"

This could not be happening. How could this be happening?

"—found a silk stocking in the room when they went in after!" finished Sir Percival triumphantly, snickering as he nudged Alexander. "And as I know *I* haven't had the pleasure."

"But I tell you, man, neither have I," snapped Lord Gascoyne with a puzzled frown. "Lady Marjorie is a mystery to me. And if I *were* to bed a woman with that kind of dowry, I sure as hell would make sure the act had been done under my name! That's a guaranteed trip to the wedding altar right there. I wasn't looking yet, but for *that* kind of money…"

Silence fell between the three of them as Alexander desperately hoped they would not work out the puzzle.

It was far too much to hope for.

"But if I did not bed Lady Marjorie Dalton…" started Sir Percival slowly.

"And *I* did not bed Lady Marjorie Dalton," continued Lord Gascoyne, a leer creeping across his lips.

Alexander smiled weakly as the two men guffawed, the viscount punching him on the arm and the baronet leaning back his head and howling with laughter.

"Dear God, man, I half forgot you!" Lord Gascoyne shook his head as he wheezed for breath. "Well, I must say, I am very impressed."

"Oh, there's life in the old dog yet." Sir Percival chuckled as a gaggle of elderly gentlemen passed them, chattering away about that afternoon's edition of *The Times*. "So how was she, eh, Chance?"

This was a nightmare. A literal nightmare.

Damn it, he'd thought they had been so careful, but he had been foolish, indeed, to think an assignation of that type in daylight—well, *storm* light—would go unnoticed. It was a damned nuisance that there'd been people of good family and rank there. The place had appeared nothing but a locals' tavern with a few rooms and stabling.

And now the whole of Bath knew he had lain with Lady Marjorie Dalton.

Panic roared through Alexander's veins. *But this is a disaster.* It wasn't his reputation he was concerned about; thanks to his friends' exploits over the years, the news that Lord Alexander Chance had deflowered an innocent lady of Society would raise eyebrows, to be sure, but it would not bring him any greater censure than that he had already endured. Other than his parents not standing for it—but he was fine with that. He was in agreement with the idea that he needed to do right by her.

No, it was her. Marjorie.

Her name was ruined, and forever. There was no rescuing this sort of disgrace. He'd have to offer his hand first and foremost, of course, but if her parents objected... And even if they didn't, the rumors, the whispers, the looks would forever haunt her. And *he* had done that to her.

His mouth was dry as Alexander swallowed, his friends still chuckling and asking him a wide variety of questions about the bedsport he and Marjorie had shared.

This was a disaster.

"I say again, how was she?" Sir Percival said, his words somehow breaking through into Alexander's frenetic mind. "I wouldn't have thought you'd needed the money, chap, but then again, you are a youngest son. Should we expect a hasty wedding?"

Mouth dry, chest tight, mind spinning, floor spinning—floor spinning?

Alexander tried to get a hold of himself, which mostly consisted of him trying to swallow, and failing.

What the hell am I supposed to say?

From somewhere far away, Lord Gascoyne was chuckling viciously. "That bad, was she? Well, I suppose you can comfort yourself with some of that fortune."

And a desperate need to defend the woman he loved, to contradict the gloating idiot standing before him, and a total lack of sense combined to make Alexander snap, "She was the best I've ever had, you cretin! Lady Marjorie Dalton is a woman whom any man would be lucky to bed, and I enjoyed her most thoroughly!"

The gaggle of gentlemen finished passing them. Standing on the opposite side of them, clearly able to hear every single word Alexander had just said…was Lady Marjorie Dalton.

Alexander's heart stopped.

"Oh, dear." Sir Percival smacked his lips. "Now you're in for it, old boy!"

He paid them no heed.

What did he care that these friends of his, friends who had not felt like proper friends in years, thought?

The only person whose opinion mattered to him was standing six feet away, staring in absolute horror.

"Marjorie," Alexander murmured instinctively, stepping toward her.

She ran.

Well, not quite *ran*. The Pump Room was so crowded, it was almost impossible to walk even at a quick pace, but somehow, Marjorie managed to flit through the crowd, slipping through the smallest of gaps, and always keep ahead of him.

Alexander followed, lungs barely able to take in air as he forced his way through the laughing crowds, his mind spinning and his stomach twisting as he saw the hem of Marjorie's dress flutter out of the door.

That was fine—perhaps it was better this way. They certainly could not have a conversation of such importance in the Pump Room.

But when Alexander staggered out of the building into the Abbey churchyard, it was to see a milieu of people shopping, a few people leaving the Abbey, pigeons flying everywhere, and—

No Marjorie.

He halted, panting, desperately trying to catch his breath as he tried to understand what had just happened.

Marjorie. Sir Percival. Lord Gascoyne.

It had been the most idiotic thing he had ever done, engaging with them on such a personal topic, but Alexander had felt goaded. And for her to be standing right there…

"I cannot believe you."

Alexander's heart leapt. He turned.

There she was. Marjorie. She had evidently stepped out from behind one of the Pump Room columns, for she was standing right by one.

She was also standing with her arms crossed over her bosom and a furrowed brow.

"Marjorie," he said weakly, half staggering toward her.

She did not retreat from his approach, but it could not have been more clear that said approach was not welcome. "Well?"

Alexander halted a few feet from her, wishing to goodness his mouth were working. Or his brain, for that matter. "Look, you were never meant to hear that."

"Yes, I gathered that." There was a coldness in her voice he had never heard before, and Marjorie met his eyes with a cool expression. "I cannot believe it. Or rather, I should have believed it."

"Marjorie—"

"Here I was, knowing full well you were a rake of the worst degree," Marjorie hissed at him, glancing about with pink cheeks.

"And my mother and I—"

Alexander winced.

"—just had to put up with my friend and her mother revealing that they had heard—"

Alexander groaned.

"Oh, well might you feign concern!" snapped the woman he loved. "You are not the one whose life is utterly ruined!"

Alexander bit his lip. "I tried to tell you—"

"I didn't know you were going to tell everyone you met that you had ravished me, you cretin!" hissed Marjorie, her cheeks scarlet as she glanced about her once more. The other occupants of the square did not appear much interested in their conversation.

But that would not last, Alexander knew. The more this rumor—and perhaps it should not have been termed a rumor, as he plainly knew it was true—spread across Bath, the less likely it would be that either of them would be able to venture out into public without some finger-pointing.

And it would be her, Marjorie, who would suffer the most.

She was suffering now. There were tears sparkling in her eyes, and it was a dagger to Alexander's heart to see them.

"You bedded me, knowing you would—would brag about it with your friends in public." Marjorie gasped, her tears threatening to fall. "You absolute rogue!"

"No—no! It wasn't like that," urged Alexander, stepping closer to her, finding it impossible to be apart from her when seeing her in such distress.

But it had been he who had put her in such a position: him, with his inability to decline her scintillating offer and his inability to think things through.

And as for Gascoyne and Percival: cads, the pair of them…but was he any better?

"I never planned for anyone to find out, and I certainly did not tell anyone," Alexander explained in a rush, desperate for Marjorie to understand. "We were seen, apparently. I have only just heard."

"Yet it took less than a minute for you to start—start crowing about it with your friends." Marjorie sniffed, still managing to hold back her tears but not doing a particularly good job of it. "I am just one in a long list for you, aren't I? Is that why you keep saying you won't accept my dowry? Because you never wanted to marry me?"

She could not have been further from the truth, but Alexander was utterly helpless to articulate that.

He should have told her the truth right back at the beginning, in her garden when he had crept over the gate. He should have told her his name had been used by others to throw the scent off their amorous exploits…but would she have believed him then, when he'd been acting the rogue right in front of her face?

She certainly would not believe him now.

"I-I will marry you," he said, knowing it was the only way to save her. It was not as if he didn't wish to do so, anyway. "I just wanted to be my own man first."

"Oh, we can't have anything less than a *man* offering marriage!" she snapped. "Don't trouble yourself, my lord, trying to save face because you've never been caught with an unwed lady of such fortune before. Perhaps I can convince my parents to let me have my own dowry, anyway. Perhaps I don't need to marry to save myself from poverty and ruin—because I may be ruined, but I will be quite well off as *my own woman*." Her breath hitched. "Though it wouldn't have had to come to that if you had just kept yourself from boasting!"

"I did not tell anyone," Alexander said sharply, attempting to speak on solid ground. "It was not I who spread the rumor!"

"You would lie to me, straight to my face?" Her lips trembled, and she looked heartbroken at what she presumed was his crime. "You know how I feel about liars. White lies are one thing, but something so important…"

"I am not lying," Alexander said softly, trying to keep his temper calm. "Marjorie, you have to believe me!"

"I trusted you," Marjorie was saying, her voice as broken as her spirit, her shoulders slumped. "I-I came to care for you."

"And I care for you too, Marjorie. I—" And here Alexander took a deep breath. Perhaps these were not the circumstances in which he had expected to first say this, but needs must. "Marjorie, I… I love you."

Marjorie blinked at him. Weak sunlight glittered on the tear that managed to escape, trickling down her perfect cheek as she stared at him in utter wonder.

Alexander allowed a small smile to creep across his lips.

Then the petite and delicate woman before him uttered a curse so filthy, he was forced to take a step back.

"Marjorie!"

"Well, that's what I think of you and your lies and your cruelty," she snapped, turning in a flurry of skirts.

No.

The thought was singular, and it was this: Alexander could not allow the woman he loved to walk away.

"Marjorie!"

"All that time, I thought you truly cared for me, but here you are gossiping about my prowess in the bedchamber?" Marjorie snorted through her tears as she marched down the pavement.

It was perhaps only adding to her annoyance, Alexander observed wildly, that she had to take three steps for every two of his, and therefore, it was mostly easy to keep alongside her.

"Go away!"

"Not until you hear me out."

"What is there to hear? I was the best you ever had in bed, and now the whole of Society knows it!" snapped Marjorie, her cheeks growing blotchy as she allowed the tears to run down her cheeks. "I cannot believe you!"

"Marjorie, I love you!"

She halted so rapidly that Alexander strode past her and had to double back. She was glaring at him with such hatred, such loathing that he was forced to step away.

"You," Marjorie said quietly, "are despicable. Despicable, you hear? I hate you."

His throat closed up. "Marjorie."

"I *hate* you," she repeated, waving a hand in the air and never ceasing to glare at him. "I hate you, and your whole family, the whole pack of them. Stay away from me. Never come near me again. I am never going to see you again."

"Marjorie!"

Alexander made to grab her as she passed him, but she managed to slip through his fingers, out of reach, into a hansom cab that she had obviously hailed with that wave of a hand.

"Marjorie!" he called desperately, his stomach flipping over as the reality of what was happening finally struck him.

The driver urged the horses forward, the hansom cab lurched away at a great speed, and Alexander watched as the woman he loved disappeared around a corner, believing the absolute worst about him.

And the trouble is, he thought dully as curious passersby stared at him, *that although she has almost all the facts wholly misconstrued, she's right.*

He was despicable. And he was never going to see her again.

Chapter Seventeen

April 11, 1841

"Y OU ARE JESTING," said Miss Harding, wide eyed.

"I am not jesting," said Miss Ramsay steadily.

"You *are* jesting!" returned Miss Harding.

"I swear to you, I am not jesting," replied Miss Ramsay.

Marjorie sipped at her tea and wondered what on earth she had done to deserve such misery.

Which was harsh. She should have been grateful, she knew, that anyone from polite Society had been willing to visit the Daltons at the moment. Especially after *The Times* had published that awful gossip piece.

It has come to our editor's attention that a lady from a mostly reputable family has been so incautious as to lose her reputation unconditionally. This would be shameful in and of itself, if not for her elder sister, who disappeared in mysterious circumstances and vague avowals of "a weak constitution" and "the need for country air" near a decade ago and has only recently returned to Society, hale and hearty as ever. We have to wonder why a younger sister of such an outrageous woman would ever be permitted to be alone in the company of a known scoundrel— but then, there are some ladies all too desperate to lose their reputation.

Marjorie had boiled when she had first read it. *"Mostly reputable family,"* indeed!

The anger had burned away quickly, leaving her with nothing

but shame and pain.

I was the one to allow this to happen.

Nay, she had *prompted* it to happen. If she had not bodily thrown herself at a man who had quite proudly attained and maintained the title of rogue, she would not have been in this fix, her mother would not have sobbed at the dinner table yesterday, and her father would not have been walking about the place looking as though he had swallowed a lemon.

Or the lemon had entered through a different, more painful direction.

Her father had insisted he'd demand Lord Alexander make it right, that he'd speak to the dowager duke again about the matter—Marjorie had not missed the fact that he'd said "again," but she could not ask him why and when he had spoken with Alexander's father about the matter to begin with—but she had admitted Alexander had offered to make it right, and she'd refused.

"Refused? *Refused?*" her father had said over her mother's increased wailing.

"I don't need a husband," Marjorie had snapped. "Certainly not one who was never going to ask me if not for being caught. He kept insisting he didn't want my dowry, Father. Who, given the opportunity, turns down a dowry as large as mine but a man so stubbornly determined to avoid the altar? I will not have an unwilling husband. I would rather die alone."

Her mom had shrieked even more at that, and Marjorie had thought it best not to address the topic of her father perhaps allowing her to manage her dowry for a life of her own just yet.

Focusing on another enemy, Lord Dalton had drafted a sharp rebuttal to the horrid gossip piece, which he'd then sent to the editor of *The Times*. Lord Dalton had put it about town that his younger daughter had been terribly slandered by a rake who had no morals and no character, utterly forgoing any chance at a happy reunion with the Chances, and Lady Dalton had made some delicate calls to a few friends to win them over and continue to permit their daughters to socialize with her.

Neither had actually asked her if the story was true. Only the matter of Alexander making it right had been broached, because that mattered even more than whether or not the rumors were true, and she supposed enough had been said about the matter of matrimony.

It appeared, much to Marjorie's chagrin, that the whole of Bath had been swift to believe the Daltons' story. It was, apparently, much easier to believe that Lord Alexander Chance was a rogue than that Lady Marjorie Dalton was a hellion.

And so Miss Harding and Miss Ramsay had come to take tea with her this afternoon, much to Marjorie's surprise, and her penance, it appeared, was to be subjected to the worst gossip the world had ever heard.

"Nay, it is true. There will be a ball next week." Miss Ramsay beamed. "Can you believe it?"

"I cannot believe it," trilled Miss Harding, nudging Marjorie. "Can *you* believe it?"

"I cannot believe it," replied Marjorie, most honestly but perhaps from a greater place of sarcasm than either her friends had been expecting.

The two of them chattered on happily about the public ball and who was likely to be there, and whether the food would be any good, and if the dancing would be palatable, and—

"But my father has said that from now on, if I am to attend balls, I must have at least two chaperones." Sighing, Miss Ramsay rolled her eyes. "And all because of that fallen woman everyone is apparently talking about!"

Marjorie sighed in turn and sipped her tea.

When had gossiping about others become so…dull? Oh, she had never been that captivated by such a thing, but she had at least been amused by a passing listen to the news of the day.

Now all it seemed to be was cruelty and lies and the attempt to ruin another's life.

Miss Harding leaned closer. "I heard my parents talking about it, but they did not use the lady's name or let me read the article that covered the story, so I am still in the dark. I heard she was utterly unaware of the danger!"

"Whether she was unaware or not, she should never have been so foolish as to travel with that Lord Alexander Chance, and alone!" came Miss Ramsay's retort.

Marjorie dropped the piece of cake she had been holding.

"Oh, dear, and crumbs do find a home so quickly." Miss Harding smiled warmly. "But go on, Miss Ramsay, you were saying. Lord Alexander Chance?"

"Yes, apparently, he was able to find a young woman of good family who was foolish enough to let him *bed* her," murmured Miss Ramsay, lowering her voice, as though that made the gossip less scandalous.

If anything, it only served to make the whole thing sound more clandestine.

Marjorie swallowed. It was all too painful to hear the mentions of her greatest personal tragedy gossiped about right before her, even if her friends were unaware that the lady of whom they were speaking…was herself.

Miss Harding was shaking her head with wide eyes. "To think, the greatest scoundrel of them all! To be sure, he is very handsome—"

"Very handsome," Miss Ramsay agreed swiftly. "Those eyes—"

"Those hands—"

"And the way he—"

"But the point is," Miss Harding said, fanning herself hastily with one hand, "is that giving in to such a gentleman is never a good idea. Is it, Lady Marjorie?"

Marjorie blinked.

She had been listening—of course she had—but at the same time, she had become lost in the memories of that afternoon.

The rain, the carriage, the accident—her dreadful fear and the way Alexander had immediately pulled her into his arms to protect her. The careful concern, the decision to go back to the inn, and the heat that had overwhelmed her, causing her to make the biggest mistake of her life.

A mistake that she regretted. Obviously.

"She was the best I've ever had, you cretin! Lady Marjorie Dalton is a woman whom any man would be lucky to bed, and I enjoyed her most thoroughly!"

But it had been a delicious mistake nonetheless. A mistake she had greatly enjoyed making.

Marjorie squirmed in the chair as she smiled weakly at her friends. She should absolutely not have been thinking of the awful man. He was awful—just awful!

"Marjorie, I… I love you."

In any other situation, she would have been overjoyed to hear such words. To know she had captured the affections of such a man, to think her future and his were to be entwined…

It was hard to wish the entire courtship, if that were what she could call it, had never happened, when there were such sweet memories to be found within it.

"—and it must be especially difficult for you, Lady Marjorie."

Marjorie blinked. "For… For me?"

Her large doe eyes blinking pointedly, Miss Ramsay was looking at her most piteously, and why, she did not understand. "Why, yes. Lord Alexander Chance was supposed to be courting you, was he not?"

Mind blank, fingers barely holding on to the teacup within her grasp, Marjorie managed to say, "'Courting'… 'Courting' me?"

"My mama said that your mama must have been very certain of him, to allow Lord Alexander Chance anywhere near her daughter," confided Miss Ramsay, as though sharing this information were a great gift. "And after all, he has changed these last few weeks."

Marjorie blinked again, feeling the most utter fool. "He has?"

He had always seemed the same when she'd been with him.

Oh, the blustering, foppish, rakish idiot she had first encountered had been nothing like the true Alexander, the one she had gotten to know over time, but that Alexander, the second one, had been steadfast and true during their entirety of their courtship.

Delight had risen inside her just by the act of thinking of him and now it was falling, as Marjorie remembered he had betrayed her.

Betrayed her, and lied to her, and insulted her.

What sort of gentleman boasted about his conquests in the middle of the Pump Room?!

And what man lied about them, and to a lady's face?

Marjorie hardened her heart. Not a man she could ever permit to be anything meaningful in her life. She was tired of big lies, tired of people who thought it was acceptable to lie about important matters to her.

She would never permit that to occur again.

"Yes, I have heard his whole family is worried about Lord Alexander Chance," murmured Miss Ramsay, practically bouncing in her seat, no doubt over her ability to share this particular piece of news. "The man…is depressed."

It was fortunate, indeed, that Marjorie was not holding her teacup anymore, for there was no possibility that her fingers would have been able to maintain it.

Quite to the contrary, her fingers shook and her voice caught in her throat as she considered what her friend had just uttered.

Depressed.

Lord Alexander Chance? The man she had known? The carefree, almost giddy—

But no. That had been the first Lord Alexander Chance she had met, Marjorie reminded herself. The rake, the rogue, the scoundrel, he had been sure of himself and confident and…

And as she'd gotten to know him, a wholeheartedly different Lord Alexander Chance had emerged. One who was unsure of himself. Who cared what others thought of him. Who had cared in particular about what *she* had thought of him, though she had struggled to believe it.

"—refusing to leave his...*his bedchamber*." Miss Ramsay whispered the final two words as though she had spoken of something obscene.

Which, Marjorie had to admit, considering she had shared a bedchamber with the man... It *had* been considerably racy.

"No!"

"Oh, indeed," confirmed Miss Ramsay, nodding as Miss Harding gaped, open-mouthed. "Apparently, he has not left his bedchamber for days and is refusing to come out, no matter what his family says."

"But for what reason would a man like that take to his bed?" asked Miss Harding in wonder. "Alone, at any rate? Can you conceive of any reason why, Lady Marjorie?"

Marjorie stomach twisted most unpleasantly. *Conceive of any reason.* "No, I cannot," she said aloud, unconsciously placing a hand on her stomach as her mind suddenly froze.

Conceive of any reason.

They had taken no precautions, had they? And she had not experienced her flux since then—but then, it had only been three days ago, she reassured herself as her pulse raced. It was not impossible that it should come soon. Why, it might come today. There was no reason to suppose...

"I suppose he was betrayed by a lover," Miss Ramsay said enigmatically, her smile quite belying the murky tone of her voice. "Perhaps she was permitting the attentions of *two* gentlemen."

"Surely not!" Miss Harding gasped, her eyes wide, a reaction Marjorie did not quite understand until her friend continued. "What woman would even consider *speaking* to another gentleman if she had the eye of Lord Alexander Chance?"

Well, there was that. Marjorie could not help but agree, even grudgingly, that a woman adored by Alexander would have no need for another.

That had been one of the things she had so venerated about

him. When Alexander had his attentions on her, the rest of the world faded into insignificance. It simply did not matter.

And why would it, when all she needed, all she wanted, was right before her?

"Lady Romeril herself has said how astonished she is that there has been such a change in him," confided Miss Ramsay in hushed tones, as though God Himself had spoken.

Which, in a way, He had. Lady Romeril was, after all, the arbiter of Society: deciding who was acceptable and who was not, ruining a lady's reputation with a raised eyebrow, putting down a gentleman's enthusiasm with a sneer.

If Lady Romeril had noticed a change in a man, there would be no denying it.

"You know what I think?" Miss Harding leaned forward, and Marjorie could not help but mimic her as her friend continued in a whisper, "I think that Lord Alexander Chance has, for the first time...fallen in love."

Fallen in love.

Fallen in love?

"Marjorie, I... I love you."

Marjorie lurched back in her seat, cheeks blazing, even as her two friends continued to chatter on about Lord Alexander Chance and his dramatic amorous affairs.

He has fallen in love.

That could not have been it. It could not have been her refusal to accept his outlandish and abhorrent behavior that had put him in the doldrums...could it?

Her mind whirled as Marjorie gripped her hands together in her lap. It was not possible. The man had a reputation more dramatic than his entire family put together, which was saying a great deal. Surely, a slight tiff between the two of them would not cause him to retreat from the world altogether?

"Mama thinks he is lovesick—"

Lovesick. Alexander Chance?

Marjorie tried desperately to think back to their last conversation—the last conversation they would ever share together—and understand precisely whether she had been in the wrong somehow.

She could not think how. It had been Alexander who had seduced her, who had doggedly refused to marry her before he'd been forced to offer, Alexander who had bragged about such a fact, and in public…and yet…

And yet.

And yet he had appeared remorseful. More than remorseful, he had appeared to wish to make an explanation for his actions.

Marjorie snorted and flushed as her two friends stared at her. "Just… Just thinking," she said lamely.

Picking up her cup of tea to hide behind, she tried to pay attention as they continued their conversation.

"I never thought Lord Alexander would ever actually fall in love with someone!"

"After bedding so many ladies, it must have been someone truly extraordinary for him to take to his bed like that!"

Marjorie could not help it. A spurt of delight speared through her as she considered whether or not she was truly extraordinary.

She did not feel it.

She certainly did not feel anything pleasant when it came to considering the man who had completely broken her heart.

Nausea roiled in her stomach at the very thought. He had betrayed her, and in the worst possible way, taking from her dignity, her innocence, and her heart.

She had trusted him, and he had broken that trust.

"And I heard he was betrayed by those friends of his!"

Marjorie's grip on her teacup suddenly tightened as someone said, "'Friends'? What friends? From whom did you hear this?"

For a moment, she was astonished to hear one of her friends speak so boldly and directly. Then she realized, most discomfortingly, that the speaker had been her.

Both Miss Ramsay and Miss Harding were blinking at her, their mouths agape.

Heat burned Marjorie's cheeks. "How awful, I mean," she mumbled, gazing down into the dregs of her tea. "To be betrayed by a friend."

The moment lingered, silence creeping around their now-stagnant conversation, until Miss Ramsay nodded pompously. "That is just what I thought. Apparently, the two men had teased Lord Alexander about his carnal exploits, suggesting she had failed to please him"—Marjorie winced—"and to shut the two bounders up, he stated she was the best he had ever had!"

"That is no way to speak of a lady!" Marjorie could not help but say.

There was a dreamy look on Miss Harding's face. "Oh, I don't know."

Marjorie blinked, and the sudden intake of breath from Miss Ramsay told the room precisely what she thought of that sort of thing.

Miss Harding blushed and took a large gulp of her tea before continuing. "I am just saying, if a gentleman ravished me to within an inch of my bones, I would hope he would state proudly that I was the best he had ever…you know what I mean!"

Miss Ramsay continued glare, but in a strange haze, Marjorie realized that she did know what her friend meant.

Was it possible? Could it have been true that Alexander's statements had been made not in a statement of braggadocio, but instead as a defense of her and her name?

A strange defense, and it was unlikely for a lady to be thrilled at such a statement…but still. Miss Harding was not totally wrong.

Marjorie shifted awkwardly in her seat. Of course she would want Alexander to think that of all the perhaps hundreds of women whom he had bedded—and she tried not to think too much of that—she was his favorite, the one with whom he had enjoyed being the most.

But that did not mean she wanted that fact paraded about the Pump Room!

"I have heard Lord Gascoyne and Sir Percival are not, in fact, the most reputable of gentlemen," Miss Harding said in a low whisper, as though either of them could overhear her at a moment's notice. "My mama says…"

Precisely what Mrs. Harding said, Marjorie did not know. Her attention was unable to linger on such a person when there was Lord Alexander Chance to consider.

Was it possible—could it have been that he had in fact spoken lovingly about her?

Perhaps not in a way she would wish, to be sure, but when had a gentleman ever truly understood a lady's desire to be kept out of the trails of gossip?

And he was *bedridden.*

Well, perhaps not bedridden, Marjorie adjusted hastily. She could not imagine Alexander floundering in such a manner.

But he was refusing to leave his bedchamber. He was lovesick. And that had to mean—

"Were you not out walking with him?" asked Miss Harding curiously. "There was that time I was there, as chaperone!"

Marjorie glanced up, almost surprised to find the two ladies were still there. "I beg your pardon?"

"Yes, I heard tell that he was showering his affections in your direction," Miss Ramsay said suspiciously—or perhaps it was with envy. "What was he like, when he was courting you, Lady Marjorie?"

What was he like?

What a question. He was adoring and confident and unsure of himself. He was witty and charming and entirely distracting. He could kiss like the devil yet had the conscience of a saint.

These were the words Marjorie did not say.

But she did think them. She did think of the laughter they had shared, and the moments of surprise when he'd acted in a way far more befitting a gentleman of Society than the scourge of ladies' bedchambers.

"He was…wonderful." Marjorie sighed, heart singing.

Miss Ramsay raised an eyebrow. "And you went walking with him, did you?"

In that moment, the knowledge of precisely what she should do sparked through Marjorie's mind like wildfire.

It was, really, the only thing she could do. "Oh, yes." She smirked. "Yes, I went walking with him—and I did a great deal more than that."

Miss Harding gasped. "Lady Marjorie!"

Miss Ramsay narrowed her eyes. "Pray tell, exactly what do you mean by *that*?"

But Marjorie ignored them. It was not conversation with them she was desperate to partake in, but another's. Someone quite different from them in every regard.

Placing down her teacup with a clatter and rising in a ripple of silks, Marjorie rushed to the door, her pulse hammering. "And if I have my way, I'll do a great deal more with Lord Alexander Chance again!"

She had almost made it out of the house when she was halted by a face she had not expected.

At least, not at the Dalton residence.

"Rose!"

"Marjorie," said her sister brightly, her face falling as she took in the expression on the younger woman's face. "Dear God, you have a Lady Macbeth look about you."

Marjorie tried not to grin. "I thought you theater types worked hard not to say that name."

"It can be forgiven outside a theater, I suppose," Rose said brightly, rearranging her shawl about herself before returning her sharp look to her sister. "You look most strange, I will admit. What on earth is wrong?"

"Wrong? Nothing. Everything." It was not the most eloquent of speeches, but Marjorie could hardly fathom how to articulate it any other way. "What are you doing here?"

"Me?" For some reason, Rose colored as she smiled at the approaching footman and handed him her shawl, bonnet, and gloves. "I have no idea what you're insinuating."

"Don't try to pretend your relationship with our parents has been repaired. I have eyes, you know," Marjorie said darkly, crossing her arms and trying not to think about how she was still getting to know this sister of hers. "You don't have to tell me, obviously, but don't lie."

Don't lie.

It was the one thing she asked of those in her life, the one thing she had been clear about with Alexander, at least when it came to the important things. And what had he done?

Well. Not exactly lied. Just shouted loudly about her prowess.

"You're flushing."

Marjorie made the mistake of lifting her hands to her cheeks. "No, I'm not."

"You only used to flush like that when you had your eye on a young footman," teased her sister, her hand inexplicably resting on her stomach. "Who is it this time—Sackville?"

"*Rose!*"

"Or perhaps someone else, of a better name," Rose continued in a hush, and for a moment, Marjorie was swept back to those days when they had been young, and innocent, and jubilant. "A Chance, perchance? Like the one I saw with you in the drawing room the other day?"

If only her dratted cheeks would behave.

Her sister's jaw dropped. "Tell. Me. Everything."

"Rose, I don't have time to—"

"There is always time," she said ominously, taking her by the hand and pulling her into the morning room, "for sisters."

Chapter Eighteen

"ZANDER CHANCE, OPEN this door!"

"Absolutely not, but thank you," Alexander said cheerfully—that was, as cheerfully as he could.

He could not recall the last time he truly had ever been cheerful, so perhaps it was more accurate to say that he spoke with enough volume and power that it could have been read as cheerful by the untrained ear.

"I know you're miserable in there!"

His mother was not an untrained ear.

Alexander studiously ignored the hammering going on just the other side of his bedchamber door and turned back to the window. "Thank you, Frank."

"I still don't quite understand this, Zander," his cousin Frank said lightly from the garden below as she carefully winched up another basket full of food. "But it has proven a most fascinating challenge, and for that, I thank you."

Alexander attempted to smirk. "Glad to be of service."

It had been an excellent idea to ask his sister to take a note to their cousin Frank. Frank had an engineering mind, one that liked puzzles, and problems, and most importantly, finding their solutions. Always dressed in trousers if possible, always with a mechanical pencil stuffed behind an ear, Frank could have been one of the greatest engineering minds of England.

If her parents had not insisted that she stop drawing sketches for machines and act more like a lady.

Frank winked as she looked up at him, her shirt far more likely to be her brother's than one of her own. "Will that keep you for a few days more, do you think?"

"Yes, this will be excellent, thank you," called down Alexander as the thumping against his bedchamber door reached new heights. "Much appreciated."

Frank shrugged, called up, "Any time," and departed the garden.

"Zander Chance, I did not bring you into this world so that you would refuse to enter it!"

Ignoring his mother's calls through the very solid wood— thank goodness for dependable properties—Alexander perused the items his cousin Frank had chosen for his meals.

Two large pies, *excellent*, and two apples, a carton of strawberries, a cold fish sole heaped around with potatoes, *delicious*, some early asparagus, and a pat of butter.

"If you don't open this door, Zander, I shall have to take drastic measures!"

Alexander snorted. That was what his mother had said last night, and the only measure appeared to be asking his father to come upstairs and yell through the door. He had heard their muffled argument about it late into last night. In a way, it had been almost soothing.

In truth, he had absolutely no idea how he would have managed to get to sleep without it. His mind had whirled at a thousand miles per hour, making it impossible to do anything, think anything, consider anything except Lady Marjorie Dalton's face. Her expression of betrayal.

"You are despicable. Despicable, you hear? I hate you."

Alexander's jaw tightened even as he stood by the window. It was painful to realize he had destroyed any opportunity of being with the woman he loved and had done so months, *years* before he had ever become serious about her.

He should never have permitted Percival and Gascoyne to ever use his name.

That had been a foolish choice, one made from desperation to be liked and a need to fit in. A desire to befriend those who did not have the surname of Chance, a ridiculous rebellion of youth that by God, he was paying for now.

Why he had thought any good would come of it at all, he had no idea. But he could not have predicted just how much damage would come in turn.

"I am never going to see you again."

Pain seared through Alexander. He was the one who had done that; he was the one who had injured Marjorie, no one else. It had been his poor decisions and his inability to take control of his own life that had made it impossible for her to trust him in the end—and quite rightly.

Speaking of her so crudely in the Pump Room—what had he been thinking?

"Alexander Montague Arthur Chance, this is the last time I will ask," came his mother's stern malediction through his bedchamber door. "Open this door or face the consequences."

It almost cheers me, to hear my mother so passionate, Alexander thought as he heaved the basket of food over to the opposite corner of the room, where it was coolest. *After all, a lady gets to a certain age, her children are grown and are starting to have children of their own—they don't need her. Giving my mother something to do like this—*

A strange sort of screeching. A hammering. A sound like a saw.

Alexander lurched up from the bed upon which he had just been about to sit and ran over to his door. "What are you doing?"

"I told you, you were on your last opportunity to open this door," came his mother's grim voice. "Now you are going to pay the consequences."

Alexander's stomach lurched. *Consequences?* That did not sound particularly good. "But—"

With a sudden creak that sounded most unpleasant, the door was taken bodily off its hinges and was swung around to lean against the wall.

Revealed before him stood his mother, a smug look on her face, two footmen, a housemaid carrying a bag of tools, and a rather sweaty looking Nicholls.

"Nicholls!" cried Alexander, aghast.

"The man knows his way around some joinery, I'll give him that," his mother said pertly. "And remind me to have a word with your Aunt Florence. I don't think it's at all acceptable that her Frank has been feeding you like a princess in a tower."

And just in case I wanted to feel even more emasculated, Alexander thought darkly, *there it is.*

Great. Now he did not have a door for his bedchamber, and he was going to have the most awkward and uncomfortable conversation in the world with his mother.

His mother!

"You need a good talking to, my lad," the Dowager Duchess of Cothrom said happily. "And I know just the sort of person to whom you'll have to listen."

Alexander groaned. His father was many things—loving, in his own way, stoic, punctual—but his emotional range was not one of his finer features. Even after William Chance had given up his title to his eldest son, Thomas, Alexander had seen only the smallest of changes within him.

"Tell Papa I await him at his leisure," he said, perhaps more sullenly than was required.

"It was not your father whom I had in mind," his mother said tartly, stepping aside to reveal—

Alexander blinked. *Oh, hell.* "Samuel?"

"When I heard about the ruckus, I came straight over," his cousin Samuel said brightly, though there was a tension around his eyes Alexander did not like. "In fact, I've been staying in the guest chamber next door waiting for you to venture forth. I'm afraid your mother thought—"

"The door is gone! Once more unto the breach, dear friends, the door is gone!" cried the dowager duchess triumphantly.

Alexander met his cousin's gaze. The man had a determined mother of his own.

"I think I can take it from here, Aunt Alice," Samuel said quietly, stepping around her and jerking his head to the servants.

The servants understood immediately, departing with bows and scrapes. It was his mother, as Alexander had well expected, who did not take the carefully polite dismissal very well.

"Alexander is my son!"

"And I am sure you want what is best for him, and I will be sure to tell him how very angry we all are," said Samuel smoothly. "I suggest you go downstairs and have a nice cup of tea, Aunt Alice. You have done a great deal already."

And so it was with such platitudes and promises that the moment he was done speaking with her errant son he would report back to her, Samuel managed to clear the corridor.

When he looked up at Alexander, however, it was to see a dark frown.

Alexander growled. "I'm not sure I want to be lectured by a cousin but three years older than me, only to have my every word reported back to my mother."

Samuel shrugged. "Oh, I won't tell her everything. Just the important parts, you know. May I come in?"

Alexander glared, then looked pointedly at the bedchamber door, which was completely off its hinges and leaning against the corridor wall.

His cousin did not appear in any way abashed. "That wasn't my idea."

Oh, to hell with it.

He should have known he would not be able to avoid his family forever, Frank notwithstanding. There was something so...so *intrusive* about the way the Chance family was, even across branches. Samuel was only his cousin, not a brother, yet here he was to scold him.

Well, he might as well get it over with.

Alexander turned and stomped into his bedchamber, trying not to think about how much of a child this made him feel, then gestured to one of the two armchairs opposite his bed. "Please, be my guest."

"There's no need to be like that," Samuel said reasonably. "I just thought I could help, that's all."

"'Help'?" The outrage that flowed through Alexander's veins was utterly unrestrained and utterly useless, but he accepted it, anyway, as something to feel that was not guilt.

It was all he had felt for days: guilt.

"Yes, help," said Samuel quietly, settling himself on the chair and looking up at his cousin with an expression of complete calm, though Alexander was not fooled. There was that tension around the eyes again. "You might have forgotten, in all your adventures with the very willing Lady Marjorie Dalton—"

Alexander took a step forward, fists clenched. "Don't you dare speak about Marjorie like—"

"—that I am in fact married to Marjorie's sister, Rose," continued Samuel, his voice not wavering for a syllable. "Which makes me family twice over."

Alexander opened his mouth, tried desperately to think of something half sane to say, realized there were no words left in his brain, and closed it again.

Hell's bells. He had completely forgotten.

Yes, Cousin Samuel had come back from Brighton only months ago and revealed he had in fact married Rose, the long-lost daughter of the Daltons, supposedly with relatives in the country but really out living quite the adventure. It had been a surprise to everyone, including his own parents, and the frosty acquaintance between the woman and her parents had fueled the fires of gossip for weeks.

He hadn't heard anything substantial, but the fact was, the new Marchioness of Aylesbury politely acknowledged Lord and Lady Dalton in public, and he'd seen Rose visiting her mother himself, though he did not know why.

Alexander sat hurriedly in the armchair beside his cousin. "Have you seen her?"

"'Her'?"

"Marjorie, you fool. You knew exactly who I meant," Alexander snapped, hopes rising of hearing something of the woman he loved. "Is she well?"

It was his cousin's hesitation that crumpled his spirits.

Oh, he had broken her. He had destroyed her, with what he had done, and she would surely never be the same.

What woman would be? She had trusted him, his Marjorie, and he had destroyed that trust. Nothing he did or said in the future could ever restore him in her sights. Alexander knew that. No woman would accept an apology—what on earth could such an apology contain?

Hello, Marjorie. Terribly sorry to allow ruffians to use my name for years in their erotic exploits. It wasn't me, except when it was, but that was rarely, and I thought I was defending your honor when I bragged about how splendid you were at bedsport. In public.

Alexander cringed at the very thought of the words. There was absolutely no possibility he could speak them.

"Marjorie is…upset," Samuel said delicately. "At least, that is what Rose says. She saw her yesterday. While the two sisters are still getting to know each other after so many years apart, my impression is that Marjorie was quite open with Rose, and—"

"And did she mention me? Did she mention me by name—was she crying? I am sure she was crying, and I don't blame her. I just hate that I've brought her to tears," said Alexander in a stream of words, hardly able to marshal his thoughts into any coherent order. "Do you think if I visited—but no, there is no possibility that Lord Dalton would allow that…"

"I think it is far more likely that Lord Dalton would be delighted to see you call on his daughter, as long as it came with an offer of marriage," Samuel said quietly, his hands folded in his lap.

An offer of marriage.

If possible, Alexander's spirits sank lower. Well, he *had* offered marriage. And she'd refused him. Were her parents aware of that? Was that why her father hadn't demanded a proposal or a duel at dawn?

"I did offer," he said dully, his shoulders slumping. "It was…bad timing, to be sure."

Samuel arched a brow. "Let me guess. It was only *after* you'd embarrassed her at the Pump Room."

Alexander ignored that. "She refused. We'd discussed it before. Well, I think I'd *alluded* to it—"

"Oh, that's what every lady dreams of. *Allusions* to marriage."

Alexander ground his teeth a moment before speaking again. "The thing is, I have nothing to offer her. It's all right for you, with your fabulously wealthy aunt—"

"Great-aunt," corrected Samuel with a wry smile.

Alexander gestured to him in frustration. "Does it matter? The fact is that she left you over a hundred thousand pounds—"

"A hundred and twenty thousand pounds," his cousin cut in, almost apologetically. "Do I smell my mother's cook's tongue pie?"

Alexander sighed as he rose to his feet. "Frank brought it over."

"Frank?" Samuel shook his head, as if disbelieving what he'd just heard.

Alexander stepped across the room and retrieved the basket that had so recently been delivered.

"Frank?" repeated Samuel, accepting one of the pies but not bringing it to his lips. "You allowed Frank in here, but you wouldn't allow your own mother?"

Alexander grinned, for what felt like the first time in forever, and jerked his head to the window.

His cousin's eyes flickered over to it, took in the makeshift pulley system that Alexander and Frank had hooked up but days ago, and understanding dawned as his features softened.

"Ah," Samuel said vaguely. "Frank."

They sat in companionable silence for a few minutes as they each devoured their portion of pie. *And it is very good*, Alexander thought. If only he could know that Marjorie was happy, he would be able to enjoy it.

Not happy with him. He was no fool; he knew that ship had sailed a long time ago.

But just to know she was happy, that she was being cared for. That she had found some gladness in life, that she would not spend the rest of it wishing things had ended differently…like he would.

Samuel brushed the final crumbs from his lips then said suddenly, as though they were still midway through their conversation, "Rose said Marjorie explained to her that you would not take her dowry. That you were being especially stubborn about it."

"W-Well, I… It's not that I won't take it. Marjorie could have it for herself once married, perhaps even save it for our children should she so desire, but I'd feel a damn fool if I just sat back and let my wife take care of me." He also felt like a fool saying the words aloud. There would be no wife. No children. Not if he couldn't have Marjorie.

Samuel held up a hand. "I think you're stubborn, but I also understand. And so I have been thinking about your matrimonial prospects."

Alexander could not help but raise an eyebrow. "Why, Mama, you look so different in trousers and a shirt."

His cousin threw the pie wrapper at him, though its almost insubstantial weight meant it fluttered to the carpet between them. "Be serious for a moment, Zander. You know I once had one hundred and twenty thousand pounds—"

"What, spent it already, have you?" Alexander could not help but tease. "Bought an island? Or a few castles?"

"No," Samuel said steadily, though mirth danced in his eyes. "But I have invested, yes. In one way or another."

It seemed like a mightily strange topic to move onto, considering that Alexander's life was falling apart around his ears, but he supposed that perhaps even Samuel needed someone to cheer him up.

"Well done," Alexander said bracingly.

Samuel called him a word Alexander was certain his mother would not appreciate him uttering. "You know that's not why I bring this up!"

"Then why?"

"I wanted to do good in the world. Well, in my family at first, but Rose has opened my eyes. She... She truly is a spectacular woman."

Alexander tried not to smile as his cousin's voice trailed off, his eyes misting over and a beatific smile emerging on his face.

That was, he tried not to smile for at least a minute. After that, he coughed as politely as he could and said, "'Do good in the world'?"

"Right. Right, yes," said Samuel, clearing his throat. "As I said, I wanted to do things for my family as well."

"Please don't tell me you've given Benjamin half your assets or anything."

"My younger brother is proving himself to be quite capable of getting into enough trouble on his own, without money to help him," said Samuel with a raised eyebrow. "No, I thought about the Pernirth cousins."

Ah. The Pernrith cousins.

There were four Chance brothers from the elder generation. However, only three had grown up together. The fourth had been their father's bastard and had only been welcomed into the family as an adult. His daughters had no titles and no dowries, though they did of course have the splendor of the Chance name. Two had married already without those obstacles proving impediments, but they had two sisters yet unwed.

Understanding started to dawn in Alexander's mind—though precisely why his cousin was telling him about this, and why now, he still could not fathom. "You're going to give the remaining girls dowries."

"Teddy and Gwen will each have twenty thousand pounds when it comes to their marriages," Samuel said quietly. "I have told Uncle Frederick and Aunt Edie, but no one else."

"That is a great deal of your fortune," Alexander said, half surprised.

Well, that was perhaps a little unfair. His cousin Samuel had always been a kind man, and it made sense that a gentleman who had been given the title of Marquess of Aylesbury with the estate's income was not going to have many calls on his purse when it suddenly increased to one hundred and twenty thousand pounds.

But why on earth was he telling him this?

Samuel shrugged at the implicit suggestion that he was beggaring himself. "Would it mortally wound you to know that along with the cash, Great-Aunt Tessie left me sufficient properties to generate an income of—"

"Well, I am sure the Pernrith cousins will be delighted," Alexander said heavily. "You can go on your way now and feel smug that you have done your best to impress upon me the importance of having one's own fortune. I am very aware, thank you."

"I wanted to do something for you."

The statement should not have raised Alexander's hackles, but he could not help it. "If I didn't find my wife's sizable dowry sufficient to have spurred me to a proposal before it was too late, what makes you think this will solve the issue? I do not take charity."

"I know that." Samuel clasped his hands together in front of him, leaned back, and shrugged. "But Rose wanted to do something for her sister and agreed you are being stubborn to not accept a woman's dowry. However, I know you, and I can understand why. And now I can see how dearly you care for her... It is not a difficult decision."

Was it that obvious? Not that Alexander had ever really been able to hide it, not even from Marjorie.

Perhaps only from himself.

"And in truth, I have always felt...well, uncomfortable that you are the only Chance boy without an income of his own," said his cousin a tad awkwardly. "So as I said, I've talked it over with Rose, and we're agreed. I'm going to give it to you."

For a moment, Alexander allowed hope to flicker. Give him something?

Sufficient to marry?

No, that would be ridiculous. To purchase a competency for a Chance son would be in the tens of thousands, and the man wasn't made of money.

Not entirely.

"Right," Alexander said warily. "What?"

Samuel smiled. "The MacPhearsons' Municipal Manufacturing Company Limited."

"'The MacPhearsons' Municipal Manufacturing Company Limited'?" It did not sound particularly promising. "Just exactly what is that mouthful?"

"Oh, it's a factory in London. Somewhere in the East End. I haven't actually visited it yet myself," Samuel said quietly. "Mr. Todd, my solicitor, has examined it, however, and he believes that with some work and significantly better management—which I do not think you could fail to achieve—it could generate an income of eight thousand a year."

Eight… Eight thousand a year.

Alexander swallowed. It would put him on a par with Leopold and most definitely make it possible to wed without touching a penny of Marjorie's money.

Wed Marjorie. If she won't refuse me a second time.

There was only one problem.

"Go…into trade?"

Samuel chuckled. "I told Rose you'd take it like that, and she told me to tell you that you are a ridiculous, stuffy, puffed-up idiot if you both refuse to take a lavish dowry *and* won't earn an income for yourself to—"

"Yes, yes, I get the picture, thank you," muttered Alexander. "It's just…for a gentleman to go into trade, to *work*! No Chance has ever done such a thing."

There was a glitter of mischief in the man's eyes seated before him. "Yes. You would be the first."

The first.

And a flicker of delight soared through Alexander at the very idea. Well, he had always wanted to be different, hadn't he? Always wanted to rebel, to be set apart from his family. Chart his own course.

To earn his own living would certainly be a great departure for the Chance name.

And Marjorie—

Alexander's spirits sank. "It won't be enough."

"'Enough'?"

"Oh, no, I didn't mean—it's incredibly generous, and I would be delighted to face the challenge," Alexander said hastily, noting the way his cousin's mouth hung open. "I just meant... Marjorie is not going to be impressed by factory ownership, or any particular income. She's already refused me... I broke her heart, I think."

"Well, as someone who broke a Dalton's heart and lived to tell the tale," Samuel said brightly, "I suggest groveling. Lots of it."

Alexander raised an eyebrow. "'Groveling'?"

"Oh, yes." His cousin winked. "And apologies. Real ones, preferably. Rose is the only actress in the family and I rather think your speech to Marjorie should be sincere."

Oh, hell. "'Speech'?"

Samuel nodded sagely and rose from his seat with a laugh. "It's time to face reality, Zander—and with any other woman, after *your* history, combined with this foolish notion that a man shouldn't accept a woman's generous dowry if he needs it to wed, I wouldn't fancy your chance."

Something like hope flickered in Alexander. "But?"

His cousin shrugged. "But she loves you. What is more powerful than love?"

Bitterness tinged Alexander's mouth. "Betrayal."

Chapter Nineteen

April 12, 1841

WELL, THIS WAS it. The most outlandish, scandalous thing she would ever do.

Marjorie took a deep breath and almost laughed as she stood outside the Cothrom Chance townhouse.

This is madness! I can't go about doing things like this!

But she was. She had been too afraid to do so yesterday, rushing all the way here after leaving Miss Ramsay and Miss Harding and having a most unexpected heart-to-heart with her sister, but by the time she had arrived at this very spot before the Cothrom Chance townhouse front door, it was to see a gaggle of Chances entering the building, including her brother-in-law, the new Marquess of Aylesbury. The sight of so many people had shot her nerves.

Marjorie had spent half the night consoling herself that it had not been the right time, and the other half berating herself for having absolutely no guts whatsoever. It was not the most pleasant of conversations to have with oneself.

But it had worked.

She had given Tilly another chance to meet with her beau, had assured her the incident that had happened the last time they'd parted like that would not be repeated in the light of day. Besides, Marjorie felt certain Tilly was about to leave service and become a bride, so the threat of losing her job should the Marquess of Dalton find out did little to worry her. Once they'd parted in agreement at the circulating library, Marjorie had hastened over here as swiftly as she could. She was staring up at the house to which she had always longed to be invited under better circumstances and now…

Now she was trying to build up the courage to go in there.

Which is ridiculous. There would be a footman answering the door, and all she would have to do is slip the man the pound note she had borrowed from her sister—Rose being surprisingly obliging, considering Marjorie's own pin money was spent—and she would hopefully be shown up the servants' staircase to the bedchamber of Lord Alexander Chance.

Even the very thought of doing such a thing rippled panic through her, but she had to do it.

She had to ask him.

So, all she had to do was knock on the door. That was not difficult. She had knocked on doors plenty of times.

Well, now that Marjorie came to think of it, not that often. They had footmen for that.

But still! How hard could it be?

Very hard, as it turned out. Marjorie's nerves shook her hand as she reached up to the brilliantly bright brass knocker.

This was it. There was no turning back.

Somehow, the thought steadied her. She did not want to go back. Go back to what, a life with her parents that was stilted and painful? A life of rules and regulations that not only kept her hemmed in, but heaving a sigh as each day ended with nothing particularly exciting within it?

Marjorie knew excitement now. She knew what it was to long for the next day, and the next, because each one was filled with delight.

And that was with Alexander.

She knocked on the door. When the door opened, she gasped.

"Ah, Lady Marjorie," said the Dowager Duke of Cothrom formally, bowing as he strangely answered his own door. "I thought it might be—"

"Is that her?" A warmer voice erupted behind him and Lady Maude pushed her father aside with wide eyes. "You're here! You can't have heard! It's not been announced!"

"Um," said Marjorie helplessly.

"Now then, Maudey, she clearly hasn't—"

"You never know, Papa, the gossip in this town is simply dreadful—"

"What gossip? Oh, Lady Marjorie, what a delight!" The Dowager Duchess of Cothrom had appeared, pushing both husband and daughter away and beaming at a totally bemused Marjorie. "Come in, come in, you are most welcome!"

"I'm just saying, she might have heard—"

"She can't have heard, Papa, it's not been announced!"

Utterly at a loss, completely confused by what they were talking about, totally muddled as to why a duke would have been answering his own front door, Marjorie found herself half welcomed, half *dragged* into the Cothrom Chance townhouse.

It was resplendent. Never before had she been inside a property that was so…so beautiful.

Marjorie stared around her in astonishment. One would expect such things in a palace, perhaps, or some sort of manor house in the countryside, but not here. Not in Bath.

The hallway was large. Larger than the frontage of the house, which had to suggest they had thrown together two townhouses to expand the rooms. There were suits of armor and swords on the walls and paintings from Old Masters and even a golden clock that looked suspiciously French. The carpet was deep and luscious and it covered a black-and-white marble pattern, with footmen standing at every door and a scent of verbena in the air.

And just in case all of that wasn't enough…there were Chances staring at her.

Several Chances.

"I am so delighted you are here," Lady Maude said, almost impulsively as she stepped forward to take Marjorie's hand. "I will be honest, I thought Alexander had screwed—"

"Maudey!"

"—it up," continued the woman unrepentantly, ignoring her mother. "But you are here, which has to mean good things!"

"Ah, Lady Marjorie," came another voice as a couple she recognized as the new Duke and Duchess of Cothrom, the dowager duke's eldest son and his wife, stepped into the hall.

Accompanied, Marjorie saw with sinking spirits, by Lord and Lady Leopold Chance.

Excellent. All the Cothrom Chances are here.

Her hopes of being able to sneak up to Alexander's bedchamber and avoid seeing anyone save a footman had disappeared in a puff of smoke, but still, Marjorie attempted to rally.

Attempted.

"I was just wondering…" she said timidly.

"Whether old Zander is still having a hump?" asked Lady Maude with a giggle.

"Maudey!"

The remonstrance came from all directions, but it did not appear that the eldest Chance child seemed to mind.

"Well he does have the hump," she said boldly, meeting Marjorie's eye and winking. "But then he *is* the baby of the family. He must be expected to cry and carry on at times."

"Maudey!"

Marjorie wanted to melt into the resplendent carpet and disappear from the face of the earth. *They were just…just so much!* Did they have any idea how intimidating they were? How overwhelming it was to be around them? How astonishing it was that they simply continued on and on?

"I must say, Frank's inventiveness is starting to get worrying," said Leopold.

Maude tapped her foot. "I just wish she had done such a thing for me when I was sent to my room as a child."

"You, sent to your room?" asked the duchess. "I can't believe it."

"Oh, believe it, Victoria." Lady Maude smiled. "I was not the easiest of children, was I, Papa?"

"No," said her father woodenly, though he upset the stern image by allowing one of the corners of his lips to twitch. "You were not."

"Now, then. Lady Marjorie did not come all this way to hear you reminisce about your childhood, Maudey," the duchess said quietly, turning to her and smiling warmly. "She's come for... Oh. What is the reason for your visit, Lady Marjorie?"

Ah. Right. Yes.

It had all been perfectly planned out, Marjorie reflected furiously. And then the Chances had to go and be...well, *involved* in each other's lives to such an extent that she was rather astonished they didn't know the whole story already.

That was, assuming that they did not.

"I...came to call upon..." Marjorie desperately attempted to find a ladylike and respectable reason for her visit, but they were not fools, were they?

Besides, she had turned up without a chaperone, and even they must have realized how startling that was.

Botheration. She had no recourse but the truth.

Marjorie sighed with a wry smile. "I came to call upon Lord Alexander, actually."

The reaction was almost deafening. Lady Maude whooped, the young duchess and her sister-in-law Lady Leopold clapped their hands and made cooing noises, and the dowager duke muttered something that might have been, "I'll never see the day again."

"Well, yes, I...ah," said Marjorie helplessly as she was led by the hand to the foot of the stairs by the dowager duchess.

"He's upstairs, the indolent boy," his mother was saying somberly. "And making a huge fuss out of nothing, I dare say, considering that you are here to take him off our hands. You *are* here to take him off our hands, aren't you?"

Heavens preserve us.

"Um," Marjorie said feebly.

"Oh, don't fuss over her, Mama. Can't you see she needs to speak with Zander and get him to put his sense back on?" said Lady Maude as she disentangled her mother's hands from Marjorie's. "Go on up. Take a left, go all the way along the corridor, and his room is at the end."

Marjorie swallowed. *Right.*

Her original plan had been to speak to Alexander in his bedchamber, where they could have privacy…but that plan had been predicated on no one else in the building knowing she was there.

It was quite another thing entirely to be waved off by the whole Cothrom Chance family at the bottom of the staircase, as though she were departing on a long sea voyage, rather than doing the unthinkable and going to speak to a gentleman in his bedchamber.

Alexander's bedchamber.

Marjorie could not help but wonder, as she reached the top of the staircase and turned left, precisely what his bedchamber would be like.

She had never been inside a gentleman's bedchamber.

Oh, she had peered from the doorway into her father's bedchamber once or twice, while he'd been out, just because it was a part of the house that she never saw. It hadn't been particularly inspiring, but then her father was not one for the arts.

"And precisely how, I wonder, am I supposed to make it work?!"

The muttering was echoing down the corridor and Marjorie halted, the familiarity of that voice thrumming through her.

Alexander.

"Pricing, pricing, that's what I need to look at—but how to find comparative equals to fully understand the market, that's what I'd like to know!"

What *Marjorie* wanted to know was what on earth he was talking about. It was certainly Alexander—there was no mistaking that tone—but he appeared to be chuntering under his breath about something far beyond her understanding.

Comparative equals? Understand the market?

"And where is this place, anyway? A map, that's what I need. A map…"

Marjorie stepped forward as a thump and a muttered curse echoed down the corridor. What on earth was he trying to do?

Well, at least one of her questions was answered as she turned another corner and saw, at the end of it, the gentleman she adored attempting to…mend a door?

"Don't know why Nicholls can't put it on by himself," Alexander was muttering, as though an offense from one butler was an offense to all. "Take the blasted thing off easily enough, but putting the damned thing back—Marjorie!"

"Alexander."

There was nothing else to say. She had drawn to a halt merely two feet from him, almost afraid that if she stepped any closer, she would find it impossible to speak.

He did take her breath away. Shirt sleeves rolled up revealing those delicious forearms, buttons half-done and in entirely the wrong button holes, the man wore no waistcoat, no jacket, and no cravat.

It was almost the most naked she had ever seen him, other than that wonderful afternoon at the inn, and Marjorie had to remind herself sternly that that sort of thing was certainly not why she had come here today.

Even if it *was* all she could think about in this moment.

"Marjorie," Alexander repeated, blinking as though unable to believe his very eyes. "You… You are here."

"Yes, I am," she said quietly, unable to think of anything to say but the obvious. "And so are you."

"Yes, but… Well. I live here," pointed out Alexander. "For now."

For now? What did that mean?

It was infuriating how swiftly the man was able to get her to spiral out of control. If only the blasted man were not so handsome, Marjorie was half sure she would have been able to keep a tight lid on her emotions and not allow them to rule her.

But as it was, her mind now swirled with panic. Was he leaving? Where was he going—surely, he could not be thinking of leaving Bath? Or England? Perhaps even the whole of Great Britain?

Why would he leave—was it because of her? Was she chasing him out of the country?

"I am so, so sorry, you know," Alexander said quietly, leaning the errant door that appeared to be the one from his own bedchamber against the wall. "Marjorie, I'm so sorry."

"Oh," she said, a little overwhelmed.

This was not how she had imagined it in her head. No, the man had been almost impossible to get an apology out of in her own mind. She had thought he would protest, attempt to explain it away, tell her she had misunderstood.

But this…this bare-faced apology?

"I was wrong to speak of you like that. I should never have— and I never will again, no matter what happens between us," Alexander said in a rush, as though he were desperate to get the words out before he were interrupted. "You deserve—oh, Marjorie, the world, and I cannot give it to you—"

"I never wanted the world," Marjorie interrupted, her words slipping out without much interference from her good sense. Perhaps that was all to the good. "I wanted you."

It was not, perhaps, the most elegant of kisses, but then it did not need to be.

Marjorie gave a sigh of relief as she found herself once again in Alexander's arms. This was where she belonged: her palms splayed against him, her hips pressed against his, his lips on her mouth, and the knowledge that they would never be apart again.

For she would not let it happen. There was no part of her that wanted to be away from him, and no one in the world could change that.

The kiss ended. Alexander drew back, but only so he could press his forehead against her own.

Marjorie beamed, certain in the knowledge that somehow, everything had turned out right. Nothing could now—

"I have something to tell you," Alexander said in a murmur evidently full of fear.

Tension soared up her back as Marjorie's spine stiffened.

That did not sound good.

She pulled away, mostly so she could see him better, but also because she needed to look into this man's eyes as he spoke.

She had forgiven him; perhaps far swifter than she should have, and certainly before he had given any sort of reasonable explanation. But Marjorie could sense in the strain in Alexander's eyes that what he was about to tell her was something momentous. Something that he should have, perhaps, told her a long time ago.

"I should have told you this a long time ago," Alexander said quietly. "And I wanted to—I tried, a few times, but to be honest with you... I never had the nerve. I knew it would...would change the way you saw me, and I was not sure that it would be for the better."

Marjorie's breath caught in her throat as she forced a smile. *What on earth could this be?* "I-I am ready to hear it."

A twisted smile seared across Alexander's lips. "I... I have lied to you."

Her smile disappeared as her stomach dropped out of her chest. "I beg your pardon?"

"To you, to my family, to Society, the whole world," Alexander hastened to add, his brow clearly furrowed as he placed his hands behind his back. "Marjorie, I don't quite know how to tell you this..."

Marjorie braced herself.

Well, what was the worst it could be? A hidden lovechild—perhaps several with the ladies he had bedded over the years? Perhaps he had gambling debts, or a debt of honor that would require a duel? Was that why he wouldn't touch her dowry, the shame of it, the need to repay such a thing himself? Maybe he…he forged checks. Saved a prince's life? Was he planning a move to China?

Alexander exhaled slowly, glanced down at his feet as though gathering courage, then looked up into her eyes. "I never bedded all those women, Marjorie. Not *all* of them. By no means."

Marjorie blinked. "What?"

"I never bedded all those women. The reputation I have," Alexander said quietly. "It's false."

It's false. False?

"You know, each of those words individually, I understood," she said slowly. "And yet when put together…"

"I was a fool, a fool desperate to be admired, to belong," Alexander said, his cheeks pinking slightly at he admitted to what he clearly believed were faults. "And every gentleman of my acquaintance appeared to be bedding ladies quite happily, so I thought…why not?"

"I don't understand," Marjorie whispered, as she started to understand.

Alexander tugged a hand through his hair. "Two of my friends—friends no longer, I might add—I gave them permission to use my name. When they made their seductions, do you see? They would keep their family names clean, and I would gain an impressive reputation. This was before any of us was very recognizable among Society. We're all of a similar build, a similar coloring. You see?"

She did see. That was, she was starting to. "Then… Then you are not really a rogue."

"Not in the slightest," Alexander said cheerfully, though there was still worry in his face. "I will admit, you were not my first—"

"No, I gathered that," Marjorie murmured, heat burning in her cheeks as she recalled just how skilled the man had been before he'd made her cry out his name.

"—but other than you, I bedded three widows, *years* ago, and I stole a few kisses from three unwed ladies other than you, but that was all," he was saying, his voice lowering. Marjorie glanced over her shoulder just to make sure. "I never dabbled with chambermaids. I know it was idiotic, and I've regretted it the last year most especially. This reputation I have of being a rogue, a scoundrel—it was pleasant, for a time, I admit. But it didn't fulfill me, Marjorie. It didn't make me whole. Not like you."

Delight, sheer delight rose in Marjorie as she looked at the adoration in Alexander's face.

"I should have told you—I should have made them stop, and I should have told you," he said quietly. "I knew I wasn't worthy of you, even the true version of me, but certainly not with the reputation I had. All of a sudden, in a moment, I saw that the choices I had made would preclude me from my greatest desire. Being your husband."

Marjorie tried to breathe, but apparently, her lungs had stopped working. "Alexander—"

"And I know I will never truly be good enough, not really," he said quietly, not taking his eyes from hers as he slowly lowered himself onto bended knee beside his bedchamber door. "I could spend the rest of my life attempting to restore my reputation and it would still never be good enough—and I'd much rather spend that time trying to make you happy instead."

This was not happening. Was this happening? Was she still dreaming, waiting to wake up to creep up the servants' staircase in the Chance household?

It would certainly explain the nonsensical plethora of Chances...

"Marry me, Marjorie," Alexander whispered, his eyes lighting up with hope. "I don't ask to safeguard your honor. I know you could live without me, that you're stronger than Society's censure. I ask because I love you. Make me happy—give me the opportunity to make you happy for the rest of your life. I can provide. You will keep your dowry, do with it as you please, offer it to our children if you think that best, and I will still provide. I hope you don't mind a tradesman—"

"I'm sorry, a 'tradesman'?"

"Not important," he said hastily, and Marjorie could not help but smile.

That was the Alexander she knew. He was not a man interested in detail. He was a man focused on the destination: and the destination, it appeared, was her.

"Marry me, Marjorie," he repeated.

Marjorie swallowed. Then she lowered herself down onto her own knees before him, almost laughing at the astonishment in his gaze.

"Marjorie—"

"You really want to marry me?" she asked, heart in her mouth and laughter bubbling up within at the sight of his astonished face. "No, listen. I did not let you explain. I assumed the worst of you—"

"You weren't far off," admitted a shamefaced Alexander.

"—and if this marriage is going to work—and I want it to work," persevered Marjorie, "then we have to trust each other. We have to know that we are on the same side, the same team. That we…we love each other."

Were those tears in Alexander's eyes? "You love me?"

"Of course I do, you idiot," Marjorie said with a muffled laugh that might have been half a sob. "Now kiss me."

Alexander leaned forward and pressed a hot, passionate kiss upon her lips, fueled surely with relief and desire and a need to be close.

At least, that was what flowed through Marjorie's body as she grasped her future husband closer, her hands wound around his neck and her breasts pushed up against his chest. Oh, this was what she wanted; *he* was what she wanted.

Together, they could do anything.

When the kiss eventually ended, it was for Alexander to ruefully say, "And here I am, inhabitant of a bedchamber without a door."

"*Alexander!*"

"Well, you can't blame a man for hoping," he said cheerfully.

Marjorie sighed. It was a shame, but... "I must tell you that your family knows I'm up here."

Alexander's brows shot up. "What, all of them?"

"All of them," she said with a laugh, rising to her feet and pulling him up to stand beside her. "Shall we tell them the good news?"

"Not before I tell *you* the happy news," he said, most unexpectedly, with a look of calm and serious thought that was not only most unusual, but that which suited the man perfectly. "Have you ever longed, by any chance, to own a factory?"

Chapter Twenty

April 15, 1841

ALEXANDER COULD NOT recall being this happy.

"You aren't going to tell me, are you?"

"Not on your life, no," he said with a grin as he glanced over at his future wife.

Just two days—two days! It was hard to believe that in two days, thanks to so many titled noblemen in the family and a quickly acquired special license, this radiant beauty would be parading down the aisle to make a whole heap of vows, before witnesses, that she would never leave him.

Not that he wanted to tie her down or anything.

Hang on. Now that he came to think about it…

"Alexander!"

"Whoops!" Alexander carefully directed the reins back to the right, preventing the horses he was supposed to be driving from careering into the side of the road. "Sorry about that. Lost in my own thoughts."

Marjorie grinned. "I wonder what happened?"

The swift kiss he pressed on her lips, all honey and need, answered that particular question well, and it was only because he was supposed to be driving the curricle that Alexander forced himself away from the woman's luscious mouth.

"I really must pay attention," he said regretfully. "I have never been here, after all."

Their curricle rattled along the Bath streets as Marjorie said curiously, "And where, exactly, are we going?"

Alexander swallowed. "You know, in a way, I'm not sure."

It had certainly been a strangest conversation he had had last night with Lord Dalton. The dinner itself had been fine, if stilted, and thank goodness Samuel and his wife, Rose, had been able to supply most of the conversation.

Well. Samuel.

But when Alexander had smiled at Marjorie as she'd left with her sister and mother to retire to the drawing room, it was most inconvenient of his cousin to decide to take a moment of fresh air, leaving him alone with his future father-in-law.

Lord Dalton had not smiled. "So. You are to marry my daughter."

Alexander had attempted to look calm and collected. "Yes, my lord."

"Hmm. You are fortunate."

It had been on the tip of Alexander's tongue to point out that after the bizarre "disappearance" of his eldest daughter, and the relatively new title he enjoyed, Lord Dalton was in fact the fortunate to marry off his daughters not only to two gentleman of rank, but that the gentlemen had not even proven to be fortune hunters after his children merely for money. Though Alexander would still take Marjorie's dowry. So that Marjorie could control the sum and not her father. So that his wife could have some freedom at last and the sense of truly being responsible for herself.

Alexander had not said any of these things. He'd smiled weakly. "Yes, indeed. Very fortunate. Marjorie is—"

"Marjorie is my daughter and her happiness means everything to me." Lord Dalton had blinked and shaken his head, appearing to be reasonably startled at the statement that had emanated from his own mouth. "And Rosemary's as well."

It was perhaps the closest thing he had managed to affection, and Alexander could not help but be astonished by it.

Still, he'd tried not to make it too obvious. "Your care for them does you credit."

"Yes. Care." Lord Dalton had drawn himself up, his expression still wooden. He could have given Alexander's own father lessons. "When Rosemary decided to leave, she took nothing with her. I gave her nothing. Her second marriage to your cousin has left her a very wealthy woman, and I am given to understand that, though I offer my Marjorie's husband a not-insubstantial sum for the care of her, they are gifting you a...trade."

Alexander had winced. "Yes, my lord."

It was the precise reaction he had gained from Lord Gascoyne and Sir Percival, when he spoken to them—for the last time—two days ago.

"A factory? Work...with your hands?" Lord Gascoyne had shuddered.

"Well, that's put paid to it. I cannot use your name for seductions now!" snapped Sir Percival.

Which had rather been Alexander's hope. He had not told them, as the owner working with the on-site manager, he doubted he would be getting his hands dirty at all.

Still, he had trusted that Lord Dalton would have a slightly more modern outlook on the whole thing. Every gentleman had investments, did he not? Besides, the Marquess of Dalton was a new title, bestowed upon the current marquess's father...who had, before earning a title, built a fortune in trade.

"You think you can make her happy?"

Alexander had been pulled out of his daydream by a stern and gruff question from his future father-in-law, and he'd said hastily, "Yes!" Then he'd thought some more. "I will work hard to, for the rest of my life."

"That's more like it," Lord Dalton had said gruffly. "Here."

Pulling something rectangle out of his pocket that looked like a visiting card, he'd thrown it down on the table before Alexander.

Alexander had peered down at it. There'd been an address written on it. "I...I see. Or actually, I don't see."

When he'd looked up, it was to see Lord Dalton rolling his

eyes. Alexander had reached out and took a sip of wine. Anything to avoid looking at the man for a moment.

"It's my wife's old townhouse. Her childhood home," Lord Dalton had said quietly. "No siblings, you see, so when she inherited…it's been rented out these last twenty years."

"Oh," Alexander had said politely, not sure why he was being given this piece of family lore.

Lord Dalton's eyes had been stern. "And now it's yours. Yours and Marjorie's."

"Oh. Oh!" Alexander had stared down at the piece of card with fresh eyes.

A home.

Did it make him stubborn that his first instinct was to refuse it? When he had begged his own father for money, why was he so adamant about not letting his wife's father offer any help? This was to be *her* home as well as his. He wanted his wife comfortable.

And this was a home, here in Bath, a place where he and Marjorie already had so many fond memories. A home where they could build a life together. It was precisely what he had hoped for. Did it matter that they didn't have to spend the next few weeks or months searching for a place when the perfect one was already available?

Marjorie was right. He *was* stubborn and he'd been foolish. So he'd live in his wife's home. It would be *their* home now.

Alexander had looked up, but before he could speak, Lord Dalton had risen from his chair and done something that he'd never done before.

He'd been holding out his hand.

"Look after her. Please," he'd said gruffly. "Better than I have, at any rate. Which won't be hard."

Alexander had risen to his feet and seen in the man's eyes not only pain, but regret. A wish to go back and change the past, and a knowledge it simply could not be done.

He had not taken the man's hand. Instead, he'd stepped

around the table and embraced the older gentleman, ignoring the stiffness and the mutter of surprise and hugging the man tightly.

"Thank you," Alexander had said clearly. "For giving us the best possible start in life."

When he'd pulled away from Lord Dalton, the man had been dashing tears from his eyes. "Say nothing of it. My solicitor will contact yours about the transference of the rest of the dowry."

"Excellent. I am sure Marjorie will do great things with her fortune."

"'Her' fortune?" His future father-in-law had scowled. "I'm offering an ample dowry to ensure my Marjorie lives a comfortable life, with a would-be tradesman son of a duke or not."

"And she will live comfortably, I promise you. But that money will be hers. Our children's, perhaps. Just as your wife has given Marjorie this home."

"My *wife* didn't—it became mine when we married."

"Oh, did it? You'd deny your wife the chance to have a say in the inheritance of her own home? Shall I ask Lady Dalton what she thinks about that?" Alexander had smirked, but he'd hoped his future father-in-law would know he hadn't meant any harm in it.

"All right, all right. The dowry will be yours to do with whatever you please—even if that means making it Marjorie's responsibility." Lord Dalton had muttered something under his breath, but Alexander could only pick up something like, *"Women of fortune and tradesmen lords. What a time to be alive."*

Alexander had turned to give the future Lady Alexander Chance the good news.

"Don't—Don't tell her."

Alexander had stopped. "Lady Dalton? I was only teasing."

"No, don't—don't tell Marjorie." Lord Dalton had sniffed and picked up the newspaper currently on his desk. "She knows about the dowry, but there's no need for her to think I'm spoiling her even more."

Alexander didn't think it his place to insert himself in the relationship between father and daughter, which was why Alexander was drawing his curricle to a halt before a beautiful though slightly unkempt townhouse on the outskirts of Bath, and wondering what on earth he was going to tell Marjorie.

"Where are we? Do we know the people here?" Marjorie leaned forward curiously, staring up at the house. "It's rather pretty, isn't it?"

Alexander's delight swelled. "Yes. Come on. I have a key."

She cocked her head. "You have a key?"

"Let's take a look at it."

From the instant that Alexander had opened the door, it felt like home.

It also felt like someone else's home, someone who had not done a very good job at looking after it and had left in a hurry. He supposed Lord Dalton would send his staff here to clean the place up a bit before Alexander and Marjorie moved in. There was dust all over the mantelpiece in the hall, and an old umbrella had been left behind by a coat rack. The rug had seen better days, as had the wallpaper, which had peeled near the front door where the window beside it let in the sun.

Marjorie stepped forward and the echo of her footsteps meandered around the house. "It's very spacious."

It was not very spacious compared to Alexander's home—but then, that was his parents' home. This was something completely different.

This was his and his wife's own.

"And what's in here—oh, a dining room. West-facing, how lovely," Marjorie said quietly, peering her head into the room. "Incidentally, are you going to tell me at any point why we are creeping around another person's house?"

Alexander stifled a laugh as he opened the next door and found a drawing room, perfectly proportioned and with a dusty chandelier hanging from the center. "It's not another person's house."

His future wife appeared at his side and gazed up at him

curiously, her eyelashes fluttering. "It's not?"

"No," he said quietly, twisting so that she had to turn and lean against the doorway to keep his eye. "It's ours."

Marjorie's eyes widened and her lips parted. It took her a moment to croak, "'Ours'?"

"Ours," Alexander confirmed, hardly sure how he had managed to seduce and secure such a beautiful woman. "A, erm, generous benefactor, no one you know—"

"But my father always said this house would be Rose's, as the eldest," Marjorie interrupted with a wry smile.

Oh, damnation.

That's the trouble with incredibly clever women, Alexander thought furiously as he tried to think of a way to get out of this one without lying. The woman hated liars! And he had promised himself, hadn't he, that he would never lie to her again.

Even if he wanted to.

The trouble was, this put him in a slightly complicated position. On the one hand, Lord Dalton, his future father-in-law. On the other hand, Marjorie, his beloved.

Alexander smiled. It wasn't complicated at all. "Your father asked me not to tell you."

"Yes, that sounds like him," Marjorie said ruefully as she stepped out of the doorframe and back into the hall. "And what's down here?"

"You did not suppose that it was my own father who had gifted us this home?" Alexander called after her as she stepped into what turned out to be a small yet perfectly formed library.

"I recognized it immediately. I don't think I've ever stepped inside of it, as it's been let practically my whole life, but Mother pointed it out plenty of times." Marjorie's snort echoed around the room, which was devoid of books, though lined with bookcases. "Yes, I know I was lying to play along with the charade, but I will admit I've been a bit harsh about liars. It's not as if I don't tell harmless lies all the time. No more, though. Not unless it's in the pursuit of teasing." She took Alexander's hand

and squeezed it, and Alexander felt himself melt. "I'm sorry I frightened you so, with my harsh judgment of liars."

"I know why. That was no minor lie your parents told you."

"No, it was not." She sighed, then giggled. "Another thing. If this were a gift from your father, he would have just come out with it. He might even have accompanied us to look at it, half or more of the Cothrom Chances at his heels. My father is not that sort of man. My family is not that sort of family."

"No, he's not," Alexander had to admit. "They're not. But they do all love you, you know."

There was perhaps too much brightness in his woman's eyes as she whispered, "I know."

"And your father seems to have warmed up to me," he continued, turning away and giving Marjorie a moment to collect herself. "In fact, my own father appears to have warmed up to me. I am not sure what I have done to suddenly gain everyone's approbation, but—"

"Oh, you know full well it is the restoration of your character that has done it," Marjorie said brightly after wiping her eyes with her sleeve surreptitiously and striding out of the library to investigate further. "You should have known that would happen when Lady Romeril made that announcement at that card party!"

Yes, it had been strange, and sudden. Alexander still had absolutely no idea who had told her, but the very day he and Marjorie had formed their engagement and announced it to close family and friends, mere hours after he'd confronted the scoundrels and finally convinced them to stop via his association with trade, Lady Romeril had apparently attended a card party that very evening and told everyone with whom she'd played that she had discovered Lord Gascoyne and Sir Percival's scandalous ruse.

The whole of Bath was abuzz about it, and the upshot appeared to be that Lord Alexander Chance was now one of the most respected—and sought-after—gentlemen in the whole of England. Why, he wondered if even his own few flirtations and tumbles would be regarded as the work of the other rogues and not him. Not that he would ever lie about it if pressed—but who would press him on such a matter?

Strange how these things worked out.

"I am glad I was able to secure you before the truth came out, and not after," teased Marjorie as she started up the staircase. "I wonder how many bedchambers—"

"You honestly think you could have lost me to any other woman in the world?" asked Alexander incredulously, following her hastily up the staircase. "There is absolutely no one else in the world for me but—oh. You are teasing me."

His future wife's giggles echoed across the landing. "Only because you are far too easy to tease, my love."

Alexander's stomach jolted. *My love.*

It was strange how deeply wonderful it was to be spoken to in such a manner. Whenever he wondered how he would ever live without her, he realized that he could not.

After wishing to rebel against his family for so long, it was rather startling to find a person whom he wanted to rebel *with*.

Nobly born factory owners who had consummated before marriage, a wife with a fortune that was all her own, with his scandalous past and her scandalous sister…perhaps they were a perfect pairing.

Alexander grinned as Marjorie curiously stuck her head through every doorway on the landing. *Just perfect.*

"You know, I think it's because you have shown your true colors," she said conversationally, as though he would be able to follow her thoughts.

A frown furrowed his brow. "What do you mean?"

"Well," Marjorie said lightly as she stepped into a room. Alexander followed her to discover it was a light and airy bedchamber with a bed, a chaise longue, and an empty trunk lying open in a corner. "For years, your family has considered you a…a…"

"Rogue?" Alexander supplied hopefully.

"A reprobate," Marjorie said with a wicked grin as she stepped over to the window and tugged the curtains aside to peer through the glass onto the street below.

"'A *reprobate*'!"

"Something of that kind, yes," she said vaguely. Her expression sharpened as she turned to him. "And here we all are, discovering you are in fact a man with a huge heart who could not say *no* to his friends, who had never done a terrible thing in his life."

"Well," Alexander said awkwardly, trying desperately not to think of the remarks he had made about Marjorie's bedsport rankings in the middle of the Pump Room. "Mostly not terrible."

Her laughter was a balm to his soul. "My point is, it is as though they are all getting to know you again. The real Alexander."

Staying away from this woman was never particularly easy, and Alexander found himself being tugged by an invisible rope to step closer to her.

"But I knew the real you almost from the beginning of our better acquaintanceship this year," Marjorie said quietly, her smile not teasing now, but warm nonetheless.

Alexander groaned. "'Almost from the beginning'?"

"I do believe you wrote me not one, but *two* very scandalous letters at the very beginning of our, and I am terming this loosely, our courtship." She laughed as Alexander pulled her into his arms. "I'm assuming the second was as bad as, or worse than, the first. Though I—Alexander!"

"I was so nervous sending you those letters," he admitted, swinging her 'round and glorying in her delighted screeches. "I'd never written anything like that before."

"Never?"

Marjorie's feet returned to the ground as Alexander halted, nerves twisting in him at the revelation he had just accidentally made.

Bother. See, this was one of the many reasons why he had

come up with the idea with Lord Gascoyne and Sir Percival in the first place. No gentleman wished to appear ignorant of such matters. He was supposed to be…well, worldly.

Not shy and embarrassed at the very idea of writing a suggestive letter to a lady. Which he had been.

Marjorie's lips were parted in clear astonishment. "I… I was your first love letter?"

Affection welled within him. "I suppose you were."

"Oh, Alexander…"

He welcomed the kiss eagerly, desperate for any opportunity to taste of this woman. They had agreed, which meant that Marjorie had stated and Alexander had groaned but knew he had no choice but to agree, that they would save any conjugal relations of that kind for after their wedding.

"After all," Marjorie had pointed out with pink cheeks, "what's done is done, to be sure, but we don't have to do it again until we are married."

So it was moments like this, intimate connections like this, his hands in her hair as pins cascaded to the threadbare carpet, Marjorie's scent in his nostrils, and his pulse wildly thumping—

"You know," murmured Marjorie as she broke the kiss, gazing up into his adoring eyes. "We are not expected back for afternoon tea for almost an hour."

Alexander blinked, his mind hazed from passion. "Yes?"

Marjorie rolled her eyes, then turned and looked pointedly at the bed. "I hardly thought I would have to be the one explaining this to Lord Alexander Chance, of all people."

"But you said—you said we shouldn't—"

"I changed my mind." His beautiful future wife grinned. "Do you mind that I changed my mind?"

"You want to—you want to?" He could not quite keep the excitement from his voice, and his beloved giggled as she tugged him over to the bed.

"Only if you agree to be quiet."

"Yes, yes, I can do that."

"And if you don't tell anyone about this."

"Obviously, no, I won't."

"And," said his wicked future wife, Alexander's manhood stiffening with every syllable that she uttered, "if you bring me to climax at least three times before taking any pleasure yourself."

Alexander smiled. "It would be an honor."

Epilogue

May 1, 1841

"Now, HANG ON," Marjorie said hastily.

"That is exactly what I mean—hanging, it's absolutely barbaric!" Lady Lucy Chance said passionately, slamming her hand on the table so forcefully that the teacups rattled. "Whoops, sorry about that."

"It's fine," said Marjorie, trying not to think about the previous afternoon when she and Alexander had become so amorous, so quickly, that they had not made it successfully upstairs and had instead accidentally tipped the entire tea service onto the carpet. "But honestly, Lucy, I do not think you need to worry about such things."

"If it is not for people like myself, who are not a part of the oppressed classes, then who is to speak for them?" Alexander's cousin said passionately, brushing dark curls from her eyes and lifting her teacup to her full lips and almost taking a sip before she continued. "If prison reform is not started now, there will be countless people unfairly treated, hanged for crimes they did not commit, transported thousands of miles—"

"I told you not to get onto this topic," pointed out Alexander happily from the sofa on the other side of the room. "But you did ask."

Marjorie chuckled at her husband just as their guest glared.

"And it's people like you, Zander, who care so little for the unfortunates in the world, who comprise most of the problem! Evil unchallenged is almost as bad as the evil itself."

"Well, that is quite the accusation. I'm just saying, it is not seemly for a lady to involve herself in such things," he stated fairly.

At least, fairly in Marjorie's opinion. By the way that Lucy swelled up indignantly, she obviously did not appreciate the point.

"And *I* am just saying that until fair trials and a system of judicial review is enacted…"

Marjorie allowed the noise to wash over her.

Oh, it wasn't that she did not agree with her new cousin in many ways. The justice system in England was still in many ways medieval, and it was pitiful to see so many people taken away on ships to the far reaches of the Earth merely because they had stolen loaves of bread with which to feed their families. And while Rose still would not speak to her sister of the worst times in her life, she knew Rose was well aware of the indignities of poverty. It was part of why Rose challenged Samuel to do better with his fortune, and why she was advising Marjorie to do the same with her own. Her dowry—her own fortune now—invested properly could provide a secure future for her children *and* allow her to help the poor where she could. *How* she could.

Because Alexander was also right. It was not acceptable for a lady of Lucy's rank and position—daughter of an earl, no less—to be speaking so openly about such things. To desire to be so hands-on *involved* in such things.

She was actually attending rallies, apparently. Now *that* was only going to get her into trouble.

"And what's more—"

"There are a few good causes that the Chance family supports, aren't there?" Marjorie said desperately, eager to escape the topic of prison reform that had constituted their entire conversation from the moment Lucy had arrived over an hour ago.

Lucy waved a hand. "Oh, yes, there's Thomas's orphanage. It's doing very well, but—"

"And there's Samuel and my sister's retirement home for

actors and actresses," Marjorie said enthusiastically, relieved to have found slightly a more palatable conversational direction. "I hear that the building they have purchased in London is very suitable. Rose and I have been discussing, too, involving ourselves in more charities for children and widows of little means. Not *all* widows have the luxury of playing around with the latest strapping lord to have just finished up at Eton."

She glanced at Alexander, who cleared his throat quietly and stared at his feet. She tried to stifle a giggle.

Lucy didn't notice. "But don't you see, that is why I have to do something for the prisoners!" Lucy's face was beseeching, as though Marjorie alone could fix every problem in the world. "Every Chance has something, and this is my something!"

Marjorie's face softened. She could well remember—after all, it had been only weeks ago—when she had sought something in the world to make meaning of her place within it.

To be fair, she had found a husband and at the same time, a sense of purpose, both because he'd given her control of her own fortune, whereas her father would not, and because of his own undertaking. She and Alexander were going to take that factory and turn it into something wonderful. Not just something profitable, though naturally that would come. But something meaningful. A place where women, for they were nearly all of the workers there, wanted to work. A place that understood that real life came first, not the amount of money one made. A place where women could find friendship, and joy, and a place for themselves in the world. She'd even come up with the idea of hiring nannies, out of her own fortune if need be, to watch the workers' children at a building nearby during their parents' shifts.

Perhaps Lucy needed a project... A project better suited to a lady.

"—and if I can make a difference, a difference to one person's life," Lucy was saying passionately, "is that not worth some discomfort? Is that not worth risking myself just a little?"

Try as she might, Marjorie could not help but glance over at

Alexander.

Worth risking myself, just a little.

Yes, they had both had to risk themselves a little to find the bliss they now had together, and Marjorie was under no illusion that it would not take continuous work to maintain. The best things, it appeared, were those which required hard work.

She didn't fancy their chances without it.

"You might find that your parents have a slightly different view on the matter," pointed out Alexander.

Lucy immediately scoffed. "Oh, what do they know about it?"

"Well, I think the *Earl and Countess* of Lindow might—"

"Just because they have titles, that doesn't make them better than anyone else," interrupted his cousin with pink cheeks. "It's just a coincidence of birth!"

"You sound radical, Lucy," Marjorie said quietly, hiding her smile behind her teacup.

Another lady of Society might have taken offense at such a tone, but as Marjorie had known she would, Lucy burst into a warm smile. "Really?"

"Really," said Marjorie with a chuckle. "And I would have thought, given the time you have as an unmarried woman—"

"Oh, goodness, is that the time?" Lucy jumped up, scattering crumbs from the cake she had not eaten—her mouth otherwise engaged in extolling the many dangers of the current state of England's prisons—all across the carpet. "I'll be late for the rally!"

"Now, then, your mother made me promise," Alexander said in a warning tone, looking up from his book. "I'm your chaperone should you go anywhere else today."

His cousin merely laughed. "Don't be silly. The whole family knows you can't be trusted with that sort of thing. I'm sure she really meant that I was definitely to go to the rally, don't you see?"

Pain panged through Marjorie as she saw the hurt cross her husband's face.

"But, Lucy—"

"I'll be home before dinner, and that's far more than anyone can expect from Benjamin," she sang out cheerfully, ramming her gloves on and curtseying briefly to the pair of them. "And I'll send that petition round as soon as I can for you to sign it before we leave for Brighton. Goodbye!"

She was gone in an instant, a whirl of skirts and pamphlets that flew around the room, and Marjorie could do nothing but laugh.

Goodness, she liked this family. She had liked them from afar when she had first encountered them, and only now that she was officially a member—officially Lady Alexander Chance—did she realize how much she *adored* how dramatically different they were.

"I must apologize for my cousin," came Alexander's chuckling voice from across the room. "She is rather an acquired taste."

"She's not!"

"Oh, I'm not saying that some man won't find her obsession with prison reform charming," her husband said with a shrug. "But how many gentlemen would permit her to carry on with such a thing? Her parents don't like it *now*. In fact, they'll kill me if they've found I've let her run off without chasing her down."

"I don't think you could catch her if you tried."

He chuckled. "Tell that to any prospective suitors looking in her direction. No, she's not for everyone, our Lucy."

"I think she's marvelous," said Marjorie tenderly, and she meant it. "After living as an only child for a third of my life so far, it's pleasant to get both my actual sister back and to acquire a number of siblings and cousins through our marriage."

The last two words appeared to be the only ones her husband heard as he repeated, "'Our marriage.'"

Heat spread through Marjorie as she smiled at the man who had made her so happy.

Not an easy happiness. One they'd had to work for, fight for.

Even now, married with the support of their families, they

would have to work hard to stay within Society's good graces. The idea of a duke's son being so involved in one of his investments, even if that work mostly stretched to reading over accounts and agreeing to pay for additional safety features at the factory, had made the rounds as gossip in all polite Society and made the two of them…well, not exactly pariahs, but something close. There was also the fact that their hasty marriage had only solidified the rumors that he had deflowered her at a lower-class inn, despite Lady Romeril's revelation about all the other affairs Lord Alexander Chance was now free of. For example, the Misses Harding and Ramsay had yet to accept an invitation for tea at her new home.

And Marjorie did not care. How could she? There was nothing she wanted more in the world than Alexander Chance, and she had him.

That was, she'd had him last night, and this morning…

"Come here," Alexander said with a smirk, patting the space on the sofa beside him.

Marjorie did not require much more of an inducement. Being apart from her husband in any way, even by a few short yards, was painful. Why would she wish to be away from him even for a moment?

She rose, skirts swishing as she stepped across the short distance, and lowered herself onto the sofa.

Well. Mostly the sofa.

"I do believe your hand has got lost," Marjorie said in a mockingly stern voice as she glared at her husband, who grinned utterly unrepentantly.

"I don't think so."

She squirmed, reveling in the sensation of the man's palm and curling fingers around her buttock. "Yes, it's definitely in the wrong place."

"Strongly disagree."

"Alexander!"

"Fine, fine." He sighed, removing his hand but only so that he could wend it around her waist. "You know, sometimes I cannot believe you agreed to marry me."

Marjorie fixed him with a severe look. "Neither can I." But she could not retain the seriousness for long. "Neither can I."

Her repetition was softer, warmer, and she stared into the adoring eyes of a man whom she now knew would do anything, absolutely *anything* for her.

It was overwhelming at times, the sheer force of the love inside the man beside her. Lord Alexander Chace did not believe in doing anything by halves, and here he was, busy loving her with all his energy in the world.

There was nothing they could not do together, nothing they could not be. With every day that went by, Marjorie wondered whether the heights of his affection, or hers for him, for that matter, would ever be reached.

That day had not yet come. In a way, she hoped it never would.

"I managed to convince Lady Marjorie Dalton to marry me and be my wife," Alexander murmured, brushing a kiss against her cheek. "And that makes me the wealthiest man who ever lived."

"Yes, well," Marjorie thought delicately, pulse racing now at the thought of what she was about to say. "I think you would have had to."

"'Had to'? That's certainly right. There is no living without you," Alexander said, nuzzling into her neck.

It wasn't just the precursor to him ravishing her that was making Marjorie's heart pulse faster, though it wasn't having *no* effect at all. What she needed to do was stay calm, that was it. Stay calm, and state the facts plainly.

There was no need to lie today.

"Well," Marjorie said delicately, "I meant more that you would have had to marry me to…to avoid a scandal."

That gained his attention. Alexander sat up straight, brow furrowed as he looked at her in confusion. "'Avoid a scandal'?

Look, we've been over this. I know I asked you to marry me the first time at the wrong moment, and it seemed I'd only done so because we'd been found out. But I *wanted* to marry you from the moment I met you. I was just too stubborn to let it happen earlier."

"I know that," she said. "That isn't what I meant. Lord Alexander Chance, the rogue, the scoundrel? Did you really think none of your affairs would lead to a woman caressing a babe in her arms less than a year after?"

Alexander blanched. "I-I was careful those few times. I haven't gone about getting any lady with child!"

"That," Marjorie said quietly, hardly able to think as she sought out his gaze, "is what you think."

The words hung in the air, heavy and…well, pregnant with meaning.

For a moment, Alexander did and said nothing. He just stared, unblinking, as though he were waiting for the rest of her sentence.

The longcase clock ticked away in the corner, the sound of the carriages and horses outside their home continued to chatter away, and other than that, there was no sound.

No sound at all save for Marjorie's breathing. That was all she could hear.

Then there was a strange, strangled sort of noise that made her immediately frown. "Alexander?"

"Agrhghhh," was the response.

It was not much of a response, but thankfully, another type of response came swift on its heels.

Alexander's kiss would have lifted Marjorie's feet from the floor, had they been standing. It was a toe-curling, heart-stopping, stomach-twisting kiss that spoke of promise and joy and shock and delight and all the emotions that scattered across her husband's face.

When he leaned back, it was to stammer, "B-But you are sure? You are well, the child is well? We should call a doctor—"

"I am quite well." Marjorie laughed, delight rising within her. "I—"

"But we have not been careful—we have continued to—well, that sort of thing stops now," Alexander said severely. "No more—"

"If you attempt to forbid *that*, I shall leave you and never come back," Marjorie said lightly, still laughing as she took her husband's hands in hers.

"But the child, and you, we must be careful with you!"

"Well, I don't think I can become even *more* with child," she said wryly.

Alexander gave out a laugh that sounded nervous to her ear.

Nervous? Her Alexander?

"You are well, though," he said quietly, looking into her eyes as though he could see into her mind. "You are taking care of yourself?"

"I am taking care of myself, and most importantly, you are taking care of me," she said lightly. "It's… It's wonderful, isn't it?"

This was the moment.

Oh, they had spoken of children in the future, but neither of them had expected—neither of them had *thought* that it would happen so soon.

Alexander's smile was warm, and genuine, and it reached to the very depths of Marjorie's soul. "I could not be more pleased. But I tell you now, I don't envy you with your parents tomorrow!"

Marjorie groaned. "Do we have to tell them?"

"I suppose not. Why not keep it to ourselves, just for a while longer?" Alexander whispered, and her joy leapt as he leaned forward for another kiss. "Goodness, I love you, Marjorie. I must never, never do anything so foolish as to lose you again."

"And I love you," she whispered, her heart soaring, knowing she had everything that she had ever wanted on this very sofa. "Though I don't fancy your chance of ever losing me now."

A Short Letter From the Author

Hello! Thank you so much for reading *Don't Fancy Your Chance*, the twelfth novel in my The Chances series. I truly hope you enjoyed it and fell in love with Alexander and Marjorie just as much as I did.

If you've read the first eleven books of this series (which I strongly recommend!), then you'll have seen the four uncles fall in love, and many of their grown children. I had always wanted to write a series of brothers, but I could never "meet" the characters who were quite right. After waiting years to meet them myself, I have had a lot of fun writing the four Chance brothers—and now we're diving into their children. Make sure you go back and read them!

If you're desperate to read the happily ever afters of Alexander's siblings, then you'll want to look out for Book 5, *A Chance in a Million* (Thomas's story); Book 8, *A Sporting Chance* (Leopold's story); and Book 17, *Let the Chance Slip By* (Maude's story). Our next Chance adventure is going to jump to a different branch of the Chance family, and you'll meet Lucy's happily ever after...

Being an author can be a lonely business, but knowing that there are readers from all over the world who are going to adore my stories makes it all worthwhile. Thank you for support, and I hope you love reading more of my books!

Happy reading,
Emily

About Emily E K Murdoch

If you love falling in love, then you've come to the right place.

I am a historian and writer and have a varied career to date: from examining medieval manuscripts to designing museum exhibitions, to working as a researcher for the BBC to working for the National Trust.

My books range from England 1050 to Texas 1848, and I can't wait for you to fall in love with my heroes and heroines!

Follow me on twitter and instagram @emilyekmurdoch, find me on facebook at facebook.com/theemilyekmurdoch, and read my blog at www.emilyekmurdoch.com.